SIERA LONDON

CONVINCING LINA

A BACHELOR OF SHELL COVE NOVEL

ACKNOWLEDGEMENTS

It may take a village to raise a child, but it takes dedicated minions to produce a published body of work. My gratitude to my critique partners, Tammy and Soni, they are kind even when my manuscript is a hot mess. And to my amazing editor, Rebecca Martin, you make me shine and I value your friendship. The Formatting Fairies and the talented, J. Cupp, I am so glad I found you. The women and men of the Washington Romance Writers District of Columbia chapter, I would not be a published author without your mentorship and education.

Thank you to Cherlyn, Gayle, Jershonda, Devri, Mom, Michele, and C.H. Gideon and Lina's story is better because of you.

My writing career would not be possible without the loving support of my husband, family, and friends. Thanks for giving me new material for my stories every day. Your limitless patience and encouragement are my foundation in an ever-changing world. I love you.

CHAPTER ONE

For the second time in a week Lina James contemplated assault and battery as a viable option. Each word complemented the other, like cheese and crackers. Or peanut butter and jelly.

The sun heated her exposed arm and she sank further under her lounge chair's protective awning. Sipping her Arnold Palmer through a peppermint striped straw, she sighed as cool rivulets of condensation trailed between the glass and her skin. A gust of warm air blew from across the water, lifting her thick tresses off her neck, blowing tendrils forward dancing before her eyes. Cool mornings with a light breeze should be mandatory in January. Even in Florida.

Eyes closed, she took another deep breath. Her abdomen expanded to maximum capacity, she relaxed into the breath as a sense of resolve settled over her.

Yes, that's it. Assault and battery was the better choice because killing was a sin. Experienced psychiatric nurses de-escalated stressful situations with practiced control. That skill set would not be utilized this morning. Killing would be considered escalation. And Lina refused to add to her long list of recent missteps.

The rattling and musical chime of her doorbell for the twelfth time in ten minutes dampened the peaceful quiet of Sunday morning in Shell Cove. The man having the physical altercation with her front door was a bargain basement remnant item she'd tried to turn into a showroom spotlight. Slow inhale in, exhale out. The breathing exercises prepared her for the impending showdown.

"Jace Harper, if you remain at my door there's going to be bloodshed," she yelled over her shoulder.

Her new and improved self didn't have emotional floor space for anymore male shenanigans. She wanted a life filled with a husband and children. Unfortunately, the universe had a penchant for hurling cosmic crap in her direction at lightning speed. Fool me once, no opportunity to fool me twice. And today marked three months plus one day since Jace Harper had made a fool of her. Couple that with six weeks of dates with bad breath, bad manners, and bad math. The last guy stuck her with the dinner bill, where he ordered a bottle of wine, an appetizer, a main entrée, and dessert to go. She was done with dating.

"Lee-na, please open the door." Hearing the singsong quality he added to the first syllable of her name had her breathing in a hiss.

No man would have the opportunity to abandon her, because she was on a thirty day man-fast. No new relationship baggage allowed. The purge would be complete on her twenty-seventh birthday. The next man that professed to care about her would have to write his declaration on a stone tablet in blood. Bishop was the only exception. The man at her door was a one hundred and eighty-five pound human splinter. Old baggage. Excising him from her life was the first item on the sacrificial table. Failure was not an option. Unlike the men in her life, Lina never let herself down.

Swinging her feet to the ground, she leaned forward in her seat placing the petal pink vinyl bag she held on to the matching Adirondack table. The wide, dark pink shoulder strap snagged on the armchair pinning her in place. With care she dislodged the strap, gently folding the length over the bag's zipper. Inhaling the salt filled air, Lina pushed to her feet. The cool ocean breeze kissed her dark skin. She raised her face to the sun with a smile.

Sundays spent with the sun and sea was her favorite weekend past time. Ignoring the cacophony of fist pounding intermixed with cascading chimes, she spread her arms wide, allowing the seagulls' serene to usher in calm. The noise at the front door climbed another octave squashing her tranquil state.

"I know you can hear me. Open the door." She let her arms fall to her side. Time to discard the baggage. Turning around, she stalked through the open balcony door, crossing the glass and steel dining kitchen combo room en route to the front entrance. At the incessant knocking and unrelenting buzzing she reached for BETAS, the smooth hardwood stick she kept by the door. Jace would be the first person to experience the power of her wood deterrent.

A leather tie long enough to slip over her wrist held it suspended by a j-hook on the adjacent wall. She was thankful the beveled glass inlay door separated her from the intended target. Standing in her foyer, she offered him a final opportunity to walk away from her welcome mat.

"I have BETAS with me and we both agree it's in your best interest to get away from my door." Grateful it was Sunday morning, her neighbor usually slept until noon. The thought of Estrella witnessing a live breaking news event, she could do without.

"Betas. Who is Betas?" Steam that could rival a tea kettle rolled off her at his tone and inflection. He abandoned me and he had questions? Not in this lifetime, buddy.

"Lina." The singsong quality was gone. His voice was sharp with disapproval.

Lina grabbed the door handle, turned the lever, and pulled the door open a fraction. Jace's lean frame darkened a sliver of her doorway. For a moment, they both regarded each other, without exchanging a word. He stood in his white, long-sleeved button down collared shirt paired with a navy sweater vest. The dark blue and green pinstriped tie she purchased for his birthday knotted to perfection at his thin neck. Khaki Dockers and black oxfords completed the ensemble. She felt her brows bunch and her lips purse. The unwelcome intrusion had her fist tightening on BETAS.

The morning breeze carried the floral amber scent of his cologne through the partially open door. It was seventy-seven degrees in the shade. Most native Floridians would consider that hot for an Atlantic coast January. Coupled with the mid-morning humidity, the smell was about as welcoming as a park trash can. Bile rose up in her throat and she swallowed in succession. Gastric disaster averted.

"It's about time. I'm melting out here." Beads of sweat dotted his forehead and the bridge of his nose. The dark brown mess of curls plastered to his forehead were a sharp contrast to his pale blue eyes and reddening skin.

"Then go home." He moved to step inside her condominium, but her full-figure blocked his path. Considering she was two inches taller in her bare feet, he was the one to halt. He regarded her, irritation clear on his boyish face.

"Does he know I'm at the door?" He had the audacity to be territorial after the crap he'd done to her.

"Who Jace?" An image of her curling her fingers around his tie, pulling him close flashed in her mind. Feeling the warmth of his breath on her chin, while she inched the knot higher up his neck. Watching as he turned a kaleidoscope of colors before losing consciousness brought a smile to her face. To kill was sinful, but to choke was divine payback. Right?

"Do I know Betas?"

"No, but he wants to meet you," she gave a saccharine smile. The stick resting at her side seemed to pulse against her palm. The leather lariat around her left wrist felt tighter. She glanced downward, and he tracked her movement. His eyes came to rest on the stick in her hand. Eyes wide in alarm, he took a cautionary step back. Yep, caution warranted. She'd had enough of his drop by visits.

"Meet BETAS, my beat-that-ass-stick." Jace took a step back. "If I raise this stick above my kneecap, he doesn't go back on the wall until somebody gets their ass beat."

"Lina, be reasonable." Was he reasonable the night he ended their relationship? When he told her they were too different. From her wide nose to her, full lips, and even fuller hips, Lina was unmistakably an African American woman. According to Jace, being seen with her garnered too much attention. Negative attention.

"You at my door, gives me a reason to club you across the head and shoulders for every second of my life wasted." Looking him square in the eye, BETAS had his name in queue.

"It doesn't have to be like this between us."

"How would you like it to be?"

"I want to see you, sometimes. What will it take to convince you I'm the man..."

She interrupted his futile effort at this point in their non-relationship.

"Convince me you're a man by leaving, never to return." It was his decision that created this reality TV episode at her door.

"We can come to an agreement that suits both our interests."

"I have zero interest in a man that dumps me on our anniversary."

"Technically, I suggested we explore other dating options, but continue caring for one another's needs."

"You are going to need critical care if you continue," she hissed. "You could have told me it was over before you lured me to my favorite beach hide-a-way."

"I wanted you to be relaxed." This was her punishment for dating a clinical psychologist. Listen to the sound of crashing ocean waves, take deep breaths in and out while he ripped the beating heart from her chest. BETAS started inching upward.

"You are considerate," she offered with a smirk.

"I think I am." His shoulders dropped away from his ears as his hands relaxed at his side. Sarcasm wasted.

"You thought of everything, except that I wouldn't welcome you to my bed while you explored other options." The vanilla icing minus the chocolate topping on Jace's surprise after six months together—she was too curvy, too pigmented, and too ethnic for them to have a long-term commitment. All the attributes he claimed to love about her when they'd met. Of course, that was before the second glances and off-color remarks from his family. So why was he at her door? Ah yes. He wanted on-call booty privileges.

"It was never my intention for us to end. What is it going to take for you to forgive me?"

"Forgiveness was an option before you had me removed from my nursing unit." Scarlet crept from under his collar and spread to his face.

"You upset me by not taking my calls. I don't want things to end between us. We were good together." Now it was her fault that he sabotaged her career.

With damp palms, she squeezed BETAS, focusing her rising anger into the tense muscles in her arm.

"It's obvious Jace, good was not good enough." She stepped back to close the door and he reached for her.

"It's not like I had you fired." The hand gripping BETAS moved faster than her conscious thought, the horizontal plane of the wood made contact with his open palm.

"You don't get to touch me ever again," she hissed.

"You were fine with me touching you, before I said I didn't want to date you anymore," he drawled. There was a look of smug satisfaction on his face. Seriously? He challenged her because she refused to give up her goodies. She'd had her fill of this conversation.

"Insightful, but it will never happen."

"I miss you." Harsh laughter gushed out of her, spilling over them both.

"Did you miss me before or after your hand got tired?" She saw him drinking her in from head to toe. Blessed with Jill Scott curves that men craved, and then cursed to suffer the fallout once the novelty disappeared. She was fifteen the first time a man compared her figure to the Rhythm & Blues songstress.

Regret shone on his face. "Lina give me a break."

She was disappointed when their relationship dissipated, but to say she missed him would be a lie. Six months with Jace, paled in comparison to the single kiss she'd shared with the just-her-size psychiatrist on staff at Shell Cove Medical Center. She still wanted to drop her panties faster than the Falcon's Fury Free Fall ride at Busch Gardens theme park just thinking about Gideon. It was in her best interest to steer a wide path away from any man for which she held a remote attraction. The men in her life never stayed.

"You're right. I'm being snarky." He beamed at her comment. No doubt thinking he'd won her over.

She hadn't seen Jace's abandonment coming, but she should have.

"Finally, we are speaking the same language." What conversation was he a part of? For the first time, she had the opportunity to give a man his walking papers.

"Good, then I only need to say farewell once." She should have an online certificate mounted on her wall for a four-point grade average in mending a broken heart.

"What?" Jace questioned, his voice high pitched. Never one to leave a loose end, Lina looked him in the eye, as she launched the second strategic deterrent in her male detoxification plan.

"One more thing before you leave. Stop sending those awful white roses." His perplexed look made her ire rise.

"White roses symbolize innocence, chastity, everlasting love, and sympathy. The first three are inapplicable, and I don't need your sympathy, so stop sending them."

"But, I'm making an effort to..." She leveled him with a vicious stare. He stopped talking. She thought about the effort he put into planning their break-up. It was ingenious really—dinner, dancing, and a remote corner of the beach on a starlit night. Perfect.

"I have a new mantra thanks to you," she let a peaceful expression cover her face.

"What is it?"

Using the singsong voice he favored, she said, "No effort, no entry, and definitely no more jackassery." His mouth gaped out in silent outrage.

As if queued by some offsite director, Estrella's South American accent reached her ear before she heard footsteps.

"Lina?" Her new food buddy's warm olive face, bare of make-up and framed by shiny ebony locks came into view. She stood shoulder to shoulder with Jace, whose scowl resembled a petulant two-year old.

"Is everything okay?" Eyes rolling heavenward, Lina exhaled a large breath willing herself not to push Jace over the stone railing. Embarrassed, she turned to address her friend.

"I'm fine, Estrella. Dr. Harper was just leaving."

"I was not. We still need to talk."

"I should call the police." Though offered as a sign of support, Lina could hear the hesitancy in the other woman's voice.

"No, you should not," Jace said, in a raised voice. No doubt offended that she would suggest such an action.

"No worries, I have a friend here with me that's itching to make contact with Dr. Harper."

Taking in the added pallor to Jace's complexion he recalled that BETAS was ready for action.

"I wonder what would happen if BETAS accidentally…" Jace interrupted before she could finish her sentence.

"This is the way you want it to be between us?" She nodded.

"I'm done with you, boo boo."

"Colorful, Lina. You might change your mind."

"Too colorful for you, remember. Get off my doorstep before you have a leading role in the live adaptation of Misery." Jace smiled, but his teeth were clenched tight and his face had reddened tenfold in the past five minutes. Unsure if the burgeoning redness to his face was from the heat or heightened emotion she was tempted to offer him a bottle of water before she sent him on his way.

"I'll see you at work in the morning," he said. Now why did that sound like a threat?

CHAPTER TWO

A killer didn't belong in a hospital. In reality, he didn't belong anywhere or to anyone. Compliments of his tour in Afghanistan, Doctor Gideon Rice had more experience as an instrument of destruction, than as a psychiatrist, but failure was not an option. That's what his colleagues expected of his Wounded Warrior Recovery initiative.

Gideon stood at the psychiatric clinic's check-in desk looking out at the patient waiting room. Uniformed personnel filled the seats to capacity and he needed an experienced nurse in the next forty-five minutes. The clinic couldn't maintain this length of volume without appropriate staffing. He glanced down at the clerk seated in front of dual computer terminals.

"I'm going up to the inpatient unit. I'll be back before clinic starts with a new clinic nurse." The stout, gray hair woman winced before offering a wavering smile. He should be used to folks having low expectations for him. But after surviving a war and going on to complete his medical degree the snubbing stung more than he cared to admit.

The program allowed active duty Marines and sailors to receive mental health services in civilian outpatient facilities. Although the military worked hard to dispel perceptions, many combat veterans believed seeking mental health care within the military healthcare system ended their careers. The WWR initiative was the first civilian–military mental health collaboration between Queens Bay Naval Hospital and Shell Cove Medical Center.

The WWR was his baby, but delivering a healthy program with sustainable growth was proving more challenging than he ever imagined. The SCMC administrators never questioned the validity of his program, but rather the viability in a civilian healthcare setting. Marines were trained to be authoritative. Unfortunately, that behavior didn't take a back seat in group therapy. Several of the clinic staff members had requested to be reassigned before the first group of patients completed the program. He would find the right staff mix to help him save the clinic if it killed him.

Gideon released a sigh of frustration. Monday mornings at Shell Cove Medical Center were the equivalent of contracting a chickenpox infection one day a week and this morning was worse than most. He maneuvered through hallways of organized chaos responding to greetings from medical clerks, lab technicians, nurse practitioners, and a few physician colleagues along the way. If he broke stride or made eye contact for more than two seconds the clinic would start late and his patients would suffer the price.

Being a chatty Kathy, or whatever the male counterpart was, maybe a Talking Thomas, meant late appointments, angry patients, and long nights at the office playing catch up. The speed and focus he learned in uniform was applicable in the hospital. The doors to the psychiatric unit were in view when pediatric surgeon, Logan Masters approached with a day's worth of stubble covering his jaw and chunks of rusty blonde hair standing on end. Had he slept in the last twenty-four hours? Almost made it to the other side. Seeing his friend in distress Gideon came to a halt. The sun shaped replica wall clock with the eclectic blue hospital logo, read seven fifteen.

"Logan?" Gideon waited until the other man's eyes focused on him.

"Had to pull three slugs from a sixteen year old boy last night. The trauma team found an ounce of Galaxy in his pocket." At the haunted expression behind those blood shot eyes, Gideon felt the urge to start an impromptu therapy session. Galaxy was a combination club drug with the effects of both ketamine and GHB. Ketamine caused sight and sound distortion, with an out of body experience for the user. The amnesiac side effect meant it was a choice drug in sexual assaults. Gamma-hydroxybutyrate known as GHB on the club scene, could be mixed with alcohol or snorted. In high doses the drug could cause prolonged sleep, coma, or death.

"Was he a user?"

"He didn't have that sickly, sweet smell the users tend to radiate. He'll live, only to spend his life behind bars for dealing. It's the third Galaxy related shooting in four months." The drug had infiltrated the high schools, suburbia, and the military community. The potent combination coupled with easy access and low cost was both addictive and deadly. The affluence of the waterfront city wasn't impervious to the drug trafficking activities through the Southeast corridor of Interstate-95. Logan shattered the stereotype of a mild mannered gray hair pediatrician. The man was demanding, stubborn, and a control freak to boot. He wouldn't respond well if Gideon suggested they talk about his feelings or coping mechanisms.

Instead, he said, "How about we team up against Darwin and Graham this week on the basketball court or the golf course? Your choice." Gideon and Logan, along with his younger brother Darwin were frequent visitors to the local golf courses and basketball courts. Graham, an obstetrician gynecologist at the SCMC beach location was Logan's best friend since medical school. Johns Hopkins University graduates, the two men completed their residency program in the Baltimore, Maryland hospital.

"Can't this week," Logan replied. "Our engagement party is in two weeks and I want everything perfect for Ava." Logan's love for Ava was so intense, Gideon felt its presence whenever he was near either one of the lovebirds.

"How's the transition from civilian nursing to being a Navy Nurse going for Ava?"

"She's taken to military service like a sailor to the sea. I on the other hand, feel like a private escort when we're together and she's in uniform." Logan huffed out a laugh, a smile covering his face. Logan liked control. Ava dressed in her naval uniform would definitely shift the balance of power to the public eye.

"You're the doctor, but she's the naval officer. That makes you arm candy. Some men have a difficult time when the woman is in a position of authority." Logan's smile broadened.

"I'm looking forward to the day when I can say, my wife is ordering me around."

"Let me know if I can help out." Logan shook his head, his smile faltered.

"I might take you up on your offer. The rift between Darwin and Rebecca had an adverse effect on Darwin's disposition. A salt covered slug would be more helpful." Ouch. It was Gideon's turn to laugh. Darwin was the best man for the upcoming wedding. The grimace on Logan's face said he didn't appreciate Gideon's laughter.

"Graham would be happy to step up to the plate."

"That was the old Graham. Yvonne has his head messed up."

"Who's Yvonne?"

"Exactly."

Gideon, confused by Logan's comment gave him a dude I need more information look. Logan got the message and proceeded with an explanation.

"She's a doctoral student he met during his assistant professor gig at Howard University. They got close, then she disappeared on him."

"PhD students are a select, close knit group. He should be able to locate her."

"Great minds think alike. If she had given him her real name, I would agree with you."

"That's messed up."

"Yes, it is," Logan chuckled. "You are the only one out of us without trouble of the female variety." At the reminder of his single status Gideon masked a grimace. When the nightmares allowed him a reprieve to dream, one woman starred in his dreams. There was one woman he wanted to fill his home with their children. A curvy, cocoa beauty with an intelligent wit, and doe eyes. He hadn't found a woman willing to hitch her wagon to him for the long haul, including the one occupying his dreams. Lina James.

"How goes it with the ladies planning the wedding?" Gideon hadn't imagined it possible, but Logan's face darkened at the mention of the upcoming wedding.

"Both our families are planning the reception, except for my mother."

"Ouch." If Emma Rice was alive, she would be front and center to see one of her boys' tie the knot. She'd set up a candlelight vigil outside the honeymoon suite until an ultrasound confirmed a new addition to the Rice family was in the oven. Mothers were not created equal.

"Gideon, her hatred towards Ava is irrational." The pained expression on the other man's face made Gideon's chest tighten. Family was drama. Gideon understood that better than a lot of his colleagues with their traditional childhood. Unlike him, they could probably trace their heritage back to the Mayflower's pilgrim voyage.

His brother's phone call two hours earlier, urging Gideon to relinquish the title to his home, was the first chicken pox of the day.

"Let's get together after I give Ava her special day."

"You bet." Logan strode past him and Gideon continued on, family in the forefront of his thoughts. He had informed Ian, the lawyer of the family, Hell's Angels with grenade launchers would not get him out of his house. He would never give in. Though he no longer wore the uniform, a Marine never surrendered. His dream of a wife to share his life with and children was poured in the very foundation of that house. His custom designed home was a sharp contrast to the dilapidated shack of his early childhood. He'd created a new life for himself. Known associates and his previous life was a time capsule he'd buried years ago. In some ways, his current existence was similar to wearing a tailor made suit over well-worn jeans and a faded cotton shirt. He looked the part of a respected psychiatrist, but with less finesse, more bulky, and a lot of discomfort.

Of his five brothers, Ian was the one to force the family's stick together motto, followed by D.Wright, who was the oldest in the bunch. Gideon answered his phone if one of them called, that was enough of a family tie for him. His life was in Shell Cove. The taint of his previous existence was best left in the past. The only remnant he held sacred from his old life was the antique scrolled band around his neck.

Chicken pox number two was a lengthy text message he immediately forwarded to Ian. He wasn't going to read it today, or any other day in the future. The sender was dead to him. A skeleton recalcitrant to cremation, that refused to remain entombed. A bony shard stuck in a fleshier place than his backside. It had taken him years to block her name and image from taking shape in his mind. When she jetted on him, he never looked back to see where she landed. He wasn't the kind of man to run behind a woman.

The third chicken pox, he had the power to fix. An inexperienced nurse was assigned to his psychiatric clinic again. Her high-pitched, trembling laughter along with the smiling, rainbow colored daisy scrub top was indication enough that the woman was a poor fit for his patient population. The fact that she kept peering over the check-in desk with wide stretched eyes at each patient like she expected them to attack confirmed his assessment. Her discomfort was not missed by the waiting room occupants.

Considering a significant number of his patients were Marines, fresh from combat zones, they seemed to feed on her anxiety and patrolled the clinic like prison guards. This was the first civilian military collaboration of its kind at SCMC. His proposal received rave reviews, however, identifying staff members comfortable and competent to work with his unique patient population was tenuous at best. He'd lost two psychiatrists to transfer requests and more nurses than he could count.

Pushing through the safety doors, he scanned the inpatient psychiatric unit for the nurse in charge. The blare of ringing phones and the nasal quality of the overhead paging system filled his ears. He approached the nursing station. A stoic woman with thin blonde hair pulled in a severe ponytail was seated at the central monitoring station. She was red faced with an apple shaped body, stuffed into a camel colored knit cotton set.

"I need another nurse assigned to my clinic in twenty minutes." At the woman's vacant stare he rephrased his request.

"Good morning," he tried again. Her expression remained unchanged. "Get another nurse to my clinic in the next twenty minutes." That got her attention.

"I'm sorry Dr. Rice. There isn't another nurse available this morning. Check back after lunch."

"Lunch," he repeated incredulously. "My clinic ends at two o'clock," he ground out.

"That's the best I can do." Did she actually do something to help? He missed it.

"Call the nurse manager." Olivia Tran was the new manager at SCMC. No one asked how a woman of Vietnamese descent spoke in a distinct British accent and had a caramel colored complexion. Her penchant for dressing her wafer thin body in men's clothing to include a necktie and Rockport oxfords, pretty much assured it would be awhile before most women on staff would work up the courage to ask.

A throaty, soulful voice vibrated in his ear. His body tightened in response. He could identify Lina James' voice through the hum of morning activity. When his gaze landed on the statuesque beauty, he lost sight of everything except her. He stood still, as his brain short-circuited and the pox of the day gave way to the memory of their one kiss. He remembered the taste of her sexy bow shaped lips. The flavors of Georgia peaches, warm brown sugar and an exotic blend of sweetness unique to Lina. Recalling the warmth of her generous breast pressed against his chest, his gut twisted. He craved, dreamt of quenching his thirst with her intoxicating juice.

Blood roared through his veins, fueling his hunger for her. And the feel of those full hips snuggled into his groin had his fingers curling into fists at his side. At his six feet five inches it was a precious gift that Lina fit his height to perfection.

"I will not work in Dr. Harper's clinic. Find someone else for the position," he heard her say. His instincts signaled this was the prime opportunity to meet the needs of the clinic, take care of his patients, and get closer to the woman with the sweetest lips he'd ever tasted. Moving around the nurse's station he narrowed the distance between Lina and Olivia Tran, the nurse manager.

Lina wore a purple silk blouse draped across her generous breasts before tapering to her smaller waist. Black dress slacks rounded to her bottom tastefully, then slimmed over those hips that a man could hold onto for days. Black leather kitten heels with a peep-toe completed her professional, but all-woman ensemble. Her hair was in its customary chignon perched high on the crown of her head. Sexy full-figured pin-up girl. His groin hardened with each passing second.

Both women were focused on their conversation. When he spoke they both startled before turning to face him.

"Lina can work with me." He received surprised expressions from both women, but then confusion registered in Lina's dark brown eyes.

"Gideon?" He watched as she licked her full bottom lip. Her tongue charting a slow course of wetness caused the pressure against his straining zipper to increase. His world seemed to quiet looking down into her almond shaped eyes.

"I need you." The desire to help her overwhelmed him. He breathed in her sweet scent, smiling when he heard her voice hitch. Yeah, she felt the connection between them. He'd found a cure for Monday mornings.

CHAPTER THREE

She should have clubbed Jace over the head before he had the opportunity to cause her more trouble. Gideon Rice was man-fast kryptonite. She wasn't fooled by his polished psychiatrist persona. He was raw masculine power in dress pants and a lab coat. A body coated in warm sunshine, with waves of sun-kissed brown hair that never touched his collar. Edible panties naughty. She wanted to slide him over her curves in torturous slow motion, nestle him in tight enough to feel her heat, and then wear him all day until he was drenched in her scent. Her Cricket, aka her clitoris did a back flip before taking a position at the top of the high dive. Preparing to take the plunge into Gideon infested waters. *Stop it.* She broke in a silent rendition of her man-fast chant. Man-fast, man-fast, got to last. His body seemed even bigger standing between her and Olivia. The other woman was unaffected by his presence, while Lina's pulse pounded in her ears. Daily contact with Gideon was a temptation she hadn't factored into her successful male detoxification plan.

"Well, RN James you are in high demand this morning." Olivia's smile was genuine and Lina gave her the benefit of the doubt. The woman was unaware of Jace's antics over the past three months. His request had the appearance of a career enhancing move, but Jace only helped himself.

"How is that?" Gideon questioned in his rich baritone. Olivia squared her shoulders, faced Gideon head on, and smiled. Despite her masculine dress, when Olivia smiled her face was radiant.

"One of the psychologists has requested Lina by name for a permanent staff assignment." Pride was evident in her voice.

"Lina, what's going on?" Energy charged his words, a flicker of menace flashed in his eyes, then vanished.

The unit manager answered for her.

"I failed to convince her this is a wonderful opportunity." Lina gave an unladylike grunt.

"Lina thinks otherwise, Ms. Tran." The rumors about her and Jace must have reached his ears by now. Was he intervening because he felt sympathy for her? She didn't need his pity.

"The underground salt mines of Kansas would be more appealing." His brows drew together. He regarded her with open curiosity.

"I agree with you, Ms. Tran." Traitor. Lina leveled him with a vicious glare. "An outpatient assignment is an excellent opportunity for RN James," Gideon continued.

She ignored his conspiratorial wink and broad grin.

"Lina will work with me starting today in the WWR clinic." Her eyes shot up at him. And up. Gideon offered her a solution. "I'll have the nurse currently assigned to my clinic report to Dr. Harper immediately." Lina raised an eyebrow at his directive. He had an air of comfortable authority. A man with a history of giving orders. Less than twenty-four hours into her man-fast and the universe had plopped a warm, honey bun with mesmerizing gray eyes in her path.

"Go on, I'm listening." She hoped she sounded casual. Those stormy gray eyes fixed on her along with that sexy voice had her mouth watering.

"I need a seasoned psychiatric nurse to work with the pilot program between Shell Cove Medical and the Queens Bay Naval Medical Center." The specifics of the program she hadn't been privy to, but Ava worked with the military community health initiative at the treatment facility.

"I've heard about the program." She'd heard the Titanic had less staff jumping ship. "How are you involved with them?" She was interested to know how he was connected with the military community.

"I served in the United States Marine Corps before I went to medical school." *That is not an answer, Doctor.*

"Do you have combat experience?" Lina asked. His jaw tightened at her question. Hit a nerve with that one. She could see him grapple for the right words.

"I have an in-depth understanding of the psychological effects of deployment, physical injury, and personal loss on mission readiness." He'd said a lot, but she heard what he didn't say. The pain in his eyes said he had experience with injury and loss.

Maybe she should take her chances with Jace. There was zero chance of her falling prey to Jace's efforts at seduction. With Gideon she was in real danger of her man-fast going down in a fiery blaze, minus the glory. She could accept Jace's chicanery or face Gideon's temptation. Was she ready to accept the challenge of rescuing a worthy community health project on the brink of collapse? It was a chance to deliver herself from Jace's reach at the risk of her professional reputation and career.

"So, do you want to take me on, Lina?" Her breath hitched. Knees weak, limbs even weaker, she reached for the strand of pearls at her neck for support. *Don't answer that.* She and her man-fast were in trouble.

She wanted to take him on, but not in the way he was offering. Getting involved with another doctor she worked with was not a mistake she could afford to repeat. This was a possible win-win for her and Gideon.

"Which days are your clinic and what time would you need me in the office?" Heat flashed in his eyes, but it disappeared so quickly. She must have been mistaken.

"You will be with me five days a week, from eight to five." She was the one to look surprised. His patient profile was that large?

"Ah, I didn't realize your clinic was...," What was the word she was searching for? "Robust."

"Do you need more time to make your decision?" She would not start questioning her judgment today.

She swallowed at the thought of working with his taste bud teasing scent eight hours a day. That was five hundred and forty minutes of inhaling warm cedar and mountain air. Thirty-two thousand, four hundred-seconds being close enough to taste his flavor. She moistened her lower lip with a slow sweep, only to sink her teeth into her bottom lip to stop herself from smacking at the delicious thought. Gideon's throat clearing pulled her back into the conversation.

"I'll take the job." The angles in his face relaxed, she hadn't realized his tension until this moment. Did he really want her to work in his clinic? Was this about more than helping her out with avoiding Jace? She hadn't forgotten their kiss at the Preserves fundraiser. True it was for charity, but there was nothing charitable about the way he'd taken her mouth. She'd been hanging around the smooch booth with Ava while she worked alongside Logan. Gideon had approached the booth with the bribe of a substantial contribution to the pediatric medical innovations project. A project that funded Logan's Wound Care program. Gideon had his checkbook in hand when he approached the booth wanting a kiss from her.

The kiss started long before his lips made contact with hers. She heard the scrape of his shoes across the gravel as he stepped closer to her. Then she felt his heat when he closed in on her, the cool of his breath as it caressed her cheek, then he bent that six foot five frame to meet her six feet, willowy and waiting. Yep, she felt petite pressed into his mountain of packed muscle.

Thank goodness, she had worn her three inch sandals. She was at the perfect height when Gideon pulled her into his well-muscled, sun-kissed tan warrior, of hard man and closed his arms around her ever so gentle. Her nose settled perfectly at his neck, and then she tilted her head up and slightly back to claim her prize. And what a prize it was. If his big hands weren't at her waist, she would have dropped every pound she carried like it was hot.

Her blood sugar sky rocketed kissing that man. He was a Georgia peach cobbler and a slice of Florida pecan pie all rolled into one.

"We'll be good together." His deep, panty wetting tone pulled her back to the present and had her stifling a moan. She forced the air back into her lungs. Did he know what he was doing to her? He regarded her a moment longer, before he turned his attention to Olivia.

"Let's discuss the details of Lina's transfer. She'll be with me until…"

"Slow your roll, Dr. House. I'll be involved in any discussions involving my assignments." He might as well learn what he was getting. No one was making decisions for her. If he wanted a Florence, (the original) Nightingale, Florence of the Brady Bunch, or Florence from the Jeffersons, he needed to pick another nurse to work in his clinic, because she wouldn't last one day.

"I meant no offense."

"None taken, but I'm responsible for confirming my work assignments." He studied her now. This was it, he was going to withdraw his offer. More of the same, would any man take her the way she was?

"I trust you to work out the details. Just make sure no one will take you away from me." When both she and Olivia looked at him with wide eyes, he seemed to become aware of his word choice.

"The clinic. I mean." He cleared his throat several times in succession. "Excuse me, I will inform the current nurse that she is to report immediately to Dr. Harper's clinic." Olivia wiggled a disapproving finger at him. "Point taken, I will inform her to call you for further instructions."

"Thank you, Dr. Rice. I'm glad that we arrived at an acceptable solution for both you and Dr. Harper." Lina grinned as Gideon looked at the woman. How would he handle this? Gideon nodded in acknowledgment.

"Lina, I'll expect you within the next ten minutes." A gentleman.

"You can count on me. I'll be there for you." His jaw tightened. Steely gray eyes bore into hers. Was it something she said?

CHAPTER FOUR

Gideon wanted to kiss Lina for giving him the best Monday clinic of his career. She was the perfect fit for the clinic. And his life. The woman on the other side of his office door warmed him more than the sunlight streaming through his window. She considered saying no to his proposition, a voice whispered in Gideon's head. A sigh of relief left his body when Lina agreed to take the job. It felt like she was saying yes to him and the clinic. Sharing his day with her was somewhere between a godsend for his patients and an exercise in restraint for him. Images of him pressed into her full curves, suspended against his office door while he drove into her invaded his thoughts. Crazy as it was, his brain registered this as a step in the right direction. Lina James would be a permanent fixture in his life. He still looked at his life through the eyes of a Marine. Though he had only served one tour in the Corps, Marines went after what they wanted because life could be short. Short, sweet, and satisfying. Maybe he'd invite her for dinner. He wasn't ready for their day together to end. Finished with the day's medical documentation, he'd just settled back in his chair, when he heard raised voices at the print kiosk adjacent to his office.

"Go away, Jace."

At the mention of the other man's name, Gideon felt the tick in his jaw. He took in a breath, willing himself to remain in place. Confident Lina could handle herself. However, she was his now. His clinic nurse. He stood, and walked to open his office door. What greeted him when he rounded the partition wall made his breath stall. Lina was bent at the hips, lifting a file box. Jace stood behind her, his eyes wide in appreciation of her full derriere on display. A lavender purse, with a coordinating lunch bag were at her feet. The urge to throw a colleague out of his clinic had never been so strong.

"You working in this clinic is temporary. I'll get you back one way or another," Jace said at her back. Lina tossed an annoyed glance over her shoulder.

"And I want a sandwich, but you don't see me harassing the lunch truck guy."

"Dinner is an excellent idea. I could come over tonight. Cook whatever you like."

"You are expecting me to cook for you?" Gideon looked on as Lina abandoned her task. She stood up, and spun on Jace.

"It's not a requirement." Jace was an arrogant dung pile.

"The only thing I'll ever cook for you will be concocted in a cauldron with a league of Blair witches chanting around it like the Ya-Ya sisterhood." Good girl. Gideon loved her sassy mouth. Time to dispense with the banter between the two.

"You have two men at your disposal. What do you need moved?" Gideon took in Jace's offended expression that he was included in the daily man count for manual labor. Lina rose to her full height, and he smiled as each delectable inch stacked up perfectly over her rounded backside.

"Ah…Gideon, I should have realized you were behind Lina's failure to report for duty. You needed another passenger on this train wreck you call a clinic." Condescension filled his tone.

"Sore loser when another man beats you at your own game?" Gideon returned with a cool air.

"Think again, Rice," he spat. "You are a ruse, and I can see through your facade." A fissure opened in Gideon's calm and the man he once was reached for purchase. The psychiatrist in him said to defuse the situation, but the Marine said bring it on.

"Join me in my office, Jace. I know we can reach an understanding if we put our heads together." Gideon wasn't a violent man anymore, but he silently urged Jace to make a move. Give him a reason to wipe that smug expression of his against the tile, stone, and hardwood surfaces surrounding them.

Jace paled and took a step back. Gideon had to admit, the psychologist in Jace was good at reading subtle changing in body language.

"I'm leaving, but this is far from over," Jace said. The man knew when he was about to get a dose of Marine Corps medicine.

"Jace, RN James is a member on my staff." More if she let him. "My expectation is all your interactions with her are to be of a professional nature. You make sure of that or you stay gone when you leave."

"I beg your pardon?"

"No begging necessary, keep it professional or keep it out of this clinic."

"Look, Gideon."

Gideon advanced, until the other man was forced to take a step back. The look on his face communicated all he needed to know about Dr. Jace Harper. He never expected anyone to come to Lina's aid. It was a miscalculation on his part.

"Don't come in my clinic again upsetting Lina. Do we understand one another?"

"Lina and I have a history."

"Exactly," Gideon continued at the other man's puzzled expression. "You are history." They stood staring each other down. Jace broke eye contact, then stormed out of the clinic without saying a word.

He looked over a too still Lina. Was she upset with him?

"You okay?"

"Of course, thank you for standing up for me, but I can handle Jace." She shouldn't be thanking him. No man should stand by while a woman was bullied.

"I know you can, but you don't have to fight every battle alone." Her lips compressed as if she wanted to say more. Silence stretched between them.

"What does he want from you?" She released a sigh.

"He's on a hobbit's journey to get something he can never have." He laughed. It had been too long since he heard his own laughter.

"You are a funny lady, Lina James." She smiled up at him and his arousal shot from zero to sixty in under one nanosecond.

"You think so?"

"I do." Rubbing the back of his neck, he hesitated before broaching the subject of the clinic. "Lina, about the clinic's longevity."

"We are not going to fail, Gideon." The words held such conviction he found himself nodding in agreement. "I wouldn't give Jace the satisfaction of gloating." So it was about Jace, not them building something lasting together.

"You want him back?" Why had he gone there? Because the thought of her pining for Jace Harper had his fist clenching.

She frowned and he knew he overstepped a professional boundary.

"Not ever, but I wouldn't allow him to snub you. It's been challenging to remain in the department since Jace started wielding his authority against me."

"You are trying to protect me," he released a grin. A woman on his side—that was a first.

"I suppose I am," she teased him. "Doctors are trouble left to their own devices."

He reached for her hand. Manicured, square cut nails pressed into the backside of his hands. She was holding on to him, too. That had to mean he had a chance with her. "Let me take you out for dinner." Interest flashed in her eyes at the exact moment her smile vanished. She pulled her elegant hands from his grip.

"I can't do that," she said backing away from him. The pained look on her face was a mirror of what he felt at her rejection. She was looking at him when her foot made contact with her purse. He reached for her, but it was too late. The contents of her handbag spilled onto the floor.

He bent his long frame to help gather her things.

"I don't need your help." Her tone sharp, too sharp for the situation.

"You don't, but I'll help just the same." The purse had vomited the entire Nordstrom's cosmetic counter. She hastily tossed items into her oversized bag. He gathered a sunglass case, her turquoise ear buds and tube of *Kiss My Buns* lip color. Heck yeah, kiss her buns, her lips, her…

Distracted with fantasies of tasting every inch of Lina he was delayed in handing over her belongings. By the time he regained his common sense, Lina gazed down at his bounty, then up to his face. What she saw had her drawing in a sharp breath.

"I'll take that." She took the objects he held in his hand, then rose to her feet.

"I'll walk you to the elevator."

"No, you won't," she averted her eyes, tossed her handbag over her shoulder, and power walked toward the elevator bank. How had he messed that up? He dropped his head and a purple sparkle caught his eye.

"Lina," he called out. He heard the ding of the elevators ushering her away from him. Reaching down, he scooped up a rich purple, crocodile skin wallet with a smile. Had fate blessed him with an evening in Lina's company, after all?

Lina's hasty retreat to the safety of her man-fast bat cave came at a high cost. Her wallet with all her cash and one credit card was missing in action. It would either be on the clinic floor in the morning or one of the evening shift housekeepers would deliver it to lost and found. Either way she was screwed. Her gas tank was a hair's breath from empty and a jar of mustard was the only edible thing in the house. The confrontation between Jace and Gideon had her mind reeling. After the way Gideon stepped up to Jace, it's a wonder she hadn't left her panties and her wallet. Gideon was pure sex on a jumbo peppermint stick. One hundred percentage edible. She had never seen the two men standing together. Gideon was about nine inches taller than Jace. He had an additional forty pounds of solid muscle attached to his frame in all the right places. Jace was fit. Next to Gideon, he looked like Steve Rogers, before the Captain America transformation. Gideon was masculine perfection. But right now, she really did need that sandwich she mentioned earlier.

Usually Estrella had a dish ready on the stove, but when Lina knocked on the neighboring door it went unanswered. Who could she call to remedy her temporary hobo status? Her mother was in the midst of a major audit at work. Glancing down at her watch, Lina groaned, it would be another couple of hours before her mom was home. How much mustard could she eat before she got sick? Who else could she call?

Lina padded back to her condo. Entering her unit she collapsed on the couch, hugging herself as a feeling of isolation washed over her. There was no one she could call to help her. Lina turned a longing gaze at the kitchen, then an option occurred to her. She could call Janna.

Navy Nurse Corps officer, Lieutenant Janna Williamson was the third link in the dynamic trio. She'd flown into Shell Cove from Okinawa, Japan to help with Ava's engagement party. And Janna was scheduled to pick up Ava and Logan's engagement party favors from the engravers at six. If she called now, Janna could bring a gas can and take out dinner before her appointment. An independent woman creates opportunities for herself. She grabbed the phone from the cocktail table and dialed.

Lina jumped when the musical chime of the doorbell rang out. If Jace had followed her home, she was going to take a bite out of him. She'd left a message on Janna's cell before disconnecting the call. Placing the cordless phone back in the cradle she glanced at BETAS, before opening the door. Lina was not prepared for the man that greeted her.

"Hey, I thought you might need this." Gideon's powerful body filled her doorway and his long fingers had her wallet ensnared in his grip. Stay calm. Because of that dratted wallet, temptation had followed her home. His dark mane seemed to harness the sunlight. He looked like a fire god with sun rays silhouetting his body. Full lips and a chiseled jaw covered in a five o'clock shadow that softened the sharp lines of his goatee made her heart thud. His six foot five frame was clad in charcoal gray slacks with a light blue dress shirt hugging his broad shoulders. Perfect door ornament. She shook her head. Friends don't stare at friends' expansive chests. Her fingers tightened on the door knob. She forced herself to meet his eyes.

"Gideon, you brought my wallet." She smiled tentatively hoping he hadn't noticed her slow perusal of him.

"I didn't want to leave your identification and credit cards in the office overnight." She reached for it, only to have him pull it back.

"You gonna give it to me," she joked with him. Poor word choice.

"I wanted to take you to dinner first," he grinned showing pearl white teeth.

"You are funny, but I just ate some…" Her stomach growled so loud it rivaled a freight train leaving the tracks. Busted.

"I made reservations at Drury's. Do you want to change?" Of course, he chose her favorite restaurant and piano bar. The place was owned by Rourke and Gage Alexander. Two brothers, smooth as gourmet chocolate and just as sinful. Drury's boasted an open air terrace overlooking the northern coast of the city, which meant it was a hit with locals and tourists.

"Presumptuous much?"

"I'm rarely this close to the beach and I'm hungry. It's a win-win." He took a detour for her?

"I parked underneath the building, next to you. How long before you are ready to leave?" Her Camaro was three months new, how did he know what she drove?

"How do you know my car?"

"Are you serious? It's a purple Camaro and the tags say DIVA904." Should have seen that one coming.

"Enough said."

"Are you going to invite me inside?" This was her first man-fast challenge.

"Nope," came her high-pitched, quick reply. He smiled, those perfectly straight teeth with that come hither grin.

"You are serious about leaving me outside in a Hades heat wave?"

"I'll meet you at your car."

"Guess you like your men sweaty." She sucked in a breath. *Your men?* What did he mean by that? Was that a general statement, men in the vicinity of her person? Men in her life? Didn't matter. Twenty-nine days of fasting. No men-period.

"You're used to it, Marine."

"I promise to be a good boy, no touching." Too late on both counts. His voice was lapping at her senses like ocean waves caressing the shore. Touching all her neglected places. Everything about him was naughty, she liked it.

"I didn't bump my head when I left my wallet. We barely know one another. You want me to let you in my house while I'm in a state of undress?" Mock outrage apparent in her tone.

"I've kissed you once. Where I come from we're practically engaged." Her lips parted, and a sigh escaped. Just like that she was swept back into their kiss all those months ago. The weight of his lips pressed to hers. The warmth of his hand around her waist. His long fingers curled in a gentle hold around her nape.

"Oh," She was tempted to ask where he was from, but that would unlock Pandora's Box on her detoxification plan. Sensual heat warmed the front of her body, he had closed the distance between them. A growl filled the air, but she wasn't sure if it came from her mouth or her stomach.

"You're hungry." He had no idea how true a statement that was. "We can get to know one another starting tonight. Invite me in."

"I want to, but." Honesty hadn't got her far with men, but she couldn't change who she was. *What you see, is what you get.*

"Do it, Lina." He was the only man that had this effect on her. Lina James didn't suffer indecision. Just tell him you're on a man-fast and he can't come in… because he was in danger of her riding him like a rhinestone cowboy. The moment was too intense.

"Why do I get the sense we are talking about more than you entering my house?"

"We are." His matter of fact tone, surprised her.

"That sounds ominous."

"Not at all. I want a chance to win you." Her stomach dipped, flipped, and tripped.

"I'm not a game to be played with."

"No, you are a prize. I'm willing to do whatever it takes to bring you home." Everything she wanted to hear. Her soul cried out that he was the one for her. The man she'd longed for all her life. To man-fast, or not to man-fast, that was the question. Her next action would seal their fate.

"Give me my wallet. I'll meet you at the car in fifteen minutes." She plucked the *precious* from his extended hand before he reneged. She closed the door on an open mouthed Gideon. Man-fast, man-fast, how was she going to last?

Lina stood him up. Bold move considering he parked in the lot underneath her building. She would have to look him in the eye if she wanted out. Didn't mean he would give her a get out of dinner free card.

He delivered a single thud to the wooden frame.

"Lina, open the door." Thirty-five minutes and two trips around the parking lot to keep the air conditioning humming and she still hadn't exited her condo. He heard the click of the door lock. She must have been immediately on the other side, because the door opened and he was so confused he forgot to be annoyed.

"Why the heck are you wearing that god awful house dress?" Small metal snaps started under her chin and converged down to the floor where small clusters of butterflies became a winged swarm pooled over her feet. Unbelievable. Uncle Fester looked more attractive.

"I can't have dinner with you. I have a scratchy throat...cough thingy." She conjured up a feeble cough to support a lame, blind, and crippled excuse. He aimed a narrowed stare at her.

"I'll tell you what I think. You are trying to back out on me with a psychiatric patient cough routine. It's not happening." Her chin rose in defiance.

"You're entitled to think whatever you will." He raked his hands through his hair. Shaking his head to ward off the impending headache. All this to avoid sharing a meal with him. Would he ever be worthy? They could eat at her front door for all he cared, but he was not leaving.

"I'm not good enough for you to sit down and eat a plate of food with?" He pushed his words out through a clenched jaw.

Defiant chin now on her chest, she shook her head in denial, but he didn't believe her.

"Gideon that's not true. You can't believe that I would treat you that way." She reached for his hand, but he jerked away.

"Try me," he muttered. "Your stomach sounds like you're giving birth to a foal, but you feed me this brush off line." When would he accept his fate in life? Not today. Not with this woman.

"I don't think I can do it, Gideon." She looked down, but her expressive face looked grave. Why was she sad? He was the one being ditched.

"Unless I need to drive you to the emergency room, go grab your stuff. We can pick up cough drops on the way to dinner."

"Gideon...please."

Here comes the hard ball.

"I never took you for a coward, Lina." Her intake of breath was so sharp it singed his ears. Her spine stiffened. He leaned against the doorjamb, goading her.

"I'm not a coward."

"A shy, wallflower, then?"

"I'm not one of those either."

Gotcha.

A slow smile spread across his face. She handed him the advantage he sought.

"I dare you."

He saw the thrill of a challenge flash in her eyes, before she straightened to her full height meeting him eye to eye.

She curled each hand around the center closure of that hideous contraption and yanked the coat thing open. If it wasn't for the doorjamb he would be at her feet.

She wore a baby blue wrap dress trimmed in a thick band of bone white. And he noticed that her almond shaped eyes were rimmed in a cobalt blue that was purposefully smudged at the corners. Her hair was still perched high on her head, but the luxuriant strands hung loose, from a jeweled hair accessory.

"You look radiant, Lina." She hid behind pants and a lab coat at work. But this was the woman, not the nurse. A glow lit her cheeks. A subtle smile graced the lips that invaded his dreams.

"Thank you, Gideon." The soft, breathy quality of her words gave him the impression compliments were rare. Good heavens, the woman smelled of warm sunshine and a cool breeze. High heeled sandals with blue and white pearls were attached to the sexiest pair of legs he'd ever seen. He couldn't pull his eyes away from her. "And my face is up here."

He dragged his gaze up her full silhouette. "And what a pretty face it is." He gave her a wink. "Let's go."

Her face blanked and she gave him a stiff nod. She turned to walk away, but he grabbed her hand.

"What made you change your mind?"

"You issued a challenge. I never walk away from a fight."

"No, the first time. You are all dolled up for dinner, but you greet me with a Madea special on your back."

"Madea?" She was obviously surprised he knew of the grandmotherly movie character, that was in reality, an African-American man in a wig.

"When you're on deployment you watch what's available, when you have a free moment." The perplexed look she gave him was too adorable.

"For your information, that house dress was a gift from Jace." Why would a man buy his lady the ugliest garb he could find?

"And this has the sounds of an epic tale. We are both hungry, let's talk in the car."

"Let me grab my purse and a lozenge from the counter." He suppressed a laugh when she pushed out another pathetic cough. She released the door handle, which she gripped like the last life preserver, leaving it ajar as she moved through an elegant great room decorated in shades of purple and gray.

"You do that." He watched as she approached a bar height counter. She returned without incident.

"Your legs are gorgeous. Why do you hide them in pants?" She looked stunning, but her legs were game changers. They were just as curvy as the rest of her. She had curvy, full legs with feminine ankles slimmer than her calves. Lina was blessed with Betty Grable or Tina Turner one million dollar insurance policy legs.

"You're spreading it on kind of thick, Gideon." She tossed a smirk in his direction.

"Hey, whatever it takes," he grinned. "It's worth it for dinner with a beautiful lady."

"Whatever," her voice shook.

"You are nervous and there's no reason to be."

"Speak for yourself." She pulled the door closed, and moved toward the steps without a glance in his direction. She was feisty. Perfect.

CHAPTER FIVE

Dinner with Gideon was a mistake of epic proportions. A secluded table for two with candlelight and soft jazz was detrimental to the man detoxification plan. Why couldn't he be a lactose intolerant ogre who belched green gas that cleared a room? Instead, he was attentive and listened when she spoke. It was the best date of her life. An emergency man repellent plan was in order. Gideon was on the terrace taking a call from the hospital. *Think.* Hard muscles and smoke gray eyes wouldn't topple her man-fast resolve.

"The lovely Lina James graces us with her presence." Gage Alexander's husky voice resonated in the private alcove. Lina jumped to her feet and walked into his open arms.

"Hmm…it's wonderful to see you." She squeezed him tight. Rourke stood less than a foot behind his brother grinning like a loon. Both men were tall, with hulking shoulders, and clean shaven heads. Mischief sparkled in Gage's nut-brown eyes. Rourke the more watchful of the two, had eyes that rivaled the black diamond stud in his right ear lobe.

"Save some for me, Lina." She waved a dismissive hand over Gage's shoulder.

"There's plenty of me to go around."

"Not if my big brother has his wicked way with you."

"Both of you are terrible flirts," releasing Gage she moved past him to hug Rourke.

"Come here, you," he said pulling her in a grizzly bear hug. "You disappeared on us for months and all I get is a hug?"

She laughed but the sad truth of it was, she had stopped coming to Drury's. She had invited Jace to brunch in the early stages of their relationship, only to discover he hated jazz. He had looked uncomfortable for most of the performance. His lukewarm response eventually led to choosing more of what he referred to as mainstream entertainment. Mainstream translated into museums, live theater, and water sports, though he knew a boulder swam better than her. After their break-up it was all too clear he had issues. Drury's was another small piece of herself forsaken for a relationship with Jace.

"So true." She placed a chaste kiss on his cheek. "Is my debt paid in full?"

"We're in the black," Rourke teased her.

"Hey, I didn't get a kiss and I own the place."

"And you won't." Lina felt a band of steel around her waist before Gideon hauled her up close to him. He pressed her back in tighter to his solid wall of chest muscle as she stared up at him.

"What the flagnoid?" She tried to free herself, but wiggling would cause a scene. Plus it was impossible. His arm kept her welded to his body. This was ridiculous.

She twisted her neck to see Gideon glaring over her head at one of the brothers. He looked like a pale Godzilla preparing to terrorize small villages and the Upper West Side.

"Lina darling, who's your humanoid companion?" Gage wore an arrogant smile. Startled by the growl at her ear, she took a cautious glance over her shoulder. Gideon's handsome looks were replaced by a bull about to burst through the confines of its pen.

"Don't flirt with her." Gideon's voice was filled with gravel.

"Oh my goosebumps, play nice in the sandbox Gideon, please." She rubbed his arm anchored around her waist. All three men were locked in a Wild West standoff.

"Gage and Rourke are my friends," she whispered. Even with her feet on the ground, she felt as if Gideon was moments from carrying her off to his cave.

"I don't care if they are your priest. No one hits on my…you."

"Darling, this patient field trip was a bad idea." Gage was waving the proverbial red cape at the bull.

"Gideon is not my patient, Gage. Please be nice to my friend."

"That depends."

"On what, pray tell?"

"Did this guy eat the previous one?" Rourke joked.

Never one to back away from a difficult task, Lina raised her chin and answered the question. "The other one liked the packaging, but the flavor was too intense for public consumption. Catch my meaning?" Gage and Rourke regarded her with stony expressions. Both men treated her with sisterly respect. Admitting what had happened between her and Jace was difficult.

"And this one?" Rourke angled his head at Gideon.

"This one has an affinity for chocolate. Anymore questions, Rourke?" Menace laced Gideon's words. She had to add an estrogen burst in this sea of testosterone.

"Guys, Gideon is my new boss. It's not what you think."

"Says the woman with her feet barely touching the ground. Is your head in the sky, too?" Rourke had a valid point. Why didn't she think of that? Smiling at the men in front of her, she tried to still her lips as she spoke.

"Let me go," she murmured. His hold tightened. Warm lips touched her ear and she felt the caress of his breath. The mint on his breath tickled her nose.

"If you flirt with them, I'll toss you over my shoulder and walk out the door." She hoped that was a joke. Their gazes locked, and she recognized his determination to follow through on his threat. He eased her feet to the ground, but kept a hand at her waist.

"Gideon, you have a last name?" Gage was equally determined.

"Gideon Rice, and you are?"

"Last name is Alexander. My brother and I own the place."

"Is there a new hospital policy that every nurse receives this level of professional attention?" Gage eyed Gideon with suspicion.

"My concern is Lina. Only Lina." She couldn't contain her nervous laugh. Gideon was going all alpha male over her. Where was a news camera or the paparazzi when they were needed?

"It was wonderful to chat with you both. Gideon and I should finish our meal. We have an early day tomorrow." She moved to hug them both. Gideon bent over her left shoulder and spoke in a tone only she could hear.

"Fireman's hold, your choice." She halted in her tracks.

"I'll come by with Janna later this week," she said.

Gideon grunted behind her. She gave him a light elbow to the gut and whispered, "Keep it together, Rambo. Where did my high polished psychiatrist disappear to?" She reached behind her, a light stroke to the area she'd delivered the mock jab. The muscles of his abdomen tightened under her touch.

"Rambo was in the Army," came his husky reply at her ear. She shivered. She heard his low chuckle as desire snaked down her spine. A sexy Neanderthal.

"Tell G.I.Janna she owes me a re-match at the bowling lanes before she leaves town. Gage pulled my *man card* after she unleashed that fast ball on me. "

"Goodnight, guys."

"Bye, lil sis," came Rourke's base. "And Gideon?"

"Yeah?" Gideon was taut at her back.

"Make sure you take care of her better than the last one."

"I have Lina." Was there some male transfer of ownership process that she missed? She turned around and looked up at him.

Gideon extended his hand to Rourke.

"Nice place, you have here." Both Rourke and Gage came forward shaking his hand before they departed.

"What was that?"

"Man speak. Nothing for you to worry about." Man speak regarding her? She had reason to worry.

First Jace. Then the Alexander brothers. A face off with three men in the span of three hours. Lina attracted men like a moth to a flame. Gideon envied that talent. He had always been more controlled in his interactions with people. It had taken years for him to master the art of conversation. At this rate, Gideon had to be war ready to keep Lina at his side. After his run-in with the male models masquerading as restaurant owners, Lina suggested they eat on the terrace. Their conversation continued with a comfortable exchange of impersonal information. Had he overreacted when he discovered Lina surrounded by two men? Unequivocally no.

Half measure didn't exist in her vocabulary. Everything about her was pure pleasure to watch. The way she savored her appetizer and the way her body moved to the beat had him enthralled before their entrees arrived. Feminine poetry in motion. Their conversation remained superficial, but not for lack of him trying.

Gideon looked at her quizzically.

"Why did you stop coming to Drury's?" The conversation came to a halt.

"Jace, that is, we decided to focus our energies on activities we both enjoyed." A waitress with a sleek, spiked hair do arrived with their entrees just as the northwesterly winds ushered in a mist of sea spray across the restaurant terrace. The waitress suggested they move to an inside table, but Lina had declined. Her countenance relaxed with each kiss of the salty breeze against her now dewy, chocolate dipped skin. He was sure she would have just as much fun if he was not there. The thought was less than reassuring.

"I take it, he didn't have an appreciation for jazz?"

"Among other things," she said through pursed lips. "The wild mushroom ravioli in white wine sauce is a great choice. It is one of my favorites."

Clearly, he needed a safer topic of conversation.

"I'm glad you approve. Have you prepared it at home?"

"There's a reason I'm a regular here and at my neighbor's dinner table."

"You don't cook?"

"Can't, is an accurate description. My mom was the original Food Network sensation. I never wanted to learn."

"No one eats out every night." Turning she looked out over the ocean. He watched as she inhaled a deep breath, pushing her cleavage up and then down. Her shoulders relaxed and so did his. Mesmerizing.

"You should eat before your food cools." Time to change the subject. Compliments get you everywhere, he thought.

"I've never seen you in a dress." He whispered across the small table dressed in black linen.

She shifted uncomfortably in her chair. Compliments rattled her. He made a mental note to rattle her more often.

He leaned down closer savoring her sweet scent.

"Your legs are man tamers." Shock registered on her face.

"What did I say?"

"You're saying too much for a casual dinner between co-workers. My legs are compliments of sixty minutes of kickboxing four days per week." He was not repentant about his comment regarding her legs.

"I am not apologizing for telling the truth. Where I come from men compliment women." He liked her bold style, her intelligent eyes, and her body. Statuesque didn't fully capture the essence of the woman before him. Everything about her was built to suit a grown man. It was reflected in her runway fashion style, the body she wasn't afraid to showcase, and the witty banter she had for one and all.

"Thank you for the compliment," she said sitting back in her chair.

"Come here."

"What?" Cautiously she leaned into him. She must have thought better of it because she then pulled back. "Just tell me from here," she tossed a sideways glance in his direction.

"With your Ali bob and weave moves, it would be better if you leaned in close. You'll thank me later."

She moved within striking distance, and he trapped her chin between his thumb and forefinger. He brushed his thumb over the left corner of her mouth. She tensed, he let his hand fall.

"There was a drop of cream on your lip." Never taking his eyes off of her, he slowly raised his thumb to his mouth and licked. "Tastes sweet."

She must've been spring loaded, the way she shot out of her chair.

"I'm going to the ladies room. If our server comes, order me a grape crush cocktail." Seeing her like this, he was tempted to burn all of her work wardrobe.

"You need a stiff one to finish dinner with me?" A strained smile covered her face.

"A woman's got to do, what a woman's got to do." Confident and poised she remained, but she was on edge. He could feel pulses of her energy tracking him.

He reached into his trouser pocket and pulled out his personal cellphone. Extending his hand, he offered her the device.

"Add your information to my list of contacts." She didn't reach for the phone.

"Come on," he coaxed her. "I want to be prepared if that cough of yours should cause you trouble." She took the phone from his extended hand.

"Do you always hand your phone over to women you barely know? You're not afraid I might find incriminating pictures of you?"

He saw her eyes stretch wide, probably at discovering her name and address were already programmed into the phone. He smiled to himself. She tried not to notice how many feminine names were in his phonebook. She was about to return his phone when he spoke.

"You only added one telephone number." *Thank goodness he paid attention to detail.* "Give me your land line and your cell." She grinned, then did as he asked.

"There," she said handing his phone back to him. "Now, you have everything." She entered the restaurant, hips swaying to an inaudible beat made just for her.

Gideon watched as men, young and old, fixed on Lina's feminine stride. Those gorgeous legs carried her away from him. She'd said that he had everything. Smiling.

"Not yet, but I will."

Her heart beat faster than the lead drummer at a rock concert. Her entree wasn't the only thing steaming hot at the dinner table. At his touch, her body transformed into an overheated chocolate fountain without a shut off switch. He made her feel desirable and special. It was a sobering thought, as all her man problems started with those emotions. She could not like Gideon. As she walked away from the table, she renewed her chant in earnest. *Do not like him. Do not fall for him. Please let a unibrow troll replace Gideon in the next five minutes,* she begged the universe.

She tried to look unaffected by his charm, focus on the musical score and the buzz of conversation around them, but her blood pressure rose with each visual caress. Gideon was a gentleman, but with a raw edginess that appealed to her on a primal level. The way he swept her into his arms and held her close, had her body pulsing with need. If Jace tried that move, they would both be on the floor, with him writhing in pain. She rounded the stone waterfall sculpture leading to the ladies' room. She opened her purse, approached the mirror, and reached for a make-up compact, while regarding her appearance. Beauty looked back at her. Beauty that men admired, craved, but never claimed. Would Gideon be any different? Her heart couldn't pay the cost to find out. When she returned to the table, she would put as much distance as physically and emotionally possible between the two of them. Numb was her goal. Let it happen, but do not feel it. Yes.

The banging at the door had her jumping for the ceiling. She did a quick check of her surroundings before looking in her purse. Keys-check, wallet-check, lipstick-check, pepper spray-check. Purse in hand, she took a deep breath, steeling her resolve to handle the rest of dinner in cool detachment. She collided with a wall of muscle as soon as she exited the door. Her feet had stopped, but the force of the impact had her body moving backward. This wasn't going to be pretty. She closed her eyes readying herself to make contact with the stone floor. An arm wrapped around her waist pulling her up short.

Gideon.

She instinctively grabbed hold of his shoulders, needing to hold onto something solid. Her nose was in the hollow of his neck and she took a deep steadying breath. He smelled of warmed cedar on a breezy summer day. Her mouth watered as his scent filled her nostrils.

"Thank you," she said on a breathy note. She allowed her head to rest on his shoulder as his scent and body heat co-mingled into a sensual cocktail.

"I've got you, sweetness." His hand stroked along her spine in a soothing gesture.

"I didn't see you standing there. It was my fault." His cheek pressed against her temple.

"Shh, it's not your fault. You weren't expecting me to be at the door."

She laughed. "That is true. I don't remember inviting you with me to the ladies' room." Through her palms resting on his chest wall she could feel the rumble of his laughter.

"You left the table fifteen minutes ago. That's an invitation to chase in my neck of the woods." She released his shoulder, to look up at him.

"Neck of the woods? I haven't heard that term in years. What part of the country are you originally from?"

"I was born and raised in West Virginia."

"Big city or small town West Virginia?" He raised an eyebrow at her line of questioning.

"They are one in the same in mountaineer country."

"You didn't answer my question."

"I did, trust me. Now, allow me to escort you back to your seat. You garner a lot of attention, Lina."

She stiffened. Had she misjudged him? Guardian angel of curvy women please don't let him be a Jace Harper disciple.

"I have to follow you around to make sure no other man snatches you away."

The tension slowly left her shoulders.

"I'm a big girl, Gideon." She gestured her hands up and down her body. "This is not a snatch and grab sized package."

"I'm a big man and I like handling a package just your size." She blushed. Thank goodness he couldn't see it with her darker complexion. She admitted to herself that she did like Gideon. More importantly, she accepted that she couldn't act on that attraction. Focus on protecting yourself. Boundary management would be her last course for the evening.

CHAPTER SIX

He didn't know what he did or said, but their connection from early in the evening was officially gone from high-speed to dial-up. Gideon could feel the distance between them, tangible as the shirt covering his back. It was a quarter past ten when they arrived at her condominium. Even the night creatures kept a low profile in the humidity. He was thankful Lina hadn't balked about him not wearing a tie. She hadn't recoiled in horror when he slipped up, responding to her question with *yeah* instead of *yes*. Gideon could be himself with Lina. He freed his second button as he rounded the car. She wasn't running to her door. That was a good sign. Opening the passenger door he extended his hand palm up for her. It warmed his insides that an independent woman, such as Lina, could defer to a man the courtesy of allowing him to get her door. She hesitated a moment before placing her much smaller hand in his. He maintained his grasp on her hand as they walked to the stairway. He shouldn't ask, but he didn't want the night to end.

The scent of flowers assailed him when they reached the landing to Lina's place. He looked down to find they both were stepping on crushed, white rose petals.

"What's with the flower covered walkway?" Lina pushed out a breath, shaking her head.

"Jace must've stopped by while we were at dinner. The roses started after our break-up. I told him to knock it off." Gideon regarded her with skepticism.

She shrugged her shoulders in bewilderment. "I guess crushing them was his way of retaliating after my confrontation."

"He seems determined." Jace's actions were disturbing. Lina didn't appear to be concerned about her safety, but he was. "Is there a chance he believes the two of you could reconcile?" He searched her face. Women could hide their emotions in plain sight. He knew that from experience.

"Not humanly possible." She formed a large cross with her forearms. Then added head nods in the negative. "He's been a brat since he dumped me." Gideon's mouth slackened. His thoughts scrambled. What man in his right mind would ever leave Lina behind?

"Jace Harper ended your relationship?" Disbelief clouded his better judgment and reached for her. Closing his hands around her bare upper arms.

"You doubt me after one night?" He liked her joking with him.

"I never doubt a lady, but it's about the stupidest decision I've heard of a grown man making in recent years."

"Keep up the flattery. It'll get you nowhere, but it's nice to hear."

"I'm serious." He looked down at her. Taking in her firm upper lip and the stubborn chin, it was clear she didn't believe him. "One man's rhinestone is another man's diamond."

She laughed, but it didn't reach her eyes. The reminder of being discarded was far from amusing. It reminded him of his own humble beginnings.

"You are good for a woman's ego." He caressed her shoulders, but the playful Lina was gone. Before he thought better of it, he pulled her into a warm embrace.

"You are worth more than diamonds, rubies, and pearls." The words whispered at her ear had no effect. What words could he say to draw her out of her head and back to him?

"In my neck of the woods, we have a saying. One man's fling is another man's future." Challenge issued. Would she take the bait?

"Oh…that's good, Gideon. The problem is every man I encounter tells me, I'm his future. The onus is on me to realize when I've been downgraded from future to fling." She stepped out of his embrace. The night seemed cool without her warmth. Words like humble beginnings had been used to describe his childhood. A camouflage for being poor and unwanted. To have humble beginnings attached to your family name was a politically correct phrase for abject poverty. It made social and economic inequality more palatable to the societal elite. In his hometown of Waverly Falls, his birth name was synonymous with worthless. That was the reason he'd taken his adoptive family's last name-Rice.

"Everything about you is pure platinum." He didn't think it was possible, but she backed up against the door creating what felt like a canyon sized space between them. He didn't like it.

"You are like a brainiac, eye candy, and a hallmark card all rolled into one. The ladies need a stealth detector around you," she said.

"I'm only interested in one lady."

She gave him an "is that so" look.

"How interested?"

"Is there anyway you've changed your mind about me coming inside?" She raised her eyebrows, eyes stretched wide.

Raising both his hands, palms facing her. "I just want us to talk." She sighed as if coming to a decision.

He pressed his luck, hoping favor rested on him tonight. "Invite me in." He sent up a silent plea to fate.

"You have about as much chance of getting inside, as me frying my brain cells with a curling iron. I'm well acquainted with that type of interest. You coming inside is a bad idea." He released a sigh.

"What's stopping you?" A crease formed between her brows. She took a deep breath, then slowly released it as if reinforcing her force field. There was one more step before she would be on the other side of a closed door. He played his hand.

"You've spent the last four and a half hours in my company. You are safe with me and you know where I work. Let me, come in." She laughed at his last comment.

"Why do I get the sense we are talking about more than you entering my house?"

"I am, but, we both know nothing will happen if there's only one interested party. So, are you interested in getting to know me?" She narrowed her eyes with suspicion before taking a step back. That first kiss must have scrambled his brain. He was sending the wrong signal.

"Why did you ask me out tonight?" The wide stance, and arms crossed over her chest said she was ready for battle. It was a mistake to hint at more tonight.

"We have a connection. I enjoy talking with you. You're no longer entangled with what's his name."

"Gideon we work together." He could see where this train was leading.

"And technically, you are assigned to my clinic. I'm not your boss." She placed both hands on her generous hips. He grinned at her. He would not make it easy for her to get rid of him.

"I never knew you were such a smooth talker. Seriously, we've seen each other every day for practically nine months and you've never shown any interest in me until today. And before you mention the kiss, that doesn't count because it was for charity."

"Wrong on both counts. You have never noticed my attentions until today and any kiss between us counts." She was looking at him with a curious expression, then she frowned.

"You know that Jace will keep trying to get me transferred at best, fired at worse." Something akin to pain crossed her face, then it vanished.

"I overheard something about that. I know things went wrong between the two of you. I did what I could to help you." Her back went ramrod straight, then she took another step away from him. He didn't like the way she looked at him.

"I don't want your charity date, Gideon. I have never needed a man to take care of me, and I certainly will not start tonight." Anger colored her words.

"I know you can handle yourself. You did a darn good job of handling my clinic, too." The smile she gave him, had him hitting himself upside the head for waiting until tonight to comment on how efficient she ran the clinic.

"Thank you, Gideon. I really appreciate you telling me I made a difference."

"You came to my rescue this morning."

"The nurse rescuing the Marine? Sounds like we both felt charitable today."

"When I look at you the last thing on my mind is charitable works." He took a step closer to her.

"Since you broached the subject. What is swirling around in that big brain of yours, if you were to get into my house? How do you see this playing out?" She pointed to herself then aimed her index finger center mass at his chest. "What's your angle?"

"I told you earlier today. I don't have the tolerance for games." His statement seemed to unruffle her feathers. Her posture relaxed again.

"I'm going in the house. Thank you Gideon, I had a perfect evening."

"Perfect. That's an interesting choice of words, how so?"

She groaned aloud. "When will I learn? I should have known better. Never say the word perfect in the presence of a mental health professional. Gideon, let's end the night without a psychoanalysis." There was a bit of hostility as she spoke his name.

"Lina." He touched her left cheek. He made slow brush strokes across her right cheek with his thumb. "Tell me what made the evening perfect, because I want to know what pleases you." He'd revealed too much, but the damage was done.

"I'm listening, Lina. Tell me what you want."

He's interested in my pleasure. He wanted to know her. Her heart skipped two beats. She parted her lips taking a deep breath to regulate her pulse rate.

"I loved our ocean view seating. I prefer water, large or small over gardens and woods." His touch was soothing, but this contact wasn't like earlier before they left for Drury's. This touch was sensual, the pressure was slightly deeper and the movement was slower. A lover's caress.

"What else did you like?" The rich tone of voice penetrated her thoughts. His fingers were strong and sure.

"It's nice to share a meal with someone who enjoys a variety of food. I like jazz and R&B, so sharing great food with live music filling the air is a heady combination for me."

"And?" He prompted.

"And...I enjoyed your company."

"So, having me near you helped to create your perfect evening?" He was stroking her lower lip now. Deliberate, but feather light. The pad of his thumb grazed the border of her lip en route to her cheek. Then he would repeat the trek.

"Yes, I suppose it did." He lowered his eyes to her mouth. His attention was on her lips as she spoke. Lina felt the hunger in his eyes, a caress as tangible as the clothes she wore. She extended her tongue to wet her lip. Lost in his eyes, Lina didn't realize she'd licked his thumb until her tongue slid off the tip. They both stilled. She cast her eyes up gaging his response. The surge of heat burning in his eyes, had her insides melting. She locked her knees together, afraid Cricket might force her to call out his name, but his arm slid around her waist pulling her closer.

"Ah, Gideon, I didn't mean to do that." This was embarrassing. Was there a rule of etiquette on how to apologize for licking a gorgeous man's finger? A very tasty finger. Now she squirmed in his arms.

"Be still. Tell me what you didn't mean to do."

"You know. The accidental tongue to thumb thing."

"That was an accident? I thought we were starting some male-female mating ritual. I stroke you, you sample me." A devilish smile crossed his face. She was grateful for the reprieve his teasing provided.

"You've got jokes. I don't go around licking men on my doorstep."

"Like I said before, I'm not trying to analyze you. You could tell me what you like, but it's better when you show me."

"Hate to break it to you, but all the questions equal an analysis." He grinned but she was in awe of the entire day. "You are not what I expected Gideon Rice." He seemed more comfortable like this, than earlier in the evening. This seemed natural, more organic. She was privy to a side of him few people got to witness. This side of Gideon was congruent with what she gleaned from the evening together. Gideon and Dr. Rice were two halves of a different whole.

"And you are more than I hoped for." She released a breath.

"I should probably go inside. Thank you again for a wonderful evening." At his raised eyebrow she corrected her response.

"The evening was perfect." She was learning.

"It was. When can I see you again?"

"Gideon, please don't feel obligated to ask me out."

"Why would you say something crazy like that? Not one thing I've done tonight communicated a hardship on my part. Accidental thumb licking or not, you like me well enough and I sure as heck like you."

She double blinked at him. "I didn't mean to upset you, country boy. Your country roots sure roar back to life when you get agitated." Some unreadable expression crossed his face before she could register the meaning. He was clenching and unclenching his jaw. She had upset him. That wasn't her intention.

"I'm just saying you don't have to get involved in my drama."

He ran his fingers through his thick, dark locks before speaking. "I'm not talking about drama. I'm talking about us spending time together."

"Gideon, I'm on a thirty day man-fast." She said it. Now he would turn around and leave. Temptation averted.

"What the heck is a man-fast?" He'd sealed her in. His large hands were planted on the beveled glass door, on either side of her torso.

"It's a suspension of all romantic involvement with the male species." The tic in his jaw was nothing compared to the sound of the grinding of his teeth.

"How long?" His question confused her. He should be walking away. Other men left her without the limitation of a fast.

"How long for what?"

"How many days until the fast ends?" His voice grated with a metal on metal quality.

"Thirty days minus…"

"Stop stalling, Lina."

"Twenty-nine days and one hour." Her voice was sure and steady.

"This thing started today." Gideon voice climbed an octave. "Cancel it."

"I had fun, but nothing can happen between us. This is the end, not a beginning." She turned within his cocoon, inserting the key in the lock.

"Lina?" She turned, letting her eyes meet his and she wish she hadn't. Firm lips pressed to her forehead and lingered. He pulled away first before it occurred to her to push him away.

"It can and it has. The story of us began the first time you let me taste those sweet lips." She sucked in a breath and with it his scent, and just like that all the well-defined boundaries of her life blurred.

"Good night, sweetness." This was the opposite of good.

She gave up the forehead on the first night. His lips had touched her body. Lina's chin fell to her chest. Not her best idea to start a man-fast following a starvation diet. She could hear him whistling a country ditty as she collapsed against the closed door. He meandered away from her door like a man pleased with his progress. *He's a good kisser.* Usher's song would be at the top of her playlist by morning. His kiss had been sure, light at first touch, then a steady increase in pressure. His moist heat lingered on her skin, burning up her insides. Why didn't she pull away? He had offered her a sample of premium white chocolate, but when she readied herself for a full portion, he had put it back in the wrapper and put it away. He would load it in a 2015 gun metal gray Cadillac sedan and drive it down the highway. He was worse than an insidious white collar criminal. Gideon Rice was a candy thief.

"It's better this way."

She couldn't contain her smile. He'd given her an unexpected gift and she felt good. No, she had surpassed good and skyrocketed to great. The reserved psychiatrist had a Casanova effect on her common sense. She hadn't lied about wanting to invite him inside for the night. Her skin still tingled from his touch. A touch that was firm, sure, and heated. There was nothing tentative about the man. And those gray eyes. They were intense and ever watchful. The kind of eyes a woman could get lost in for hours-the gray seemed to roll like storm clouds when he looked at her. She could see his desire lurking beneath his controlled exterior. Her three inch heels echoed on the tile entryway as she bounced on her toes. She could get used to utilizing her extensive footwear collection. She no longer had to consider height challenges on her dates. She halted. The realization that she had envisioned herself dating Gideon had her kicking off the conspiratorial heels, followed by the control top pantyhose. She picked up all three items, moving through the darkness toward the custom designed closet in the master suite.

She started to sing a *Linearized* of the late James Brown's "I Got You" as she undressed.

"I feel good, dada dada dada, da, I didn't know that I would." Her voice rang out bouncing off the walls in the bedroom as she danced across the floor in her bare feet. "I'm so good, so good." She gyrated her hips to the beat in her head. "Coz, I got somebody new, dent dent dent dent." Wrong. Man-fasting and considering a relationship were diametrically opposed ideas. Opening her heart to Gideon was a foolish consideration. She did one full twirl then took a deep bow imitating the Godfather of Soul. It felt good to sing again. She rose from her concert bow, she extended her right arm, pressed the room light control, and froze. Body ridged, eyes wide, she unleashed a scream that ricocheted off every object in the bedroom.

The scream slashed through Gideon's detailed plan for his next date with Lina. A woman's scream from years gone by echoed through his brain bringing back memories of his failure.

Turning, he raced back to Lina's door, as the screams intensified. Lina's condominium resembled a large, single family beach house. Grabbing the door lever, he found it locked.

"Lina!" "Lina, open the door."

Preparing to kick the door lock, he loosened his stance when she opened the door in bare feet with a long, hardwood stick raised over her head like a police baton.

"I heard your screams. What happened?" At her silence the hairs on the back of his neck stood on end. Lina didn't suffer a loss for words often.

"The scream, Lina," he prompted her.

"Someone broke into my house." Her words came in a rush. Protectiveness and anger spiked through the very core of his being. The need to protect her besieged every fiber in his body. She was blocking his entrance to the entryway.

"Let me come inside." He was thankful that she didn't hesitate. He'd alienate any threat to Lina.

"You stay by the door," he told her. This was not the time to ask politely.

"You'll get no complaints from me. It's in my bedroom." Her bedroom? She pointed to a flight of hardwood stairs that lead to a loft overlooking the living area.

He looked her over, reassuring himself that she was okay. Lina was rigid from head to toe as if preparing to attack or to be attacked.

Gideon moved in the direction she pointed. He scanned the surrounding space as he moved. Her living room combined with the dining area and overlooked a stone balcony with a view of the beach. With the hour nearing eleven in the evening the starlit night was beautiful. The house was immaculate. Her bedroom was off the far corner of the formal living area. He pushed away the fleeting thought that the intruder was someone who knew her house, and exactly where the bedroom was.

The metallic odor was the first red flag. A rectangle rhinestone studded headboard covered half of the right bedroom wall, in the center of the royal purple duvet were at least a dozen white, long stemmed roses, dipped in crimson liquid. *Blood stained roses.*

Gideon recalled what Lina told him about Jace and the roses, but breaking and entering to leave a blood-soaked message spoke to a more sinister intent. No man in his right mind would consider bloody roses a reconciliation gesture. Bending low he examined the lock on the bedroom door leading to the balcony. There were no visible signs of tampering. The hairs on the back of his neck were tingling. This stunt required pre-planning, timing, and patience.

He hadn't noticed anything out of the ordinary about the surroundings when he picked Lina up for their date. But dense woods surrounded her dual unit condominium. It would be easy for a perpetrator to hide until the opportunity to enter presented itself. He had more questions than answers at this point. He knew he wasn't leaving Lina alone tonight.

"Gideon? Is everything okay? BETAS and I are ready if you need us."

Not hearing anyone enter the condo, Gideon started towards the woman waiting for him at the door.

"Who is Betas?" Lina aimed the hardwood stick approximately the length of a baseball bat, but half the diameter in his direction. The way she held the thing, he was hesitant to get too close.

"Dr. Gideon Rice, meet BETAS." Gideon looked on as Lina gripped and released the smooth shaft of wood in comfortable familiarity. Gideon swallowed and willed his country boy thinking back into the barn.

He pointed at the stick then at the floor. She was slow to lower the wicked looking instrument.

"You named a stick?" She shrugged.

"I got it as a housewarming gift four years ago."

"From who?" He tilted his head, interested to know who would give her a weapon.

"My mother if you must know."

"It's an unusual gift, don't you think?"

"According to Bernadean James, a woman has to take care of herself." He surveyed the room during her explanation.

"I don't see any signs of forced entry from the balcony door. Who has a key to your house?"

"My mother. Oh, and Janna. She's storing Ava's engagement favors in my guest bedroom."

"Not Jace?"

"I answered your question, counselor." He held up his hands in mock surrender.

"Sorry, I know a lot of women give their boyfriend's keys to their place."

"Jace never had a key." Knowing the other man hadn't earned the privilege to enter Lina's domain at will, set a part of his mind at ease.

"I think you should alert the authorities. Is anything missing or out of place in your bedroom?" She lowered the stick and pressed the fingers of the opposite hand to her left temple.

"I'm fine and nothing's out of place. But you're right. I should call the cops. I'll see you to the door." He didn't budge.

"You have two choices. You come with me or I am staying the night with you. I'm not leaving you alone knowing there's a potential threat to your safety. I'm not convinced this is Jace's actions, maybe an unknown assailant entered your home." The roses he could accept, but to secure blood, most likely from an animal source, then dip each individual one in blood with meticulous care, led him to think a more sinister plan was at work.

"What's on the other side of the living area?"

"Another bedroom and bathroom are beyond the kitchen. I rarely use that side of the house."

"I'll go search the other spaces. You stay in this spot until I come back." He could see the protest forming with the slight twist of her mouth. "Lina, I need to know where you are in the house." He settled a determined look on her, he waited for her to accept his words. Patience earned him a stiff head nod. Reluctant, but he was sure she would do as he instructed. Gideon proceeded with his plan to ensure Lina's safety and secure the perimeter.

"Call the police, while I check out the rest of the house."

"I will, but first…"

"No buts," he said, pointing in the direction of her bedroom. "That scene on the bed is a message. A calling card. Get the police here, first, anybody else can wait." Lina James did not respond well to directives. That made for an interesting dynamic in a nurse. "Who might want to scare you?"

"First, I'm not scared. If anyone comes in this house uninvited when I'm here, they are going to get a kick from my whip ass shoes and a taste of BETAS." A fierce warrior princess. Greeting him at the door with her humanized battering stick told him she brought the war to the enemy. Just like a Marine. He would give just about anything to call her his own. Running a hand through his hair, he refocused.

"Any names come to mind when you think about pulling out the whip ass shoes?"

"Other than Jace, no," she said, deflated. "I've lived here for four years without incident." He believed her.

"Remember, you stay here, no matter what." Mindful, he made a slow approach to the closed guest bedroom suite. Even without his Kevlar boots, he kept his steps nimble, and light in his leather soled dress shoes. Out of habit, he reached for his sidearm weapon. A maneuver he'd done hundreds of times as a Marine in combat. His hands met a cell phone holster. It wasn't there. Lina's guest suite was equally decorated as the rest of the rooms, a bold mixture of texture, tone, and shades of the color purple. Both bedrooms had the look of a magazine layout for seductive boudoirs.

By the time he closed the guest bedroom closet, he could hear a car pulling into the parking area. When he walked into the living room Lina was peering through the wooden shuttered windows in the living room that faced the parking lot.

"Is it a patrol car?"

"No, it's my neighbor, Estrella."

"How long has she lived here?"

"A few months, give or take a week. She's originally from Peru, she moved here because of her job."

"Husband or children?" Huh. A woman that traveled out of the country for work. The women he'd grown up with believed in staying close to home. The residents of Waverly Falls didn't venture far from the stable.

"She never mentions a family." Neither did he.

"You know her well?"

"Well enough. She's been supportive since things went sour with Jace." Lina didn't strike him as the type of woman that needed a shoulder to cry on. He rubbed his forehead at the image of Lina shedding tears over Jace Harper. "She cooks, I eat." Ah. He could reconcile that kind of support with what he knew of Lina.

"Sounds like a good arrangement."

"It works for me. Being trapped in the kitchen with raw ingredients and a cook book is equivalent to running with wolves, risky and detrimental to my well-being. I'm not sure what Estrella is getting out of it, but it makes her happy to watch me eat."

"It would make me happy to see you eat too. You enjoy your meal with all your senses." She narrowed those chocolate eyes on him, for the second time this evening.

"There you go pouring on the syrup." He watched as she shook her head as if to remove a cobweb.

"Is that your way of calling me sweet?" He asked.

"Yeah, you are too sweet."

"There is no such thing, you just have to take incremental doses until you can increase your tolerance for what I have to offer." She rolled her eyes, but offered him a smile. He'd take it.

"Lucky for both of us, I'm not accepting any offers." Her words pulled him up short.

"There's an easy remedy."

They were facing each other when she spoke.

"Relationships are not my strong suit. I am determined to complete my thirty day man fast."

"Twenty-nine days," he corrected.

"Yeah, I may extend it. Make sure I'm good and ready for the real thing."

No way on earth would she complete and/or extend this fast on his watch. Plus he noticed her eyes darted to the left with that last sentence. Meaning it was a lie or half-truth. The observation techniques he learned in the military still served a purpose.

Watching the woman named Estrella ascend the stairs, Lina pulled the door open before he could stop her. Immediately, Gideon stepped in front of Lina.

"Gideon? What are you doing?"

"Someone could be watching you." It was a possibility he had to consider. The stalker could be watching how Lina responded to his message.

"Estrella, come inside." Estrella stopped outside the door, but didn't move inside.

"It's late chica, we can rendezvous in the morning," Estrella said.

"Someone broke into my house and left bloody roses on my bed." Estrella's tan skin, paled. Eyes wide she took stilted steps into the room. Gideon hadn't moved.

"I vouch for her, step aside Jean Claude Van Gideon." She made light, but he noticed the voice tremors when she spoke. She pushed on like a soldier, talking and moving to keep the anxiety from biting at her courage. Gideon eyes swung down in her direction, a hint of a smile graced his full lips.

"You have a gift." Lina looked expectantly at him.

"Can it be packaged or marketed?"

"Not in the traditional sense, but bringing humor to any situation is a gift."

"I find nothing humorous about having to troll the stores and hunt for a new purple comforter, or replacing my mattress."

"I didn't touch anything, but I don't think the blood soaked your mattress."

"You're crazy if you think I'm putting this body in that bed." She placed a hand on her hip to emphasize her point. He raked his gaze down her generous curves and back up. She arched an eyebrow at his obvious perusal, but he didn't miss her dilated pupils. He closed the distant between them. Her lips parted, and then her warm breath touched his skin. His own breath quickened, her lips parted, and her tongue made a slow trek across her lower lip. He saw and felt her body shift as he lowered towards her upturned face. He was going to kiss her and she would let him.

"Adios, chica, I can see where this is headed, and I'm out of here. Knock on my door when your friend is gone." Estrella's tone put a stop to what was happening between him and Lina.

Lina cleared her throat, taking a step back. The distance did little to break her spell.

"Estrella, this is my new boss." Gideon looked in Estrella's direction for the first time since she'd arrive. She merely gave a smirk. "I mean co-worker." Estrella didn't move to offer her hand in greeting.

She was tiny compared to him. Average build. Estrella maintained eye contact and held her ground, even with him towering over her. Some men took a step back when Gideon approached, but not this woman. She had her arms crossed over her chest. By the smirk on her face, as she looked up at him with a steady gaze, Estrella wasn't intimidated by his size. He gave another cursory glance, impressed with her initial presentation. Interesting woman. He liked her immediately.

"I'm Gideon. Did you see or hear anything unusual tonight?" The woman studied him. Not with appreciation, he realized, but because she was sizing him up. He wondered if he had competition from her of another persuasion. Perhaps Estrella fed Lina and liked watching her eat for the same reason he did. Gideon was ready to do battle with any man, but he hadn't considered a woman.

"You being here is the only thing I noticed that's different," Estrella finally answered. He didn't see that sledgehammer coming. What other surprises did Estrella have in store for him?

Two hours later, she stripped and changed the sheets in the master bedroom. Gideon was right, the mattress wasn't stained. But she wasn't going to lay down on anything the intruder had touched.

Meanwhile she took comfort in the fact that she wasn't alone.

When the police asked if she knew of anyone that would break into her home, she remained quiet. Jace was a pest, but she couldn't envision him violating her home like this. Gideon hadn't mentioned Jace's name to the police. So, he wasn't keen on hanging the incident tag around Jace's neck, either. After handling the majority of the police report, she decided to be safe and let Gideon stay. So there he was, under the same roof. Something Jace never would have done.

Though Gideon tried to camouflage the warrior side of his nature, his Marine Corps training was inherent in everything he did. Case in point, the man had a duffle bag in his car with a complete set of business clothes. Who does that?

"Lina?" Startled she jumped, knocking over the bedside clock. She righted herself, holding out a hand, as if to stop Gideon. It was futile to become accustomed to his help when he wouldn't be around.

He leaned against the door frame, all country swagger. Her eyes slid to half mast, her nostrils flared, and her lips parted. A little tension relief was in order after tonight's events. She was man fasting, but for the life of her, looking at his non-classical features framed by long ebony lashes, a square jaw, and a shadow well past midnight, she could not recall one logical reason why any woman would willingly deprive herself of Gideon Rice.

Her mother's warning came to mind as she stood facing off with Gideon. *No boys allowed in the house.* But a take charge psychiatrist with a dangerous edge was an acceptable exception to the rule. Doctors were allowed to make house calls, right? *No. Boys. Allowed.*

"Do you need something, Gideon?" He pushed away from the wall, he stood in the center of the doorway, a sliver of light outlining his large frame. He'd lost the dress shirt, a sleeveless T-shirt clung to his chest. Hands in his pockets of his slacks, he remained motionless in the doorway. Silently, his body language requested permission before entering her bedroom. She gave him a nod to enter. His eyes slid over her body in pure male appreciation. That's when she heard the tribal chant in her head; *man fast, man fast, man fast.* Swallowing the lump in her throat, she hoped it would squash the butterflies fluttering in her stomach.

"What can I do for you, Gideon?" He moved towards her and his scent made her all too aware that there was no barrier between them. He must have a sexy man camera slow play feature, every ripple, every flex, and every bulge of muscle was on ESPN replay. Breaking the focus on his body movements, she let her eyes drift downward, noting the carpet fibers sinking low with the shift of his weight. Now he stood in front of her.

His facial features were chiseled with just the right amount of refinement to avoid a harsh profile. His was built more for the open range than the calm surroundings of a psychiatric office. Total eye candy. She loved his Appalachian accent that he tried hard to conceal. She had noticed during dinner that he spoke with deliberate inflection on each syllable.

"I need to know that you are okay."

"Fine," came her quick response. "I don't understand what happened here tonight." She sounded stilted, even to her own ears. It would be a lie to say she wasn't upset by tonight's break-in, but the physical damage was minimal. The toll to her emotional state was still being tallied. Shoring up her spine, "I can handle it. But it's unnerving." The more she thought about it, the more she was convinced someone other than Jace had delivered the roses. Jace hated the sight of blood. He paled watching the sushi chef.

"We should look into installing a home security system as soon as possible. I didn't find a control panel when I searched the home. I will research—"

"What was it that you needed?" She interrupted. He'd been kind. But tonight, of all nights, she couldn't tolerate a promise of support that would be forgotten in the morning light. She didn't want to repay him with rudeness, but men offered her the fairytale and didn't deliver. She'd fallen for enough unicorns to last her a life time.

"I want something." Would he hit on her now? So far, he'd gotten everything he wanted from her today. *The man fast chant stopped and the booty call alert began.* She shouldn't be disappointed that he was interested in her body, but a part of her wanted him to crave her heart more than the hips. She had to give him props, he was unsuspectingly smooth and calculating. She liked him. Steeling her spine she tamped down her desire and prepared to push him away. Send him home after a lesson in urge control and keeping his priorities in order.

"A towel, beach sized if you have one."

"Towel?" He stood there looking like a super-sized bottle of sex, and she was vulnerable and ripe for the taking and he wanted a towel?

"It's a useful item following a shower, but I can air dry if you don't use them."

He missed the memo. He was supposed to be flirting, taking the edge off the evening, so she could turn him down and send him packing. *Maybe if she flirted a little, she'd close her eyes tonight and not have nightmares.* She was more than a little perplexed. Looking up at him, the deep smile lines bracketing his mouth told her that he knew the direction of her thoughts.

"Grab a set out of my closet," she said in a casual tone. She placed one hand on her hip, and then pointed to the closet with the other. He openly grinned at her then. Oh my goosebumps, he was a gorgeous specimen of manhood.

"Ooh, closet privileges," he joked. He placed a chaste kiss on her forehead before moving away. If he only knew how close she was to giving him full access. To everything. He crossed the three feet to her closet in two steps, disappearing from sight. Tempted to massage the conciliatory kiss into her skin, she started tugging at her jewelry dropping it in the footed silver bowl on her bedside table. Bothered by Gideon's lack of flirting, Lina was cranky, her skin felt too tight. Quelling the urge to walk into that closet and straight into his arms, she sank into the bedside chair. Dropping her head to her knees, she rubbed her damp palms up and down her shins, willing herself to breathe. In and out, nice and slow. She was stressed and her previous form of release was off limits for the next twenty-nine days. How could she keep it together, when her biggest temptation was three feet away and untouchable?

CHAPTER SEVEN

Gideon was born on the wrong side of the economic tracks. Once he left Waverly Falls he learned the hard way that it was easier to bury the original rails and lay down new tracks far away from where you started, than try to convince people of your worth. But frugality he learned as a child never left him. He recognized fine quality in clothing, cars, and food.

Lina's closet, on the other hand, could make a guest appearance on *Keeping Up with The Kardishians*. He had never been in a woman's closet before, hers seemed to brim with couture designs. The cherry wood shelving and glass doors resembled an episode from one of those remodel house shows.

He had shared a closet with a woman, but stepping into Lina's closet was similar to experiencing who she was through fabric and color. Her shoe cabinet was anchored from ceiling to floor on the rear wall. The shoes were color coordinated by seasons. Racks of clothing hung from light to dark according to length. Two jewelry cases adorned a chest of drawers in the center of the space. As a veteran Marine, Gideon valued organization. Being in the closet was less painful than he imagined. What struck him as out of place was a child's pink and vinyl bag covered in bows.

"Are you alright in there?" He heard Lina ask. "I roll my towels instead of square fold them. They're on your left." Grabbing a towel roll, he exited the closet.

Holding it up, "Got it, thanks. Your closet is pretty fancy."

"The custom remodel was a birthday gift from my mother three years ago."

Gideon thought about the expansive closet. Her condo had a wooded preserve view to the east and the river view to the west. This place was a stretch on a nurse's salary. Maybe her family was wealthy. A disturbing thought crossed his mind and he gave voice to it before he thought better.

"Have you ever been married?"

"No, why do you ask?"

"This location is atypical for most single women. I thought maybe, there was an ex-husband with a couple of kids in the not too distant past." A serious, almost tragic expression crossed her face. Had she given that level of commitment to another man?

"No children," she said, in a low tone. "A husband doesn't seem to be in the cards for me." She was a gorgeous woman. There was no way she believed marriage was off the table.

"You looking for a husband?" By her open mouth, his question had caught her off guard. Her brows furrowed. The blood thundered in his veins.

"I'm not sure how to answer." He knew enough about Lina, to know she had an opinion on marriage. Was she too afraid to give voice to her wants?

"Tell me what you want." Her breath hitched. His member pulsed in his pants when her lips parted and her tongue did a slow glide over that full bottom lip.

"I would like to meet a man interested in a committed relationship and the possibility of children." That was an interesting response for a woman on a strike.

"Kind of hard to do on a man-fast."

"Yep, there's a season to everything. I appreciate you helping me out, and for staying the night."

She was good at changing the subject.

"I could've gone to my mom's house, but she worries about me. Telling her what happened tonight would've sent her into hyper drive. She probably would have relocated us to an underground bunker." That stopped him cold.

"Lina, I'm not doing you any favors. Tell me why your mother would be so worried about you."

"You could have left me after the police report, but you didn't. Not every man would have made the choice you did tonight, I appreciate the whole dark knight persona you have going on." The woman was stubborn and she had not answered his question. His adoptive mother, God rest her soul would have said Lina had moxie.

"He would if his intention is to stick around." He would have pushed for Lina to give him an answer about her mom, except she looked away from him then, but not before he saw the flash of fear in her eyes.

"We should get ready for bed, I'm tired, and my new boss is a stickler for punctuality."

He watched as she walked into the master bathroom. She closed the door and he heard the lock engage. He would convince her that he was a man that kept his word. He would be the man to break her fast.

How many times had she believed a man when he said he was with her to stay? She had scoured the "sucker" tattoo off her forehead. Those words no longer held value. Words that were too easy to disregard, forget, or abandon. She knew from experience.

She exited the master suite dressed in a royal blue cotton sleep set with capped sleeves. The v-neckline was tasteful, rather than revealing. She expected to see him stretched out on the sofa when she descended the stairs from the master suite. Gideon was organized, so it was odd to think he required extra time in the bathroom. Her graphite color couch was unoccupied.

Crossing to the darkened kitchen area, she hesitated a moment outside of the guest suite. She gave a quick rap on the door and waited.

"Come in." Gideon's voice hit her ear in a perfect amount of base. Her body vibrated like a tuning fork. She pushed the door open with two fingers and regretted it instantly. Her eyes widened, probably popped out of her head, and she felt her tongue hanging. His skin was damp, the shadowy light from the bedside lamp created a glistening effect on his torso. He wore loose cargo pants, with the perfect blend of tanned ropes and corded muscle covering his back. She'd barely caught her breath when he turned then, giving her a full frontal assault. A silver cable chain hung around his neck, a thin white metal band ring dangled from it between his well-defined pectorals. A network of scars crisscrossed his right chest wall up to his collar bone. Her eyes stopped. Seeing the evidence of his flesh and blood sacrifice for his country shot her sexy man meter to the danger zone. The best looking pajama set she'd ever seen on display. He was a graduate of Defined and Sculpted Muscle University with a doctorate in body psychiatry. She certainly felt the mood elevating effects of this visual therapy session. His wrinkled dress shirt and slacks hung on a hanger hooked around the closet door. Organized Marine, to the core.

"Man, you've got to put some clothes on if we're going to stay in this house together." Lina shook her head trying to dislodge the image of him half-dressed from her royalty free stock photos.

"Stay in this room together," he responded as he pulled a loose black, cotton t-shirt over his head. She shook her head *no* in earnest for three reasons. First, to rid herself of the new image of thick biceps above his head as the t-shirt fell over his muscles. Second, to reprimand her inner naughty nurse into putting her cap back on and zip up her dress. And third, no way was she sharing a bedroom with him.

"Listen Clark Kent," because this casual look was uber sexy, "you checked the place out. So did the cops. We're safe."

"Are you my Lois Lane?" He smiled. Her breath hitched.

"Did you hear anything I said?"

"Yea, I'm your Superman." Oh goodness, her panties were moist.

"I'm ignoring you." She pointed to the door. "You are welcome to the couch."

"Unless you are on the couch with me that is not going to happen." The steel in his voice had her bristling and melting in equal measure.

"We are sleeping in this room, together," he said pointing at the glass door leading from the bedroom to the balcony. "There is a balcony entrance to every room in this place. It's like a miscreant's dream," he grumbled.

"Hey, easy with the labels. I pay a mortgage on this miscreant paradise."

"I have to be able to get to you before the threat. I can't do that if there is a wall between us and the stalker has direct access to your bedroom."

"I'll take the bed. You sleep there tonight," Lina gestured to the eggplant colored chaise adorned with atomic silver pillows.

They looked at it, then at each other. Half his legs would dangle off that thing. He raised an eyebrow at her with a slight smirk to his lips.

"If it's okay with you, I'll position the chaise in front of the balcony doors. You take the bed, and I will sleep on the floor," he said.

"Yeah, that can work, too."

"Thanks, I try to offer reasonable advice when I can."

"Don't rub it in." After a pause she added, "I'll iron your clothes in the morning."

He raised an eyebrow in question.

"Cooking is off the table, but you'll iron my dress shirt."

"Even civilian nurses appreciate a hard crease in their uniform scrubs."

"Touché. In exchange I'll make you breakfast."

"Cute and domesticated." She approached the opposite side of the bed, turned down the covers and climbed in. She observed as he rearranged the room, then settled on the floor between the glass door entry and the bed. He was doing more than staying with her, he was protecting her.

"You're a keeper," she said, before she closed her eyes.

"You can count on it."

"Gideon?"

"Yeah."

"I can take care of myself, but do you have any idea how I should proceed?"

"We will figure it out together. I'm not going to leave you, Lina. Sweet dreams." Sincerity rang out in his voice. There was a time when Jace's voice was similar, and Troy before him. Words were not to be trusted.

As she drifted off to sleep, visions of candy hearts with Gideon *hearts* Lina danced around her. Maybe, her blood sugar was too low?

During the night, Lina awoke to a thrashing sound near the floor. Her first instinct was to bolt for the door, but then the scent of mountain air tickled her nose and she remembered Gideon was beside her.

"Stay down Sergeant," he bellowed and Lina tensed. He was remembering an attack in theater. He quieted, but his lips still moved. It sounded as if he muttered a name. Did he say *Torres stay down*? His pitch dropped lower before she could decipher all his words. He was having a nightmare.

As a psychiatric nurse she was trained to avoid touching a patient experiencing a traumatic episode. It was paramount to protect yourself and the patient from physical injury. But she disregarded her training to help Gideon. Tentatively, she moved closer to the edge of the bed. Remaining on her stomach, she lowered her left arm toward the floor until she made contact with the fabric covering his chest. Delivering feather light strokes, she rubbed across his chest listening in the dark room for any sounds of increasing distress. Her touch had the opposite effect of what she saw with her patients. He quieted. With her upper body one quarter off the bed, slowly she inched her torso more fully into the bed. The room had fallen quiet once more. She stilled the hand on his chest. Sleep had claimed him. Gently she lifted her hand away, not wanting to disturb his rest. His powerful fingers curled around her hand. Instinctively, she tried to pull her hand free of his unrelenting hold. Though he was not hurting her, she tensed, squeezing her eyes closed. Anticipating the moment when his closed grip around her smaller hand would inflict pain.

The pain never came. She released a sigh of relief, then slowly opened her eyes. Lina found Gideon's storm gray eyes trained on their joined hands. Knowing better than to look at him, she raised her eyes anyway. Desire smothered in his eyes, then caught fire when he raised her fingers to his mouth and kissed each digit. Another of Bernadean James' warnings rang out in her head. *Keep your hands to yourself.*

He watched Lina from his concealed vantage point in the dense forest cover, as she entered the condominium unit and closed the door. It was too dark for him to distinguish the color of her dress, but there had been enough light to showcase her womanly curves. She'd matured into a beautiful woman. His body had pulsed with pent-up need. He took a deep breath reminding himself that she would be his soon. He would punish her for allowing another man to touch her. Anger coursed through his veins when the man, probably a date, dared to touch her skin. She belonged to him. She was a beautiful woman and he loved watching her. But watching her savor that man's kiss had fueled the barely contained rage coursing through his veins. She shouldn't let any man touch her. He hated knowing other men had touched her.

He hadn't seen her with this man before tonight. He could feel the predatory energy surrounding this new man. He'd lingered after Lina entered her house, instead of getting into his car and driving away. Now he was in there with her. This guy would be trouble. Lina sang when she was happy. He'd left his favorite look out point to conceal himself on the balcony because he wanted to see her face when she discovered his gift. Her voice had carried through the kitchen window that she never closed, smooth and soulful like the woman herself. She hadn't sung in a long time. Balling his fist in anger, knowing that this guy made her sing fueled his rage at not having her. He cracked the knuckles on each hand. He must remain focused.

He'd watched her for months, planning for this night. His plans had been ruined by this man who looked like a businessman, but moved like a trained killer. Only *he* was supposed to hear her cry out at the message he'd left on her bed. No one else. His chest filled with joy at her screams, that's how he missed the initial banging on her front door. He had barely gotten back to the parking structure underneath her unit when he heard the larger man's voice through the kitchen window.

Her bed would have been perfect for their first time together. Her sweet scent clung to the sheets. He'd pressed his face into the round purple pillow she held to her chest when she read at night. Careful not to stain her favorite pillow with his gift, he inhaled deep, pulling her essence deep into his lungs. Purple was her favorite color. A strappy, off the shoulder gown with layers of violet lace awaited Lina's generous curves in his private apartment. Not even the boss knew of its location. He'd been prepared to take her tonight, but it would have to wait. He would make that guy pay for ruining his plans for tonight and for touching Lina.

Abandoning his hiding place, he moved closer to the building. Her place went dark thirty minutes ago and the man hadn't left. Fury gnawed at his insides that Lina had settled in for the night with that man. This was definitely trouble for him.

It was getting late and he had stayed too long for his comfort level. He was good at what he did because he was always careful. Finding her gone when he arrived at sunset had thrown him off their routine. After an hour Lina hadn't returned and he had gone in search of her along the beach. She looked at peace when she sat at the shore, digging her toes into the sand. She'd never noticed him watching her, but he was always close. Sometimes, he even understood the words she spoke to the universe.

It was time for him to get home to his wife. He didn't want to worry her by staying out too late. He stalked down the stairs across the parking lot. His car was parked two blocks south. He was careful to park away from her travel routes. He didn't need her recognizing how often the same black Range Rover was in the neighborhood. Shell Coast was a large waterfront city, but her community was quaint and intimate. It was perfect for what he had in mind when the timing was right.

CHAPTER EIGHT

Bloody roses and break-ins would not interfere with mother daughter time. For Bernadean James, Tuesday night bingo was a sacred event, along with her Saturday morning wash and set at Sassy Styles Salon and her monthly reading group. It was Lina's joy to drive her mother to Big Bucks Bingo at the Riverwalk Shriner's auditorium. Every Tuesday evening Lina found herself in her mother's quaint living room. The Queen Anne sofa had been the center piece of the room since she could remember.

"Momma, you're going to lose your table." Lina collapsed into an oversized leather recliner in front of the television.

"No I won't. I talked with Willa earlier today, she's saving me a seat up front." Willamena Jackson owned Sassy Styles and was her mom's best friend in the whole world. They had argued over the same boy in junior high school. After both of them had been rejected by said boy, they became fast friends since they obviously had something in common. They liked the same type of men, and they both chose poorly.

"Why are you taking so long to get ready tonight?" Lina gripped and released her nape. The tension from last night had returned. Odd, when she was near Gideon the tightness in her muscles relaxed. One evening with Gideon sealed with a kiss, three kisses to be exact, and she had a song in her heart again. Who would have thought he wielded that kind of restorative power? Even now, she smiled at the computer printout of local home monitoring services handed to her before lunchtime.

"Lina Diane, why are you rushing me off to the wolves den? I hope you didn't take jumpy Jace back, did you? I swear, that boy leapt out of his skin if anyone other than you approached him."

Jace was the least of her worries. Thinking about the blood stains on her bed and a stranger in her house sent a shiver down her spine.

"You seem antsy tonight. What's going on with you?" Her mother had a habit of responding to a question with her own question. Lina should be used to this weekly exchange with her mother, but tonight felt different. She loved spending Tuesdays with her mother, but she craved the sense of safety Gideon's presence provided.

"You didn't answer my question," her mother called from the other room.

"I would run on a treadmill until the second coming of the Messiah, before I reconciled with Jace. And don't mention his name, he is a world class butt wipe to me." Lina hadn't told her mother that Jace was trying to get her transferred to his clinic.

"Something has changed," her mother said stepping out of the bedroom. "Tell your momma what's going on?" Her mother's voice was coming closer. Lina schooled her face into a blank expression. She didn't want her mother thinking she had jumped head first and blind folded into another male guided train wreck.

"I'm fine Momma. You worry too much about me." Bernadean's petite frame appeared in front of Lina. Unlike Lina, Bernadean preferred to wear her hair in a sleek, copper-brown full length bob that graced her shoulders. They shared a similar body build, but Bernadean was a "pint sized" version of her daughter, rather than the other way around. Lina always felt like an Amazonian warrior looking down at a little person when she stood next to her mother. She'd told her mother how she felt after graduating from high school. Her mother had looked devastated and Lina wished she could have taken the words back. Bernadean had looked up at Lina with tears in her eyes. In the middle of the Shell Cove Town center, her momma had grabbed her hand placing it over her beating heart. Her mother told her she was perfect. That she should never compare herself to another living soul on the planet. From that moment forward, Lina accepted the body that housed her soul. She was created with her own unique brand of femininity and no woman could rival Lina at being herself.

"Of course, I worry about you, Lina Diane. You are my child. I'll never stop worrying about you." Her mother took both of Lina's hands, pulled her to her feet all the while making a slow appraisal from head to foot. Lina squirmed under her mother's scrutiny.

"Surely the nights of worrying have decreased since I'm all grown up?" Lina laughed at her own joke to lighten the mood, but Bernadean remained silent in front of her.

"You'll always be my baby. I love you more than anything in the world, Lina. There is nothing I would not do to protect you." Her mother's tone bordered on somber, triggering Lina to look up and over at her mother.

"Momma, why are you getting all serious on me? I'm okay," she said, lowering her eyes. Lina hoped her mother didn't notice the telltale gesture.

"You never could lie and maintain eye contact. What's going on?" Her mother shook her head as her smile fell back into place. "What's his name?"

"Whose name?"

"The man that has you twisted up in knots." She was so obvious when it came to male interest. Lina shook her head in mock disgust.

"My pseudo boss helped me out of some trouble. I don't plan on liking him." Rolling her eyes heavenward, she sent up a silent prayer for strength to resist Gideon's pull.

"When it comes to a man, the best laid plans can be met with unforeseen consequences."

"Momma, no man talks are allowed during my fast."

"Fine, I believe you but, you let your momma know if anybody is giving you grief."

"Okay, *Original Gangster* of bingo. I'll keep you posted if anyone disrespects your little shorty." Her mother gently patted her cheek.

"See that you do that, my little Lina Diane." Her mother turned in a whirl of colorful fabric disappearing back into her bedroom.

Lina followed behind her mother taking a seat in the winged back chair nested in the bay window. Lina breathed in the familiar scent of childhood.

Her mother's house always had a soft floral scent. Her eyes settled on the antique dressing table against the far wall. What she saw there brought a smile to her face. Draped across a jewelry display mannequin was a hot pink plastic necklace with a matching bangle bracelet. Lina had bought it for her mother more than fifteen years ago. Her mother had cried when Lina had presented her with the poorly wrapped box for Mother's Day.

"Momma, why do you keep that old jewelry set on display? You can't think to wear those colors again, it would be a traumatic fashion faux pas." Bernadean glanced at her daughter, then her dresser and smiled.

"That jewelry set was the first gift you, my most precious daughter gave me. You bought it with your own money. I cried so much your father thought I was having a nervous breakdown. Only death could part me from that hot pink jewelry set. Your daddy would shake his head in dismay because I wore that plastic necklace with my Sunday's finest for six months. He would always joke that everybody was whispering he was a cheapskate."

Her mother had a pleasant faraway look. Lina never understood why her mother never had any resentment towards her father. How could you have happy thoughts of a man that abandoned you to raise a child alone? Lina could not think of one instant when her mother said a negative word about her father.

"Ready." Bernadean turned off the lights and stepped out of her walk-in closet and sashayed into her bedroom wearing a cheetah print swing dress with three quarter sleeves.

"Foxy Brown eat your heart out. Is that the latest ensemble for Tuesday night bingo?" Her mother flashed a coquettish smile.

"I have an admirer if you must know. He's a Deacon at Olive Branch Baptist, that large white brick church near the community college campus."

Lina's iPhone dinged an incoming message. She rolled off her hip to pull the phone free of her jeans pocket. The message was from Gideon.

You disappeared on me. Where the heck are you? He was so country cute with his southern dialogue.

It brought a smile to her face that he wanted to know where she was. Maybe it was the way men treated women in his neck of the woods, as he put it, but his words made her feel special. Like she mattered to him. *About to get cozy with a tanned hunk,* she texted.

He texted back, *He'd better be on the television. Get dressed. I'm coming to get you.*

How presumptuous of him to assume she wasn't dressed and didn't already have plans. She looked down at her oversized tee with a scoop neck and rounded tail, faded jeans, and sandals. Okay, technically she wasn't dressed for a night out on the town, but it would do in a pinch.

What makes you think I'm not dressed? She typed as fast as her thumbs could move.

His response-*I was just hoping.*

Lina couldn't help but smile as she mentally assembled her outfit for her second date with Gideon.

Lina responded that he could come over at seven thirty.

"A name, Lina Diane?" Bernadean's face held a knowing expression.

Lina released a slow groan. "Momma, it's nothing. He's just a friend from work."

"Is that right?" Bernadean stepped back and settled a stern look on Lina. "You come in here jumping like you just got tasered. You're impatient to get me off to bingo and don't think I didn't hear you singing when you stepped out of the car in the driveway. Now, you're smiling like Alex Trebek wrote you one of those Jeopardy checks."

"What's this friend's name and don't try to stall me because Deacon Wilson is waiting on me." Lina's shoulders slumped.

"His name is Gideon Rice." Bernadean cradled Lina's face in her palms.

"And the trouble Gideon helped you resolve?" She hoped her mother had forgotten the mention of trouble.

"Someone broke into my place last night." Her mother went still. Abject fear covered her mother's features.

"And you didn't call me?" The hurt underpinning her mother's words pierced her heart. Rising to her feet, Lina pulled her mother into an embrace.

"Momma, I wasn't there. They didn't take anything."

"The fact that he didn't take anything is irrelevant. Why didn't you come over here?"

"I took care of it. I notified the police, they checked everything but my blood pressure. I had BETAS with me, too." She rubbed her mother's arm in comfort.

"If nothing was taken, how do you know someone was in your house?"

"Because someone left blood stained, white roses on my bed." She felt her mother stiffen in her arms, but her heart was beating at a frantic pace. Having never seen her mother in this state Lina was unsure of what action to take.

"It's okay, Momma," Lina said, in a reassuring tone.

"No, nothing is okay," came her mother's whisper. Lina felt her mother squeeze her tighter, then she let go. "Never keep anything from me, Lina."

"I didn't want to worry you, and Gideon stayed the night with me." Her mother regarded her with tears in her eyes, the fear from earlier replaced with an emotion Lina didn't recognize.

"I'll meet you at the car," her mother said, dabbing at the corner of her eye. "I need to pretty myself up, again." Her smile resembled glass in the middle of an open flame, on the verge of melting away. "You tell me all about your Gideon Rice on the ride to bingo." The sudden change in her mother's mood was unnerving.

"Are you disappointed in me for not calling you last night? I didn't want to bring trouble over to your door and…"

"Those were Gideon's words. I raised you to be independent in the world, not from me. Gideon sounds like a man used to bringing the fight to his opponent." Her mother gave her a pointed look, "We depend on one another, Lina Diane. You've always told me everything. Don't let that change because of a man."

"Momma, Gideon is a nice guy. Don't think ill of him."

"Maybe, he's not as nice as you think if he doesn't appreciate the relationship between a mother and her child." Her mother's voice held a hint of concern and fear. Her mother had gotten to the root of the issue in one conversation. Lina gave her trust to men, too easily.

"I'm so proud of you, baby. Go on to the car. I'll be there in a minute."
Her mother said all the right words, but she had the look of a woman who was
handed a life sentence. Lina couldn't shake the feeling that an irrevocable
change had taken place.

CHAPTER NINE

Wednesday was a breeze compared to the Monday she and Gideon had experienced. The last patient left Gideon's office twenty minutes ago, but the man remained behind closed doors in his office. There was a part of her that wanted to wait until he came out of his office. She wanted to see him. Technically, she was still true to the man fast. But the past seventy-two hours had changed the nature of their relationship forever. He was a friend. He watched over her, supported her, and held her hand when she didn't know that's what she needed. Their relationship had a foundation other than physical intimacy. She wanted to share herself with Gideon, but she knew he would still be there for her if she didn't. It was liberating to know she did have a choice. He wouldn't walk away because she hadn't slept with him. Her inner naughty nurse whispered, *take him*, every time Lina glanced in his direction.

She completed her nursing entry for the last group therapy session, logged off the computer, and grabbed her purse. A bottle of chilled white wine was calling her name.

"Lina." Her heart rate increased at the sound of his voice. "What adventures do you have planned for tonight?"

"A little bit of this, maybe a lot of that."

"How about," he stepped closer, "you give me a do-over for last night?"

"I had a nice time watching *Empire* with you." Empire's Cookie Lyons was Lina's favorite television heroine. The way she loved her family, with fire and ice, serving up a hefty dose of either one depending on the latest family drama.

You treat Cookie right, the warmth of her love covered a person better than a mink blanket. But, if you became a threat that same love and passion would encase you in ice. She smiled up at him. "The urgent call to the hospital altered our Empire marathon plans." Every time she looked up into his eyes she blushed, though no one could see it. She felt small standing next to Gideon, dainty even. Curvy girls wanted a man that could toss them up in the air and catch them without wearing a back harness. She liked the way she felt about herself when she was with him.

"Me, too." Trying not to be presumptuous, she refrained from saying anything else. She learned her lesson about assumptions where men were involved. After Jace, the next man she welcomed into her life would have to carve his feelings on a stone tablet, in blood.

"Do you have plans for tonight?"

"And if I did?"

"Do they include me?" Heck yeah, her plans could be all about him.

"Possibly."

"How do I transition from a possibility to a definitely?"

"You could just ask."

"Miss Lina James, can I take you out tonight?"

"You sure can, but I have to meet a friend at my house within the hour. I'll text you when we're done. Spencer is fast. We should be done in no time."

"He's fast at what?"

"My new mattress will be delivered tonight, and the old one has to be out of my bedroom before the delivery service arrives."

"Change of plans. I'll follow you home. Where did you park?"

"Gideon, it's cool. Spencer is a *murse*, so no worries."

"I don't care that he's a male nurse or that he's officially in the Girls' club. To be frank, that's a dynamic I prefer not to explore. He could be the last eunuch and he would not set his eyes on your bedroom."

"I don't like what you are implying, Gideon. Spencer is my friend and a pediatric nurse. Spencer is the Mellow Yellow of the male species. He would never do anything to jeopardize our friendship."

"I know RN Hayeswood is a good friend to you and Ava. He's a standup guy. I know several of the single, female nurses consider him their resident handyman. But you have me. To my way of thinking, you can call on me for everything you need."

"Be reasonable. You and Spencer can work faster together," she huffed.

"In my neck of the woods..." She interrupted before he could start with his country caveman moral code.

"Oh my goosebumps, for someone who does not talk about his past, you are quite fond of the woods." Gideon captured her in a narrowed glance.

"As long as I have breath in this here body, I don't care if Spencer built your house with his bare hands, he's not setting one foot in your bedroom." It was eighty degrees outside and Lina could swear she saw his breath. He was livid. Time to wave the white flag. Bottom line the mattress would be moved.

"I'll grab my stuff."

"Thank you very much for allowing me to help. I'm looking forward to seeing your new purchase. Text Spencer and tell him not to come. I'd hate for you to see how much of a mountain man I can be."

"Why is that?" Snagging her around the waist, he pulled her in close.

"I want to see my future resting place." Her lips parted and a soft moan escaped. His crotch instantly hardened against her pelvis.

"Come on sweetness, let's get outta here. I want to have the mattress in the living room before the delivery truck arrives." She grinned at him.

"What's funny?"

"Nothing, it's just when you aren't thinking about it that accent of yours makes itself known."

"Actually, the family that raised me never owned any animals."

"You were adopted?"

"Yeah, I was."

"Wow, Gideon. I had no idea." Lina volunteered at Second Chance House and saw how difficult it was for kids to get placed.

"How old were you?"

"Seven." Without another word he grabbed her hand, leading the way out of the clinic.

It was after five on Thursday evening when Lina turned off the car ignition in the parking lot behind Second Chance House. Once upon a time, it had been a single story home for pregnant teenagers, but the program had expand to a multi-building complex with services for women and children ranging in age from seven to twenty-two.

Gideon didn't understand her need to work with the young women at Second Chance. Volunteering a few hours a day, twice a week was her chosen form of therapy. The end of the week was the busy days for client intakes. Staff members were spread thin with admission forms, room assignments, and crisis situations. Volunteers like Lina, augmented the counselors seven days a week.

Though Gideon talked with his patient's about the importance of maintaining healthy connections and the role that a supportive family played in the healing process she noticed he didn't apply the same rules to himself.

Lina grabbed her purse and exited the car. She took the ramp leading to the Maternal Infant wings of the facility. She was about to enter when her phone rang. The picture of Gideon she'd taken on the beach was visible on the screen along with his telephone number. He was still in the office.

"Hey, you," she said into the receiver.

"Where are you? You left without stopping by my office." His voice sounded strained.

"Did you forget?" She laughed, "It's my night to volunteer at Second Chance."

"I didn't forget, but I didn't think you would leave me without saying goodbye." Wow. He sounded as if she had abandoned him.

"I should be done here, by eight o'clock." She made her voice light, hoping it would cheer him up.

"Where are you volunteering tonight?"

"The usual, with the pregnant mothers." He was silent on the other end of the phone.

"I thought the center had a mental health unit?" Unease skirted down her spine. She hadn't pressed him when he refused to discuss his nightmares. Why did he feel the need to question where she volunteered her time?

"They do, but I want to work with mothers-to-be." She heard his sigh through the phone.

"You volunteering tomorrow night, too?"

"Yep," was her only reply.

"Alright, sweetness. I'll see you at work in the morning.

She heard the hospital's announcement system blare to life in the background.

"Duty calls."

His deep chuckle hit her ear. Her stomach did a familiar dip.

"Have fun and call me when you're headed home. If I don't hear from you I'll be at your condo with an overnight bag."

"You got it and I should get inside. Tonight is one of our busiest nights."

"Do you have plans for Saturday?" She smiled. That was the Gideon she knew. Always thinking ahead.

"Nope."

"Pen and ink me in for the entire day." Her heart rate soared at the thought of spending an entire day with Gideon.

"I'll pencil you in," she teased him.

"You have jokes."

"What can you possibly plan that would take up the entire day?" She grinned into the receiver, knowing he liked to be challenged.

"Oh, I'll think of something." Lina knew what he planned, he'd exceed her expectations.

Gideon had to be out of his mind to suggest a Saturday morning at the beach. He could barely conceal his erection with her fully clothed in the office, now he had the cooler separating them as they lazed on the beach in far less clothing. With her silhouetted curves on display, if he got any harder, the ice pack to the groin would be in his treatment plan.

They arrived at his favorite fishing hole on the Palmdale River at eight o'clock. The Palmdale was a four mile brackish tributary off the Saint Diasus River. Palm trees leaned into the water with the wear of by-gone decades, swaying in the soft breeze. The afternoon sun hung low in the sky, partially obscured by clouds. An overcast sky kept the salty air cool and light. Lina had managed to hook two medium sized whiting to add to his five smallmouth bass. They sprawled out on oversized beach towels underneath a low-lying canopy of palm trees. The beach was cozy, large for a small gathering, but they had this area to themselves.

"Thanks for inviting me to hang out with you, Gideon." She thought he was hanging out with her, like one of the fellas.

"Is that what I did?"

A family of harlequin ducks quacked in cadence for her answer.

"You got me out of the house on Saturday morning to stand on a pier casting a fishing line. I promise you, only a personal invitation would have worked."

"Hold the applause until the end of the day. This is only the first, one-third of the day. This picnic on the beach with my promise to cook dinner later had nothing to do with you accepting my offer?"

The wide brimmed sun hat shielded her eyes from view, but he saw her smile widen.

"Is it considered blackmail if I benefit from the deal?"

"No, sweetness, it's called a well-played hand." Calling her everyday wasn't enough anymore, he needed to be in her presence.

"I've lived here all my life and never noticed this private oasis. How did you find this place?" The worry lines, she tried hard to hide during the work week had disappeared. This was the woman he met last fall, the one who ignited a fire in his gut with one look.

"I'm a bit of a nature boy at heart. I like to scout out my location and learn the area."

"Spoken like a country boy Marine." He stilled. He was not that person anymore, the sooner she realized that the better.

"I can hear you thinking too hard, Gideon. Relax, you are a big time psychiatrist now, but I like my country boy Marine."

"Is that how you see me?" He asked, frustration clear in his voice.

"I see you, the boy from small town West Virginia, the brave Marine, and the edgy psychiatrist."

"And your verdict?"

"You're alright," she said, perched up on her left elbow.

"That sounds marginal, at best." He reached over placing an innocent kiss to her shoulder.

"I stopped grading on a curve. Too many losers made the cut." Her voice was strained, but light. "Does a refined psychiatrist have anything to drink in the cooler besides cheap beer?" With the heat radiating from his groin, he'd be lucky if he avoided a two degree burn.

"You hurt my heart, sweetness. A man has to drink a beer while fishing. It's the American way," he grinned down at her. She wore a sheer black beach drape, with a drawstring waist. Those gorgeous legs were on display all morning. He had yet to see her full package for the sun and sea to drink in.

Turning away he rolled up from the beach towel, he opened the lid and peered into the wicker basket packed with everything non-perishable he could find in the pantry.

"There's bottled water, sun brewed tea, and fresh squeezed lemonade." He glanced back over his shoulder when she didn't respond. At the sight that greeted him, the pressure in his groin increased enough to tent his trunks and the sand.

The beach drape lay in a heap at Lina's manicured toes. Both arms extended over her head in an ultra-feminine cat stretch elongating her curves and thrusting her ample chest heavenward. The one piece black and white tuxedo bathing suit she wore screamed take me here, take me now, and take me hard. It was a strapless number with black panels covering her breasts and abdomen. Solid white bands of material started down the side of her torso stopping at the high cut hipster. A faux white belt accented her smaller waistline. He shook his head, willing his hands to stay away from the breathtakingly, gorgeous woman who would serve as a hungry man's feast.

"Lina, is the fast over?"

"Six days and counting," she smiled.

"You wanna cheat?" He asked with a smile, but he was serious with a capital S. He saw the pulse at her neck jump, just as her breathing increased.

"I want…" she trailed off.

He placed the drinks back in the cooler. The silence stretched between them. Lina sank her teeth into her lower lip and he released a groan. He couldn't take any more. Reaching over he placed his hand on the exposed skin at her hip. As the coolness of his touch seeped into her hot skin, she hissed out a breath and his hold tightened.

"Tell me you want to cheat," her gaze dropped to his mouth. Her eyes darkened, and he knew she craved his touch. Wanted the same thing he did.

"I can't, Gideon."

He let his hands fall away from her body. Her eyes pleaded with him to understand.

He understood her need to maintain control. She wanted to complete the fast, but heck, her man-fast had become his man-fast. He was ready to eat.

"But, you want to cheat with me, right?" He didn't know if it would help, but he needed some indication that he wasn't going insane. Her only response was a barely perceptible nod. Breathing in the sea, he pushed his arousal back into the recesses of his mind. Much had been revealed today. She wanted him. That would have to be enough.

"Lina, I'm not just hanging out with you."

"Say what's on your mind, Gideon."

"Once this man-fast is over, I'm taking you home. We aren't leaving the bedroom for days."

"Is that so?"

"Yeah, it is." He grabbed her and pulled her to stand. "Know that I'm going to feast on every inch of your body." Her fingers gripped his, like she couldn't let him go. He couldn't look at her or he would lay her down, peel that suit from the smooth chocolate skin he dreamt of licking and love her all night long. "Let's go for a swim." She stiffened, but he gave her arm a tug. She fell in step behind him.

They treaded into the water up to her waist, Gideon was pulled backward when Lina stopped moving.

He turned, scooped her up into his arms. He waded into deeper water. She screeched louder than a little girl that had dropped her ice cream cone.

"Gideon Rice, you put me down this instance." She demanded. He laughed, placing a kiss on her cheek. She peered up at him, a glint of surprise in her eyes. He loved stealing kisses from her. "You keep wiggling and I might drop you." Fear flashed in her eyes, she pressed closer to his chest.

"Don't do that," she whispered. Her arms felt like she glued them around his neck.

"Hey, sweetness," he crooned, "you know I won't let you down." A furrow formed between her brows before she averted her gaze.

"Eyes on me, little warrior princess." Her face was as still as a wax figure. He needed her to look at him. Why couldn't she trust his word? Letting her leg slip from his hold he reached for her chin. Her back bowed out of the water as she jerked him forward, nearly throwing them both in the water.

"Lina! Calm down." Her legs wrapped around his waist in a wrestler's hold. Between the reverse sleeper hold on his neck and her powerful legs compressing against his midsection, he was basically breathless.

"Sweetness, loosen your hold."

"Not happening, mountain man."

"You love the water, but you can't swim?"

"Bingo, give the man a prize. We all have scars from childhood." She tried to laugh though her voice shook.

"My prize is wrapped around me just the way I like it." Her breath hitched and her hold relaxed. He nuzzled her neck and smiled when she released a sigh.

"Did I discover your sweet spot?" he teased.

"One of many…Oh my Todd, I should not have said that out loud."

"You're honest. I love that quality. What you see, is what you get." He continued to nuzzle her neck. "And I love what I see." Gideon lengthened his body in the water, forming a bed to cradle her body.

"You say that now."

"I won't change, Lina. I won't let you fall." To his point, he tilted his pelvis upward, pushing her bottom above the surface of the water. Just realizing she was afloat with him supporting her, she stiffened.

"Don't let go. I've got you. Trust me." Tentatively, her muscles slowly went lax but she never broke eye contact. His gut tightened at the small victory in their relationship.

"Say it, Lina."

"What do you want me to say?" This was her next lesson in trust.

"Tell me you know that I will not let you fall." She swallowed several times in succession before parting those full lips.

"You won't let me fall." Her eyes lit up, then he knew she believed the words.

"Say it, again." When she did he felt his erection grow, filling the space between their bodies.

"Gideon won't let me," her voice faltered. "Ah, you're poking me."

"Not yet, but it's coming."

Lina was on man-fast day twelve. The sun was shining with the radiance of the best cut diamond. If she sang any more than she did, the Apollo Theatre would be knocking at her door.

"Hey Doc, the new nurse is better than a pair of seasoned boots," Staff Sergeant Hain called to Gideon from the discharge nurse desk.

Lina had come to learn that was a primo compliment for a Marine. They walked a lot of miles, both at home and abroad, so they took great care of their feet.

Staff Sergeant Ty Hain was the socialite of the Marines transported via military van to SCMC twice a week for WWR clinic. Gideon implemented

Lina's suggestion to offer an active duty group therapy session at six thirty in the morning for the Marines assigned to Queens Bay Medical. The session was after physical training and before they got their work day started. Therapy attendance numbers were already on the rise.

"You don't have to sell me on RN James. She'll be a long standing fixture in this clinic." Came Gideon's reply.

Lina's pulse rate sped up at his familiar base. His words were filled with pride and laughter. She could almost hear his smile. Her life was good.

Thanks to their day at the beach, Gideon's naturally white smile looked brighter against his tan skin. They had returned to their beach after work twice since that picnic. He was teaching her to float on her back. It was slow going and she suspected he did more holding than she did floating. She smiled at his crisp, white shirt tailored to fit that muscled body she'd come to know as well as her own.

Amazing how often she had to touch her swim coach. A good education was fundamental to increasing her opportunities to succeed. You never know when those skills would be required.

The tradeoff for ironing his shirts, he cooked for her twice a week. Between Gideon and Estrella, her wallet was heavier and she was five pounds lighter.

"Are boots and fixtures code names for awesome?" Lina teased them both.

"Yes ma'am, a rifle, dry socks and a pair of well-fitted boots are a girl's best friend in the field." At twenty-five years old, Tynisha Hain was married to the Marine Corps. The petite African-American beauty loved her hometown of Atlanta, Georgia. She ate, slept, and drank the United States Marine Corps.

"Noticed the limp is gone this week. How's the muscle strengthening program?" The shrapnel to the leg had nearly ended Ty's career. After getting to know the woman, Lina suspected most of the emotional stress was related to her physical injuries limiting her career.

"Physical therapist says I'll be ready for the combat readiness exam within a week." The woman's chest swelled with pride. Lina mentally did a happy dance for Ty. Her emotional and physical hard work would pay big dividends.

"That is awesome news, Staff Sergeant. I'll personally add your picture to our Wall of Courage during your next deployment." Tynisha mastered each challenge presented to her. The last hurdle was in sight and Lina was proud to have a role in the woman's success.

"Ma'am, I'm focused on passing my next combat fitness test, so I can rejoin my unit. The Marine Corps is my life."

Lina could relate to Ty's statement. This clinic and caring for this patient population was woven into the fabric of her life.

Gideon's vision for the WWR extended beyond outpatient services. When fully integrated, military personnel would establish a rapport with a mental health professional before, during, and after deployment. When the full scope of the initiative was funded, combat ready Marines would have access to mental health care before and during combat. Before the psychological scars could form.

Chapter Ten

Disaster was an understatement. The Shell Cove police department picked the Saturday afternoon of Logan and Ava's engagement party to erect the police roadblock from Dante's underworld. The drug trafficking through the Southeast corridor of Interstate-95 had extended its reach into the affluent community of Shell Cove. Roadblocks like this had become more commonplace than Lina ever imagined possible in their picturesque city.

Every vendor, including the decorators, arrived at the Cove Towers Somerset ballroom sixty minutes before the event was to start. Granny Lou and Mrs. Walters helped the Towers staff with setting the tables. Janna, Lina, and Bernadean worked with the decorators to dress all fifty round tables in navy blue linens with yellow accents. The ballroom walls were covered in soft yellow silk. An elegant backdrop with the dark linen table. The live band unpacked their equipment in the far right corner. As the florist added fresh bouquets to each table, the scent of lilies and sunflowers perfumed the air.

Lina wanted the evening to be perfect for Ava. Ava and Logan's romance was far from story book, their love was hard won. Ava, the most relationship averse woman she knew, was engaged to be married. Lina had kind of pushed Ava and Logan together. The night of the Shell Cove Medical Center fundraiser, Ava found the man of her dreams, and Lina lost hers. Threats from Ava's future mother-in-law had forced Ava to leave Shell Cove and Logan behind. It took Ava weeks to muster the nerve to face Logan's wrath over her abandonment. Ava left Logan following his mother's threats to ruin them both.

"Lina." Her best friend glowed in a soft, yellow mermaid dress with a navy blue belt at her twenty-four inch waist. Lina knew that because Ava offered her a few shirts that were too big for her since joining the Navy Nurse Corps. Lina, meanwhile, filled out every stitch inlay in her clothing.

"Hey girlfriend, you look beautiful. Logan and the Navy must be treating you well." The words came from Lina's heart. Logan's love had given Ava the strength to pursue her dreams.

"Thank you, bestie. I am enjoying my first duty station and Logan treating me like a queen. The verdict is still out on his thoughts about me serving in the Navy." Lina threw her arms around her friend and held tight. They shared matching lunch boxes, matching outfits, and matching hairstyles through the years.

"Logan will adjust to sharing you with the Blue and Gold." Ava laughed, rolling her eyes heavenward.

"If I agree to another collateral duty in the clinic, he'll apply for hardship reassignment." Lina crinkled her nose in confusion.

"Collaterals are additional duties outside of my nursing responsibilities."

"Ah, I get it." Lina pulled her best friend into another hug.

"I'm in charge of staff education and training and we have an inspection coming up within the week. The prep work keeps me in the office later than Logan would like." At Ava's sniffling, Lina pulled back to look at her friend's face.

"There's no crying before the engagement announcement." Ava shrugged and dabbed at her eyes.

"I'm happier than I ever imagined I could be, but there's a weight in my chest that makes me want to run before something terrible happens."

"Ava are you ending the engagement?" Wide eyes in disbelief Ava stared at Lina.

"No. The only thing that can stop me from marrying Logan, is the heavenly rapture."

"Amen, to that."

"But, this day feels out of sorts. Aron and Zari, haven't arrived with Shaylah from the airport." Ava's younger brother and his wife had volunteered to pick up the oldest Walters' sibling. Shaylah was a doctoral student at Howard University and worked for the Department of Social Services in Washington, DC.

"I received a text alert that Interstate-95 was gridlocked courtesy of the police blockade." Lina patted her friend's shoulder.

"Don't worry about the details. You're here and Logan will forever be at your side. That's what's important." Ava's smile brightened and Lina's work at reassuring the bride-to-be was done.

"Can you believe I'm getting married?"

"Yes, I can." That's all Lina got to say before the elite of Shell Cove's shakers and movers started spilling through the double doors. Logan's family tree and social network sported million dollar homes, luxury cars, and private yachts. Ava was the middle child of a postal carrier and a school teacher. When the two looked at each other, all she saw was love. The differences didn't matter if you loved someone. That's what Lina told herself, though her reality with love was a less forgiving tale.

Gideon was her date again tonight. He stayed close to her, but gave her enough space to socialize with her friends. She hadn't uttered the word dating and neither had he. They had a comfortable weekly routine. Friends that spent every waking moment together. Of course, he had taken off to the men's dressing room to commute with Logan and his male entourage.

Lina noticed Darwin Masters, Logan's younger brother, love interest Rebecca Lynn Holbrook had arrived with a new man in tow.

"Who is the guy with Rebecca?" she directed over her shoulder to Gideon. Gideon golfed with the men of the Masters family on Sundays, so he knew more details about the Masters family. Almost as well as Lina knew the Walters' clan.

"The one with the scar along his face is Bluton S. Faraday. He's made millions creating industry in underdeveloped countries."

"He has the bluest eyes I've ever seen, but he's not the one I'm asking about. Who's the guy crowding Rebecca's personal space?" Lina touched Gideon's arm as she spoke. When had she gotten comfortable with touching him?

"Richard Ascot, his family is heavy into defense contracts. With Logan off the market, Dick is Rebecca's latest wealthy suitor."

"Dick?" she tried not to smirk, taking in the laugh lines formed at the corners of his mouth.

"Hey, that's what the guy told me to call him." Lina studied the man standing next to the perfectly coiffed Rebecca. He was lean, approximately six feet, light on muscle mass with an arrogant smile on his too thin lips. There was enough gel in his hair that it resembled a high-gloss combat helmet. At his side, Rebecca kept her eyes forward, back straight, toes pointed at twelve o'clock. She looked like she was on duty, rather than a date.

"Rebecca looks miserable trapped between B.S. and Dick Richard."

"Probably, because her father is trying his hardest to orchestrate a relationship between her and Dick."

"Please stop calling him that. I'm afraid food, drink, or both will fly out of my mouth."

Gideon's laughter filled the chilled air around her, warming her skin with a slow infusion into every cell. That warmth happened whenever he was near. She felt his stubbled jaw graze her ear before he pressed those full lips close to her ear.

"Shh, it's time for the big announcement."

"Don't shush me, I'm pouring out my fears to you," she teased. He pressed his well-muscled chest closer to her curves in response. Yep, all that man muscle and clear mountain air scent shut her up. He chuckled. So he knew his effect on her. Well, turn around was fair play. Offering a challenge test of her own, she pushed her derriere back into his groin. Smug satisfaction was her reward when she heard his groan.

"You'll pay for that later, sweetness." She hoped he was a man of his word. Nope, nope she didn't. Her head was screwed up. At the sound of a man clearing his throat Gideon increased the space between them.

Lina turned to face the stage as a smiling Logan and a grinning Ava came into view. Lina felt someone brush against her right arm, she looked to her right and down to find Lieutenant Janna Williamson at her side. Gideon stood at her side having a casual conversation with Kathryn and Cannon Quest. Kathryn worked as a nurse manager at SCMC before transferring to a similar job opportunity at Queens Bay Medical facility. Gideon's arm hung loose around her waist, heating her insides. *Friends held friends around the waist she rationalized.* Janna and Ava met at Florida Agricultural & Mechanical University, better known as FAMU, their freshman year. Janna grew up in the neighboring town of Halaskie, FL and traveled home with Ava at least three times a year during college.

"Who's the stallion with the shoulders?" Janna whispered. Lina shot a quick glance up at Gideon, hoping he didn't hear Janna's reference to him. He was occupied, talking with the man standing next to him.

Before she could respond Janna's phone dinged, signaling another text message. Lina watched as her friend, pulled the phone from her palazzo pants pocket, read the message, and promptly deleted it without responding.

"What are you talking about?" Janna zeroed in on Gideon's arm about her waist, then met her eyes with an undeniable smirk. "Mr. Six foot five, two and quarter pounds of muscle."

"You are good." Janna knew a man's height, weight, collar, and cuff length by sight. "I didn't want to come stag and Gideon invited me to be his date." Janna regarded her with a narrow eyed gaze before studying Gideon from head to toe. Lina recognized the moment Janna reconciled his name with previous history.

"Cut your losses, romance junkie," Janna said in a flat, matter of fact tone. It had always unnerved Lina how callous Janna was about the male species. Janna thought of men as a necessary evil that had to be managed.

"Is that what you're doing with the man on the other end of all the text messages you keep erasing?"

"Dawson knows the deal. He's interviewing for a joint task force billet on the narco-terrorism staff. He's trying to sweeten the pot since we are both in the area, but all we'll ever be is friends."

"Gideon and I are friends."

"Uh, huh. He's the *friend* that licked your tonsils at the fall charity event." It was a statement. Lina felt the other woman's stare and refused to look in her direction.

Keeping her eyes forward, "We are just friends. Nothing more."

"So what are you getting out of this?" Janna looked genuinely interested in her response.

"He makes me feel feminine, soft, and delicate. He appreciates more than my body," Lina whispered. "I'm the woman I've always wanted to be with him." *Cherished.*

"That's a twist on *just friends* I haven't heard until today. Did you tell this man that makes you feel like a crystal figurine, that he's just a friend? His hold on you says otherwise."

"He knows."

"I thought you were on a man-fast?"

"I am." Janna stepped back and pointed at Gideon's hand on her back.

"Is this the kind of fast that you smell the steak, lick the steak, rub the steak all over your lips, but don't take a bite?"

"I'm still ironing out the fine details."

"If you keep him around, your fast, diet planning, and calorie count is out the window."

"Besides, I don't have anybody with me."

The three women had become fast friends. Lina had considered transferring from First Coast University to FAMU with Ava and Janna, but that meant leaving Troy Lawson behind. Back then, she hadn't been strong enough to walk away from the man she loved.

"True, but you're not interested in anybody."

"I'm definitely into bodies. I'm not interested in anything else."

"Commitment phobes only need apply." Lina knew Janna's standard operating procedure when it came to men.

"Exactly, there's no room for drama between body parts." Janna said in all seriousness.

"Only if he knows what he's doing." They both laughed.

"Would you want an engagement party like this?" Gideon's question took her by surprise. When had he finished his conversation?

"You offering for my hand or is this purely academic?" She stiffened, but it was too late to retract the words.

"Are you ready to end your man detox slash fast?" Her breath caught at his heated tone.

"I want a viable engagement candidate, then I'll consider planning a party. With my track record, I'd skip the engagement phase and get him to the altar before he ghosts on me." She laughed, but Gideon just watched her.

"We'll talk about diet modification tonight when we get home." She glanced up to find an all too serious expression on Gideon's face. Home. Her cozy, condo had transformed into a home since Gideon entered her life.

Lina was distracted when Ava stopped speaking in the middle of her declaration of love for Logan. "Marcus?" That name on Ava's lips made Lina's blood run cold. Lina watched as a range of emotions flashed on her best friend's face. The room had fallen into an unnatural stillness as hundreds of people stared at the silent couple on stage. Logan was visibly scowling and scanning the crowd. Lina followed Ava's gaze and landed on the well-dressed man at the far corner of the ballroom. Marcus Grant, Ava's abusive boyfriend from college stood at the back of the ball room. What the flagnoid? Who had invited him?

"Butt wipe," she heard Janna mutter, as the petite powerhouse turned and started pushing through the crowd.

"I'm tracking him." Lina started putting an extra dip in her hip, clearing a path for her and Janna to get to the man who had nearly destroyed Ava. A nondescript man of Hispanic heritage stepped into her path, bringing her to an abrupt halt. She felt Janna bump into her rear and bounce back with the spring of a quarter hitting a military rack.

"Excuse me, ma'am, would you like a glass of champagne?" The man thrusted a fluted glass with golden liquid up at her face. The guy was enthusiastic about his job.

"All these people to serve, and you stop me in mid-stride," she took a step back and peered down at his oval, gold colored name tag attached to his starched, white jacket the man was wearing, "Moon, appreciate your attention, but not now." When he didn't move, Lina straightened her spine, showcasing every inch of her six feet, one inch in heels. Hands on her full hips, she pressed her lips together, narrowed her eyes all the while watching Mr. Moon. *Her stance said, you don't want any of this.*

"Pardon me ma'am, I apologize." It looked like he was about to say something else, but Lina was distracted yet again.

Gideon's familiar scent surrounded her before she felt a steely, arm close around her, waist, "Hey, what is going on with Ava?" Gideon said close to her ear. The warmth of his breath heated more than her cheek.

"Look to your right, the black guy in the navy suit near the rear exit is the guy that hurt Ava in college. His name is Marcus Grant."

"I thought you and Ava attended different colleges?"

"We did. She's a FAMU graduate, but I saw pictures."

"You never met him, but you recognize him based on a photo from six years ago?"

"I rarely forget a face. It's one of my many talents."

"Who the heck invited him?"

"My first guess, Ava's future mother-in-law," Lina offered a saccharine smile.

"Oh damnation."

"Yep, that about sums it up."

Lina observed as Robert Lee Masters, sliced through the crowd like the neurosurgeon he was, eyes searching frantically through the crowd.

"When Lina heard a roar from the direction of the stage, she turned in time to see Logan leap from the stage, barreling his way through the crowd." From there, mass scale chaos ruptured.

Masters men were on a rampage throughout the ball room. Of course most of the guests had no idea why Logan's fiancée was mute all of a sudden, or why Logan swept guests out of his path like bowling pins to reach the back of the ballroom. God, this had to be miserable for Ava. She and Logan deserved happiness, but it was proving to be elusive.

If she met Mr. Right and he stayed around long enough, Lina would forego all this hoopla. Get that man to the altar, and straight to a coat closet to consummate that sucker before something went wrong.

Gideon could see Ava's lips quiver as the room erupted in full on chaos. Looking at any woman on the verge of tears churned his gut. He needed to help the guys with keeping Logan calm. So, he left Lina with the icy, pint-sized Navy nurse corps officer. Janna Williamson's five foot frame draped in a robin's egg blue pant suit with springy curls flowing down her back was a stark contrast to her brusque personality. With her squared shoulders and parade rest stance, she reminded him of a female Marine. Taking in the melee, Gideon was pissed at the damage done to Ava and Logan's special day. Of course, having the groom-to-be attack one of the guests changed the tone of the party. Guests were exiting the ballroom with the efficiency of a fire Marshall Directive. Gideon breathed a sigh of relief when Lina, Janna, Rebecca Lynn and all the women of the Walter's family rallied around Ava. The mild mannered, always poised pediatric nurse was escorted off the stage before more chaos ensued.

Marcus Grant looked stunned when Logan tore through the crowd en route to him, but the man was ready when Logan aimed a fist at his face. Marcus was skilled and ready for the punch, but he'd underestimated Logan's intensity. Logan pushed every ounce of his weight into his punches. Marcus should count his blessings if all his teeth remained in his mouth. Seriously, if Logan's mom had orchestrated that cluster fubar she was one vicious socialite.

"Where's Ava?" Logan's wild gaze searched the shattering crowd. Gideon took in the blood spatters on Logan's white dress shirt, the skin covering his knuckles was crimson red and bruised.

"Logan," Gideon started cautiously. Logan didn't look at him.

"Not now Gideon, I need to be with Ava, now that the asshole is out of here. And my mother is on her way home."

"It's a bad idea to approach Ava spattered with blood." Ava looked ready to crack when her friends ushered her to the ladies' lounge. Menace rolled off Logan with the intensity of a magnetic pulse. His strength seemed unnatural as he drove through the crowd toward Ava's abuser. Darwin had pulled Logan off the bleeding man with the help of Graham.

"Not to get into your family business, but does your mother have any underlying mental health concerns?" Gideon knew he was in uncharted waters. He and Logan limited their conversations to work and golf.

"She starts her day with a drink." Ah. An alcoholic. That answered one of his questions, but not the most important.

"Why is Ava a target for her anger?" Gideon knew Maribelle's threats contributed to Ava running away from Logan at first. She'd joined the Navy Nurse corps to protect Logan and escape Shell Cove. Gideon watched as the other man ran tracks through his hair with his fingers. By his tight expression, Gideon knew whatever Logan was about to say would be a doozy.

"This is all new information to me, but, my grandfather had a mistress." Gideon shrugged his shoulders. Unclear how this information related to what happened.

"His mistress resembled Ava." Oh, damnation. Gideon raked his fingers through his hair.

"Wow. I don't how to respond," Gideon said.

"That makes two of us." Logan's face went blank. Gideon could feel Logan's sorrow. "My grandfather was involved with her for decades, until she died. Their relationship was public knowledge and a source of ridicule for my mother throughout her childhood."

Interesting. An experience from childhood had driven the woman to attack her son's fiancée. As a friend, he accepted the information as presented to him, but as a seasoned psychiatrist he knew there had to be something more recent to trigger her behavior.

"The man has been dead for over ten years. Any advice, counselor?" Logan looked at him expectantly.

Logan's mother hadn't forgiven her father.

"None that would help you today. I'd be happy to arrange an initial consultation for your mother with one of my colleagues," he offered. Logan snorted in response.

"You've met my mother. I would like a team of wild horses to drag her into a psych clinic." Or maybe one determined Marine.

"Before this question and answer session evolves into a one hour visit, I need to see Ava."

"I agree, but look at yourself." Gideon pointed at the blood spatters marring Logan's sand colored suit jacket. Logan quickly glanced down.

"I need a change of clothes."

Clamping a hand of support on the distressed male's shoulder, Gideon said, "Come on, I have an extra shirt in my car. I'll go grab it while you clean up."

Logan didn't move. Gideon met the other man's gaze, silently questioning his delay.

"I'm pissed, but I know you're using your de-escalation techniques on me."

"You'll thank me and my de-escalation methodology when you see yourself in the mirror."

"Since you're offering advice, here's some for you. I saw you with Lina tonight and I have not forgotten that kissing stunt you pulled at the country club." Gideon didn't like Logan's tone. Like he was warning him away from Lina.

"Tonight isn't about me and Lina." Gideon knew his voice was stern, too directive for the moment, but he wouldn't discuss what was happening between him and Lina with anyone.

"I know it's my and Ava's night, but keep walking if your plan is to toy with Lina."

"You ready to get your ass kicked? That's about to happen if you're thinking you can warn me away from Lina." They were at a standoff, both of them staring each other down.

Logan laughed then.

"Glad we understand one another."

"Yeah, we do."

"You know that country accent of yours shows itself when your pissed."

"Get out of here. I'll bring the shirt." Before Gideon could turn away, Logan extended his hand.

"Thanks, Gideon."

"No problem. That's what friends do."

"You're serious about Lina." It was an observation more than anything. Gideon nodded his head in agreement.

"Protect her better than I've done with Ava." Lina needed protection, but not from clawed and winged socialites. The tightening in his gut when he replayed the scene in her bedroom said danger was close. He would keep her safe at any cost.

The ladies' dressing room resembled a scene from the Rocky Horror Picture show. Ava's grandmother, affectionately called Granny Lou by grand and non-grand children alike, had a vise-like grip on Mrs. Walters shoulder, while Lina's mom, Bernadean had a similar grip on both the woman's hands. Nostrils flaring and lips thinned, Ariss Walters, Ava's mother, looked ready to rock'em and sock'em like a vintage Batman television episode. For Maribelle's sake, Lina hoped the woman had pulled an Elvis and left the building.

Meanwhile Ava sobbed in Lina's arms. Lina took in the smudged eyes, the waterproof mascara that hadn't lived up to its namesake, the puffy red eyes. It broke Lina's heart to see Ava hurting. Maribelle had wrecked her son's engagement celebration, with God and The Reserves country club members as her witness. How could one woman justify being so horrible? Lina couldn't imagine being that deliberately cruel to another human being. What pleasure was there in Ava's tear stained face and Logan's bloody knuckles?

"Marcus is gone. Don't cry anymore," Lina cooed as she hugged her friend.

"I'm not crying over seeing Marcus. He doesn't scare me anymore." Ava's statement brought a smile to Lina's face. Before Logan came into Ava's life she was terrified to question or confront a man. Sharing the same space with the male species made her uncomfortable. Lina on the other hand adored male companionship. Too much for her own well-being. If she was remotely attracted to a man, her body suited up like Ironman with a target in sight. She didn't want Gideon to get away. But get away from her, all men had.

"Then why are you still crying?"

"Because engagements and love shouldn't be this hostile. Logan's mother hates me. I'm marrying into a family where I'll never be accepted."

"All these tears and the wedding is still a go?"

"Lina, what do tears have to do with my marrying Logan?" Janna who had been a silent observer, chimed in.

"Cover your ears, Monique." Everyone looked at Monique Faulkner. Monique had been a patient of Ava's when she was on staff at SCMC.

"I'm seventeen, you can say bad words in front of me." Monique pouted reinforcing why it was in everyone's best interest if she left the room.

Lina stepped in before any one caved to the saccharine smile plastered on the girl's heart shaped face "Time for you to wait in the lounge."

"No Lina, why?"

"Because you believe there are bad words. Everyone else in the room knows there are situations where those *bad words,*" Lina motioned air quotes with two fingers on each hand, "are warranted." Peeping through lowered lashes, Monique scanned the room searching for an ally. With none forthcoming, she turned in a huff and exited the soft spring loaded door.

"Ava, the whole engagement and Masters family drama has you stressed out. I say ride that man like Seabiscuit, then cut your losses if this family thing doesn't work out."

"Language, Lieutenant," Lina chided.

"No offense Granny Lou, Deanie and Mrs. Walters," Janna said. Lina's mom beamed at the use of her nickname. Unphased by the Logan Seabiscuit comment. Lina recalled the first time she heard her father refer to Bernadean James as Deanie.

Lina had been about eight years old. Her mother had been flipping mouse eared pancakes on the griddle. Her father had walked up behind his wife, encircled her in his arms, planted a loud, smack of a kiss on her right cheek and said, *I love you, Deanie James*. Lina had looked on from the round oak table grinning as her mother had returned an equally affectionate kiss on her father's lips. The kids in the neighborhood still called her Mrs. Deanie. All these years later, that memory still brought a smile to Lina's face. That was the kind of love Lina wanted for herself.

"None taken, lil Miss Janna, but keep your equine metaphors to yourself. Our Ava is getting married and giving me some great grand babies. Your mother and I are going to have a show down with Maribelle Masters, as soon as I go get my blessing oil," Ava's Granny Lou said.

"She's not going to let you near her, Granny Lou." Ava replied, honestly. To Lina's knowledge, Maribelle had made no effort to get to know the Walters family.

"Well, I could accidentally drop the bottle on her head. Prayer works, children, even when you're unconscious." Granny Lou nodded her head to no one in particular.

"Okay, before we consider senior-on-senior violence, let's freshen up and get on with announcing an upcoming wedding." Lina was the temporary maid of honor in Shaylah's absence. No way, would she allow Ava's engagement to go do in flames.

"But, everyone is gone." Ava words sounded as sad as she looked.

"I see enough people, Ava." Lina stated.

"Come on Rebecca Lynn and Janna, let's go tell the guys."

"Did Dick leave? I don't want to go out there, until I'm sure he's gone."

"I haven't seen your date since the melee started."

"Good." Rebecca released a sigh of relief. "Hopefully, he left with the rest of the guests."

"Okay, Ms. Thang, spill the milk. Why are you here with a man named, Dick As-cot, knowing Darwin is crazy about you?" Lina asked the question they all wanted answered. Six pairs of eyes turned in Rebecca Lynn's direction.

"My father really likes Dick," Rebecca said with a sigh. Coughs, giggles, and all out laughter filled the room.

"You need to rethink ever saying that sentence again and I strongly suggest you call him, Richard." Lina said.

"Lina Diane James, enough with the sharp tongue." Her mother rebuffed.

"Oh my goodness, I just caught the meaning!" Rebecca's cheeks flamed red. She covered her mouth with her hand. They all laughed at Dick's expense.

"What about Darwin?" Ava's soft tone blanketed the room.

"What Darwin and I have is more complicated."

"Relationships always are," Ariss Walters commented.

"What Darwin and I have is more carnal than your traditional relationship."

"My motto, is hit it and quit it," Janna stated matter of factly.

"Sugar that's not a motto, it's a defense mechanism," Bernadean offered. "At my age, carnal interest and love are crystal clear. Even my eighteen-year old self recognized her soul mate in Lincoln James." Lina stilled at her father's name. It was rare that her mother even mentioned him in conversation. Lina remembered when her father stopped coming home, she remembered hearing her mother's sobs through closed doors.

A knock at the door brought the conversation to a halt.

"Sweetness, you ready to go?" She'd recognize her country boy in a saloon full of rowdy cowboys. Lina responded to his call without a second thought.

"Give me fifteen minutes." Lina looked up to find six pairs of eyes trained on her.

"When did you become *sweetness* to Gideon Rice?" Ava questioned.

"He's helping me sort out some personal stuff." Lina would not make Ava's day worse by mentioning she had a stalker.

"What kind of stuff is going on with you that requires Gideon to be at your side frequently enough that your name is now synonymous with powdered sugar?" Janna asked in a low tone, her eyes serious.

Leave it to Janna to ask the pivotal question. Lina looked to her mother for guidance. The sadness in her mother's eyes was beyond disturbing. It made her heart ache. She could tell her friends about the break-in or she could do her part to save the day. Ava's day.

"It's nice to have a man's assistance with some things." Lina said, with a coy smile.

"Lina *Independent Woman* James is allowing a man to help her. You never let us help you, but by some miracle, Gideon gets the honor." Ava gave her an incredulous look. "Who are you? And what have you done with my best friend?"

Ava's statement was an uncomfortable truth. A fist tightened around Lina's heart and she swallowed the lump that formed in her throat. She needed to stay in control of her emotions and refocus on what they were dealing with at this moment. Ava and Logan. She glanced around the room to find all eyes on her. She schooled her features in a mask of composure.

"I don't ask for help, because I can take care of myself," Lina stated. "Besides, I didn't ask Gideon for anything. He won't take no for an answer." She prayed a lightning bolt did not strike her down, because the truth was she had grown accustomed to him being there for her.

"Nice save, Lina, but you better get going. Gideon is probably missing his sweetness by now," came Janna's voice. The room erupted in laughter, Lina felt anything, but joyful. She'd begun to depend on Gideon. What would she do if he decided to walk away?

CHAPTER ELEVEN

She still wasn't dating Gideon. The connection they shared was beyond dating. It was a deeper connection, more intense, all-consuming. The clinic day ended for the rest of the staff two hours ago. Her SCMC process improvement meeting took her away from the clinic for the better part of the afternoon. She managed to restructure the clinic appointment templates to expand availability during the morning hours. Freeing up an hour in the afternoon for each provider left time in their schedules to document patient encounters, make in-patient rounds on their recent admissions and leave the hospital at five o'clock each evening. She however, hadn't faired as well in the deal.

Lina wanted to get home, soak in a verbena scented whirlpool bath, and eat whatever Gideon or Estrella prepared for dinner. She couldn't remember a time in her life when she felt more cared for.

Gideon's door opened and the man she saw walking away from a neutral faced Gideon nearly brought her to her knees.

She must have made a sound of distress, because both men looked down at her. Now she saw an equal measure of shock register in wide stretched chestnut colored eyes. He was the first to speak.

"Lina?" God, the tears started flowing unbridled down her face. He shouldn't be here. This couldn't be happening. But he was real, because she felt his arms curl around her back, pulling her into his comforting embrace.

"Bishop?" Resting her head against his firm chest she let the tears flow. Her fingers curled into the fabric of his shirt, she pulled at the material trying to pull herself together. Seeing him here, changed everything.

"I'm fine, baby girl." If he was back in therapy his words weren't true. Bishop had been an active duty Marine during Operation Enduring Freedom. His time in Afghanistan had changed him. He'd seen too much and done too much to stay alive. Knowing that he was now Gideon's patient, spoke volumes to what he'd experienced in the conflict. She'd read enough medical records on their patients' nightmares, thoughts of violence, escalating over minor offenses.

"Keep your tears for someone important." Loosening her hold around his waist, she tilted her head back, raising her eyes to meet his.

"You're important to me," she said before dropping her head to his shoulder.

"Thanks, baby girl," he said planting a kiss on the top of her head. The soft strokes he delivered to her back did little to soothe her.

"What are you doing here?" she asked, her face now buried in his shirt. Maybe, she was overreacting. Gideon was a Marine. Hoping Bishop and Gideon were battle buddies was probably asking too much of the universe. She sniffled, and the stroking to her back increased.

"Doc and I met through the WWI program at Queens Bay Naval Treatment facility." Fledgling hope blossomed in her gut. Bishop wasn't Gideon's patient. "Some heavy stuff is going down in my police precinct because of the increase in Galaxy drug activity and missing persons reporting."

"But why are you here? Meeting with Gideon in private?" It was unprofessional to use Gideon's given name with a patient, but her thoughts were scattered. "The crime scenes triggered memories from my time in Afghanistan."

That's when Lina noticed Gideon stood stalk still in the door to his office. He watched her and Bishop. He looked downright menacing.

"Gideon," Lina called his name. He turned his steely gaze to her and she saw the storm clouds brewing in his eyes.

"When did you start working in this clinic with Doc? The last time we talked you worked on the inpatient unit." She should've never left the unit.

"How do you two know each other?" Gideon's tone sounded accusatory. What was the matter with him?

"Gideon is everything okay?" He couldn't think she was involved with another man. She spent her days and evenings with him. Granted he hadn't stayed with her since that first date, but he knew her.

"Bishop is my…" She looked at Bishop then, questioning if she should disclose their relationship before he was ready.

"What is he to you?" Even Bishop pivoted on his heel to look in Gideon's direction. Gideon's voice was low pitched, feral.

"It's okay to tell him."

"Tell me what?"

"Bishop…he's my brother." Their relationship was fragile and she would do anything in her power to protect the budding kinship with her father's firstborn.

"No." That single syllable word spoke volumes to their immediate dilemma. It was unethical to become involved with your patient's sister. "You don't have the same last name." Judging by the furrow between Gideon's brows his statement was more of a question.

"Lincoln James and my mother were married for less than two years. When my mother remarried she gave me the Cardar family name." Bishop's jaw was tight and Lina knew it cost him to disclose that information in her presence. It still bothered him that he didn't have a choice in keeping his father's last name. She didn't know Bishop well. Their kinship had been strained most of her adult life. Her father, Lincoln and Bishop's mother had ended their marriage long before Lina was born. With her father gone, and her mother rarely acknowledging his existence, Lina didn't learn of her brother until she had prodded her mother for information regarding her heritage.

"Why does it matter? Your job shouldn't be in jeopardy because I'm a drop in patient of Doc Rice." If only it were as simple as Bishop presented it.

Lina straightened her spine and proceeded to do what she did best. Make everybody happy. "I'm proud of you for recognizing you needed help and for seeking out Dr. Rice. He's one of the best at what he does." She could feel the heat seeping out of her body. The cold settled into her limbs. She wanted to go home. Lina watched as Bishop looked from her to Gideon.

"You both look as if my coming here is worse than a six shooter in a combat zone."

"I see finding humor in any situation is a family trait," Gideon offered.

"What are you not telling me?" Bishop directed his question at Gideon. Typical, Marines questioned Marines.

"Lina and I are dating." He'd said the "d" word.

"We must have decided that while I was sleeping." Gideon didn't take his eyes off her when he spoke. Lina refused to look away. Dating had never come up in their conversations, their time together was a natural progression they both accepted, but never validated with a label. She wouldn't sacrifice her family, for a man. Family came first. She didn't know how much Bishop would allow their budding kinship to flourish, but she was sure it would last longer than one of her relationships.

"Bishop, I'll call you in the morning with a plan for moving forward."

"Sure thing, Doc." Lina wouldn't look at him. Too afraid that she would change her mind, if she met his eyes. Bishop pulled free of her embrace.

"Walk me to the elevator, lil sis."

"Sure."

Lina's voice a whisper in the room, had the affect of a cymbal in her head. She couldn't continue *dating* Gideon if Bishop was his patient. There were other psychiatrists in Shell Cove, but none that were veteran Marines. Lina knew after witnessing one of Gideon's nightmares that he struggled with his own demons from combat. She understood that Gideon could help veterans suffering from combat fatigue and post-traumatic stress disorder beyond the average mental health professional. He'd walked in their shoes, literally. He survived pain and loss. His body bore the scars of his sacrifice.

"Sis, you need to leave the Doc alone." Shocked was the only word to surface in her head.

"You're the patient, and you think the doctor is crazy?"

"You don't know him like I do."

"I'm the one dating the man." For all of five seconds, but hey, he'd been the one to let the cat out of the bag.

"And I'm the one that knows what drives a Marine. How his mind ticks. As in ticking time bomb. We all are."

"Well, we're not going to see each other anymore."

"Doc said you were dating."

"And what did I just say?"

"Marines have a short half-life. If he says you are with him, I'd take him at his word."

"He's not a Marine anymore."

"Once a Marine, always a Marine. Never forget." That was the problem. She couldn't forget Gideon. Not now.

The dresser hit the floor with a crash, sending the etched purple vase filled with two dozen white roses careening to the floor. A special order for their first night together. Glass shards, framed photos, and perfume bottles skittered across the carpeted floor. Where was she? For over an hour, he waited patiently in her bedroom. Tonight belonged to him. He never took anything from the boss, but Lina was his prize for faithful service. He earned her.

"My Lina." He roared, rage tearing a chasm inside him like a caged animal clawing for freedom. She was with him. Images of the man touching her that first night, flooded his mind.

He spun, grabbing the bedside lamp, he yanked the cord from the wall. He hurled the bulbous glass base at the wall art, watching as they both shattered. Debris rained down, joining the soppy mess on the floor. She would pay for ignoring him. He would make them both pay, for every touch. For making him watch.

She's mine.

He pulled at his hair, gripping his head as he stormed in the bathroom. The counter top was organized with containers of various sizes. Things to make her beautiful. Beauty she gave to another man. With a furious swipe of his bulky arm everything on the counter took flight. The sound of glass hitting the tiled-floor fueled his rage. Sweet fragrance filled his nostrils and he remembered Lina's dark almond shaped eyes the first time he'd seen her. He glanced down eyeing the glass waste bin, he picked it up, measuring the weight. Seeing his reflection in the mirror, hair standing on end, eyes wild, he hurled the object at his image. He didn't flinch when small cuts burned on the exposed skin of his face and arms.

Lina was unfaithful.

He turned and strode into the bedroom. Reaching into his back pocket he pulled out his blade.

Gideon waited until he heard the ding, signaling that the elevator had started its descent before he moved in Lina's direction. Whatever Bishop Cardar, now Bishop Cardar James had told Lina he knew it involved her ending what they had found in each other. She stood, staring at the closed elevator doors, no doubt contemplating how to give him his walking papers.

"Lina, I'm not giving you up." The fire in her eyes, at his words, made his heart soar, then the reality of their situation brought it crashing to the searing, hot Florida pavement.

"You're not. I'm walking away."

Lina grabbed her purse, and moved toward the elevators. "Man fast, remember?"

"And I recall telling you, not on my watch. I'm hot on your trail, sweetness. Expect me tonight."

Lina stepped in the elevator when it arrived and kept her eyes trained above his shoulder until the doors closed. Gideon returned to his office, logged off his computer and grabbed his keys. Lina was not walking away from him. He wouldn't survive it.

Something bad had happened at Lina's condominium. Gideon arrived at Lina's complex to find the service road partially blocked by three police vehicles. Blue lights bounced off his windshield then lost their vibrancy amid the dense forestry.

He pressed the brake pedal, slowing to a near crawl, snaking his way through the haphazardly parked cars. The road was clear of pedestrian traffic. An ambulance was parked in the center of the parking lot, both rear doors opened away from his field of view. Assessing the scene Gideon concluded the police had parked on the road leading to the complex to leave the ambulance a clear path out of the parking lot. What the heck was going on?

His heart pounded in his chest. He needed to find Lina. She would've arrived home within the past fifteen minutes. Had this scene happened since she arrived or had she been greeted by flashing sirens? Pulling his car in front of an abandoned squad car, he killed the engine, pocketed the keys, and set out on foot.

Lina's condo came into view. Two men dressed in dark blue pants with short sleeved shirts were wheeling a gurney out of Lina's floor door. His heart sped up. He ran toward the building yelling her name.

"Lina!" Had Lina been hurt? Fear and rage swelled with the force of a crashing wave. First he had to know what happened to Lina. Then someone's family would need a priest and a black suit. Seeing Lina's metallic purple Camaro, parked underneath her building in its designated parking space, ratcheted up his fear for her safety.

Approaching the gurney, Gideon was floored to see a bruised, bloody, but conscious Estrella.

"I tried to stop...him." Gideon scrubbed one hand over his face at the sight before him. Vivid purple bruises covered Estrella's face. Her left eye was swollen shut.

"Mo...man came," she panted. As she talked fresh blood coated her teeth. Gideon took a breath, reining in his fury. What kind of animal would beat a woman?

"Danger, get away." Estrella's skin had an ashen blue hue and wheezy sounds followed each syllable as she spoke. Her words were non-sensical. Each breath seemed to drain her strength.

"Estrella, save your energy. Don't talk. You need medical attention and I'll get Lina someplace safe." The effort to nod her head siphoned her remaining energy. Gideon turned his attention to the paramedic when her eyes slid closed. "She's a friend. Were there signs beyond a physical assault?"

"She was fully clothed when we arrived." Gideon nodded his head in acknowledgement. He needed to lay eyes on Lina. A man capable of hurting another person like this, would do more than physical harm if given the opportunity.

"Lina?" Gideon shouldered his way toward her, making steady progress through the crowd of onlookers.

"Gideon, I'm here." The fear in Lina's eyes unleashed buried memories of another woman who'd depended on him to have her back. Seeing her quelled the storm brewing inside him, but that's where the calm ended. On slow approach, he noticed the fine tremble to her lower lip and he wanted to gather her in his arms and erase all her hurts. Reaching for her, he tightened his arms around her. Peering over her shoulder, her condo looked like a bomb had been detonated at center mass. The glass doors were smashed. All the artwork was broken or dumped in the center of the living area. Slash marks covered the soft cushions.

"You okay sweetness?" Her tremors vibrated through his chest causing anger to coil in his veins like a cobra ready to strike. When he found the man responsible for putting that fear in Lina's eyes Gideon would make him pay.

"No." He searched her for injuries. Her exotic scent blanketed him and he held her tighter. Breathing her in soothed the beast in him wanting to break free. The one ready to hunt the man foolish enough to target Lina. How far would he go to protect her? He'd kill to protect his woman. And Lina was his. He would take her home. There would be no compromise on this. He needed to keep her safe. Everything in him said she was his to protect. Capturing her chin between his thumb and forefinger, he raised her head until their eyes met.

"You were hurt?" The sadness in her eyes was so foreign for the vibrant, confident woman he knew.

"I wasn't, but Estrella…they are telling me I can't go with her to the hospital. Why is this happening to me?" His jaw tightened. A roar sounded in his head. She asked questions he wished he could answer.

"Sweetness," he said cupping her delicate features in his big hands.

"Who are you?" Gideon felt the arms around his neck tense. He lowered his hands, but kept a possessive hand on Lina's waist. He heard her inhale a deep breath before she turned to face the officer. She often did that deep breathing thing when she was stressed.

"He's my," she glanced over her shoulder in his direction, "I meant he's… Gideon what are you to me?" He'd never seen her so lost.

"I'm all hers," he heard himself say. "What happened here?"

"Beachcombers called us," the uniformed officer offered. He was past his prime, with a thick waist, a ruddy complexion and a dirty brown comb over that failed to conceal the baldness.

"Did anyone see anything?"

"Nothing much that I can tell. Appears there was a break-in. The neighbor heard the disturbance. The neighbor went to investigate and was physically assaulted by the perpetrator."

"When I arrived she was lying on the kitchen floor, beaten and barely conscious." Lina's voice shook worse than before as she described Estrella's condition. Tremors raked her body as she spoke but she didn't seem to notice.

"Did you notice anyone, a car, anything large or small Lina that could be important?" Looking at him, she shook her head no and Gideon recognized the emotion. Guilt.

She would've looked away, but he held her shoulders steady.

"What happened here isn't your fault."

"Isn't it?" Her voice climbed higher. "That beating Estrella took was meant for me." A panicked expression crossed her face before she schooled her features into a fragile mask.

"You don't know that," he said in a firm voice. The self-reliant woman in her balked at his tone, the terrified little girl was relieved he was there and she didn't have to face the big, bad wolf stalking her alone.

"He's right, ma'am. There is no way to know how the person or people who did this would have reacted to your presence."

"I don't want to hear anymore. I'm going with Estrella to the hospital."

"We'll follow behind the ambulance, then you are coming home with me."

Chapter Twelve

Shocked and scared witless. The roses, the vandalism, nothing made sense in Lina's world. Not wanting to completely crumble, she stared ahead as Gideon drove in silence. The warmth of his large fingers curling over her hand, nearly undid her. She'd never been great at accepting help from other people, especially men, now Gideon's touch was the only thing keeping her together. She was an independent woman capable of taking care of herself, but she didn't know how to protect herself from the monster that nearly beat her friend unconscious.

"I need to call my mom." Her hand shook as she pulled her purse up between her feet where they rested on the floorboard of the car. Rifling through the depths of her tote bag, not seeing the phone only served to heighten her anxiety. Not finding it, her breathing rate increased, she felt like she was suffocating, panicked. She wanted to scream.

"Can you lower the window, please? I need some air." Gideon briefly glanced in her direction and what he saw must have alarmed him, because he hit the right signal light and pulled over onto the shoulder of the highway. The passenger window lowered and humid air rushed into the car.

"Lina, breathe," Gideon's voice was firm and directive. The tone a drill sergeant would use with a grunt, she realized. His face was closer to hers, but she couldn't see any details of his face. The sound of tires against the asphalt intensified, and each vibration penetrated her body, and settled in her chest until she felt as though she was coming apart at the seams.

"I'm trying." She felt his hand tightening on hers, but it did nothing to alleviate the pressure in her chest.

"Look at me." The mental images of the blood stained roses, and slashed furniture, the broken glasses slammed into her mental strongholds. Near toppling her defenses. Someone wanted to scare her. It was working. "Look at me, now." Holding her left hand securely in his grip, he cradled her cheek in his large palm angling her face toward him.

"I've got you. You're safe. No one will get to you as long as you're with me." God, she wanted to believe him. But they didn't know what or who they were fighting. How was she supposed to defend herself? He leaned across the center console then, pressing a gentle kiss to her cheek.

"I'll keep you safe. I promise." She didn't realize what she was doing until it happened. She pulled her hand from his, snaked it around his neck, threading her fingers into his lush, dark curls. Pulling him close she pressed her lips to his and took what she needed to quell the fear rising in her. He wasn't resisting her, but he didn't respond to her touch. Rejected. She wouldn't let the tears fall. Not here, not for him, not ever. No man would have that type of power over her again.

She moved to pull away, but his hand around her nape kept her in place. She lowered her head, embarrassment competing with the fear for purchase in her overtaxed brain. She felt his fingers caress her cheek, before he lifted her chin, turning her face in his direction. The pads of his fingers were calloused but not abrasive. Her skin tingled and heated where his warm breath fanned over her.

"I want your sweet taste in my mouth," came his low rumble. "Kiss me back if you want me beyond this moment, and then take whatever you need." Fire lit his smoke gray eyes as he bored into hers. The evening breeze lifted her hair blowing strands into her face. Lina closed her eyes when he brushed the hairs from her face and tucked them behind her ear. Biting into her lips, she savored the moment, the feeling of connection was unlike anything she'd shared with another man.

His lips claimed hers. The kiss was slow and sensual, but not gentle. His mouth was hungry on hers. His lips were soft. He caressed her lips with his own over and over, until she surrendered and he pressed inside.

Once inside, he teased her tongue, delivering long strokes that she felt down to her toes curling in her shoes.

"Take, Lina," he spoke into her mouth. His willingness to give was so unexpected, emotions she had long ago abandoned in a relationship stirred deep within her. Pleasure she hadn't realized was possible flooded her senses and she reached for it and held on.

"Yes," and that's what she did. Took what she needed, had denied herself too long. She drove into his mouth like a drowning woman reaching for a life preserver. And he answered her demands with his own. When she felt his strong fingers over her breast, she jumped, breaking the kiss.

"I'm too old for back seat of the jeep escapades." She ran her trembling fingers across her forehead, "kissing you was a major man-fast violation."

"We both needed that kiss." He flashed a wick grin and winked as he released his grip. "Sweeter than my dreams. You wanted that kiss as much as I did."

"Half way to the finish line, I can't quit," her voice rose.

"You know and I know, that there will never be another man in your life. Or in your bed." Her eyes flew to his, dumbstruck.

"What are you saying?"

"You can deny yourself anything you want, except me." She shivered, picturing all of Gideon's hard muscles over her, driving into her. The endorphin release flooded her system and her insides quaked. Yeah, he was definitely an escape from her current state of unrest. Releasing her, the car engine purred to life and they ate up the miles in companionable silence. His house. A house that she probably shouldn't think of as a refuge. But, she didn't want to be away from him. She trusted him to keep them safe. She trusted him with her life.

"You are safe with me, but you're never too old for good loving." She was vulnerable to another type of harm if she stayed with him. How could he save her from her own desires? She wasn't sure she wanted to be rescued anymore.

Lina is mine auto played in his head the moment he pulled into the circular drive in front of his home. Gideon would never let her go. This was the first time a woman had crossed the threshold to his home since... Not wanting to go there, Gideon focused on the fact that Lina was here with him, finally. Sharing his home. The home that he had commissioned an architect to build for his family.

Unlocking the front door, Gideon reached for the dimmer switch on the lighting panel. Warm light washed the sunken formal living room in a soft, yellow hue. White washed oak furniture had been artfully placed by an interior decorator. Chenille throws and pillows were added to give a cozy feel of provincial country living. He could have brought Lina into the house through the attached garage that led to the mudroom, but he wanted her to view the house as a guest might. He didn't want to be alone anymore, and he'd do everything in his power to impress her, have her stay with him, and make it a home.

She was motionless behind him. Her feet planted under the brick arched entryway, indecision was clearly written on her face.

"Come inside with me Lina." He reached for her, but didn't go as far as to touch her. This had to be her decision. They both knew this moment would change everything about their relationship. And it was a relationship. Recalling the situation with her brother, he'd transferred Bishop to another psychiatrist on his team. Gideon could serve as a consultant on his case if needed, but no way in hell would he stop seeing Lina.

"Gideon." The vulnerability in her voice tugged at his heart. A heart that was beating again because of Lina. She looked better than during the ride over, but a sense of panic, confusion, and fatigue surrounded her.

"Yeah, sweetness." He could see her gracing his bed. Opening herself to him as he explored every nook and curve of her beautiful body.

"I'm really vulnerable right now. What happened in the car was wrong. I used you to ease my own fears and I can't promise I won't accost you again." He released a low chuckle.

"Your type of abuse is my favorite kind. What else do you need me to ease, tonight?"

"I'm being serious."

"So am I. Now, come on in the house. I know how to protect myself from a she-cat."

"I've got your she-cat."

"I'm counting on it, sweetness. Get it here, you need to eat and get some rest."

"A hot bath would be nice."

"I can arrange that, too." He led her through the family room into the first floor guest suite.

"There's a walk-in shower and linen closet to your left. The large soaking tub is in the master suite. You're welcome to use it."

"Thanks, I will. I don't have any clothes with me. The cops wouldn't let me take anything from my house."

"I have something that will fit you." Preferably him, between her legs, open in invitation. "We'll worry about tomorrow in the morning. Let's get through tonight."

"Your house has feminine touches. Any secret girlfriends lurking in the bushes?" His spine stiffened.

"No. If you don't like this room you can choose from the four upstairs. My room is on the opposite side of the front office."

"Hey, Gideon," she touched his cheek as she spoke, "I didn't mean to offend you. It's just most guys, don't have a six bedroom house fully furnished. Your house is beautiful, a bit monochromatic for my tastes, but it will do in a pinch." She thought his house was boring.

"We can change it more to your liking." Lina looked anywhere other than his face. Slow down, she'd be running for the hills if he was more obvious that he wanted her to stay.

"Your house is fine. I'll take you up on the swim in your tub. You lead the way." She followed him through double doors that opened into the master suite.

The master suite was divided into a sunken sleeping area, a raised wet bath area with custom cabinetry built around a 65 inch flat panel television. The back wall held a double sided fireplace flanked by paired arched doorways leading to a sunroom and a patio.

"Wow…you built all this for yourself."

"For my family."

"I'll join your family plan." His strong arms circled her waist pulling, until their bodies were meshed together. The pulse in his neck thrummed at a rate matching her own. She swallowed and his eyes tracked the movement. Licking her lips, she could almost taste his heat.

"What are you doing?"

"Welcoming you to the family." His breath caressed her mouth for a brief moment, then the pillage ensued. His tongue swept into her mouth, seeking, savoring, probing. He tasted fresh, and warm, like hot buttered bread from a brick oven. And she wanted more of him. Her fingers curled in the fabric covering his chest, anchoring him in place. He couldn't pull away without taking her down with him. The candy thief had met the master chocolatier. She returned his ardor with an urgency that bordered on savagery. She pulled at his dress shirt, tugging the hem free of his slacks. Pushing the fabric upward, she made contact with hot, hard muscle. She moaned and he capitalized on the opportunity and drove deeper into her mouth. His erection dug into her pelvis and she ground her heated mound against him, hating the clothes that separated them. Gideon broke the kiss. The cool room air touched her moistened lips and she mourned the loss of contact.

"End your fast." That pulled her up short. Why was she setting herself up for heartbreak? *Blood loss and stone table, remember?* Words were easy to spout, she needed proof of Gideon's feelings for her before she gave her heart again. She wouldn't survive Gideon's abandonment.

"No." Hurt shone in his eyes. It saddened her to know she had caused him pain, but she wanted a man's love, not lust. He stepped back, breaking their connection. His stance said he accepted her decision, but his eyes, and that stubborn jaw said he didn't agree with denying what they both wanted. Determination. That's what she saw.

"I'll draw your bath and make you something to eat while you get cleaned up." He pushed past her without meeting her eyes. He pushed through a set of frosted glass doors to a breathtaking bathroom suite. A marble roman style tub occupied the center of the room. The backside of the tub was encased in glass with an oversized shower nozzle hanging from the ceiling. Two additional shower heads extended from the left and right glass wall. Wow. The sound of water filled the room and she waited until he exited before she moved into the bathroom and closed the twin doors.

Soaking in Gideon's tub reminded her of arriving at the community pool in her mother's neighborhood before anyone else. Heaven. Inhaling the tropical fruit scent that filled the room, Lina sank further into the tub until the bubbles covered the swells of her breasts in fragrance and warmth. Her body was hot after the kiss-athon with Gideon, the bathwater cooled her off, allowing her hormone levels to return to near normal. Even though she was in water, she knew there was a different kind of moisture gathered between her legs.

A single bathroom door swung wide, Gideon's hulking frame filled the entryway.

"I brought you something to eat." The food smelled good, but he smelled great. He'd traded his dress shirt and slacks for well-worn jeans that hugged his thigh muscles and a faded green tank. *Lip smacking delicious.* And whatever he carried in on the plate smelled fattening too. A man bearing food was a dual temptation. Caught up in the package delivering her nourishment she forgot her nakedness until she saw the slow perusal Gideon gave her poorly covered curves. Bubbles did little to hide her breasts, belly, and hips.

"I'll be out in a minute," she said sinking down in the tub. The water level increased a fraction, to just below the tub rim.

"Your food will be cold." He crossed the room planting his fine ass too close to her mouth. Lifting the sandwich to her mouth, "Bite." He was thinking about a sandwich, but she contemplated taking a bite out of him.

Staring at his offering, she said, "Looks like a square ham and egg muffin."

"It's prosciutto, egg, and parmesan cheese on white country bread."

"Eat, woman." He patiently fed her every bite until nothing was left. The combination of the water's warmth on her skin and a full stomach relaxed her. The tingle along her spine reminded her that she was naked and Gideon could look his fill. Goose bumps formed over her body and her nipples tightened. She waved her hands through the water making rippled angels, at peace with her world.

"That good, huh?" He studied her, the gray of his eyes darker, with a predatory gleam.

"Great," she smiled up at him. Not feeling the least bit self-conscious about being naked in a room with a man she wanted to surrender to. Then it occurred to her, Gideon had returned to her within twenty minutes.

"Did you eat, Gideon?"

"I'm about to." His voice was a low caress that heated her and the bathroom temperature by another ten degrees. Those long jean clad legs stepped into the tub. She gasped as he bent low. He descended over her with the surety of a conquering lord and he didn't stop until his hips straddled hers. He didn't move. His eyes fixed on her parted lips.

"I want to taste you." She nodded her head because the primal look in his eyes silenced her words. He slowly lowered his hands into the water, then she felt them on either side of her waist. He skimmed across her abdomen, leaving warm ripples to caress her flesh and tease her nipples. Then two warm hands cupped her breasts and she moaned as her back bowed and pushed her aching globes further into his palms. The fullness of her breasts pushed between his spread fingers as he kneaded with a gentle tug at her nipples. She hissed as the pleasure tightened her buds to the point of pain. He stopped then, removing his hands from her breasts, searching her face. He recognized her answering hunger, because what he did next floored her. He plunged into her mouth, pushing deep into her throat. She sank deeper in the tub, water sloshed over the rim, waves splashing onto the floor.

"Gideon." His added weight displaced more water. "You'll need flood insurance if we keep this up," she said.

He ended his oral assault.

"I don't care."

She sat upright and pulled each arm free of the tank, throwing the sopping wet material on the floor.

"Touch me, Lina."

Tentatively she started low, where that happy trail of dark hair disappeared behind his zipper. It was his turn to hiss. Caressing the muscles covering his abdomen, flank, and back she watched as the muscle contracted and released under her touch. The bulge in his jeans expanded to press into her round stomach. He pulled her hands from his body. Her gaze shot up wondering if she had touched him in a way he didn't like. Holding her wrists in his larger grip he bent her arms until each of her hands rested on her breasts. *Okay, this was an interesting time out.* At her confusion he leaned forward his hot breath caressing the shell of her ear.

"You have me under your spell."

"I'm not a witch."

"I know, but your kisses are magic."

"I can live with that," she beamed up at him. His eyes dropped to her breasts. His eyes darkened to a molten gray and she bit her lip to trap the moan threatening to escape.

"Present your breasts to me." His voice a sensual whisper that caused her insides to quake with need.

She was a big woman, and handling her breasts was a two-handed evolution. She cupped both her breasts, spreading her fingers wide underneath each for support. Gideon leaned down covering both her hands in his big grip, his long, strong fingers covering the tops of each breast, his thumbs stroking her fingers.

"That's it sweetness, give me a mouthful." Thank goodness the tub supported her back. When his hot mouth closed around her right areola, she sucked in a ragged breath. Closing her eyes, she groaned and thrashed like a wild woman, keeping a firm grip on her breast. He dropped his hips pinning her in place. Unable to pull back from his attentions, incoherent sounds spilled from her lips, filling the moist air with sounds of satisfaction. He lavished his attention on each breast with equal fervor. With a wet popping sound he released her breast. A shiver ran down her spine as he circled her left nipple one last time.

"That's enough."

She whimpered when his mouth left her heated flesh. It sounded like a cascading waterfall when he stood. Opening her eyes, she saw he had a hand extended down to her. Reluctantly, she accepted the help to stand, but disappointed that there wasn't more in store for them. Not wanting him to see how he left her wanting, she kept her head lowered as she lifted her right leg to descend the few steps leading to the wet floor. His hand at her waist halted her tub exit.

"Where are you trying to go?" Looking up she saw that devilish grin of his.

"I thought…"

"You thought wrong. Plant this," he cupped her bottom in both hands, "on the edge of the tub and lean back against the glass." The zing of excitement raced through her. Oh ham sandwich, she was about to get it. The look in Gideon's eyes said he was about to give it-in double doses. He moved forward, forcing her to move back until the tub hit her calves.

Sitting down, her face was at eye level with a very aroused man. Looking up, Gideon's eyes were narrowed on her.

"Not tonight. Tonight is about you." A man who was focused on pleasing her. She must have chosen the blue pill in a parallel universe that converged into a sexual Matrix, because this had never been her reality.

"Open your legs." He waited, giving her the opportunity to renege.

Watching him, she leaned back onto her elbows, opening her legs wide.

His eyes stretched wide, a greedy smile covered his face as he stared at her hairless entryway.

"Love the look, sweetness." He licked that full bottom lip that she loved to suck between her teeth. "Is it all for me?" She nodded her head, afraid she would say he could have whatever he wanted if she opened her mouth.

"Say it." She could do this. Just look him in the eye, tell him there's no one else, then she could get her freak on.

"There's no one else." Eyes narrowed, jaw tight, Gideon dropped to his knees. Warm water splashed around them both. He didn't flinch. His eyes stayed focused on her. Pushing between her spread legs, he pushed two fingers into her waiting heat. Stretching her, teasing her. He didn't stop until his knuckle rested at her entrance. Her head fell back, her eyes slid to half mast and she moaned in delight.

"You're a smart woman Lina, and that was the wrong answer. I'll give you another chance." He trailed wet kisses down her exposed neck. Licking and nipping between kisses. She clamped her muscles around his fingers as he drove into her with long, sure deliberate strokes. "Is everything I touch and taste on your body mine, Lina? Because I'm all yours, sweetness." He rotated his wrist left and right, stroking her slick walls, tunneling into her core, driving her inevitable climax higher.

"I-." She couldn't fall for this again, these were just words. Words she liked hearing, but nothing lasting. He plowed into her faster. Panting she tried to put some distance between his very knowledgeable fingers and her straining muscles.

"Not going to work, sweetness." His left arm wrapped around her butt, and he pulled her in to meet his thrusts.

"I'm a Marine, we don't quit." He claimed her mouth once more, mimicking the unrelenting rhythm of his fingers in her feminine heat. She could feel her wetness on her thighs and pooling under her bottom. "Tell me, Lina. Who do you belong to?" He pushed deep, hit her g-spot, and held the position. She flew apart and she screamed, "You." more times than she could count.

He slowly withdrew his fingers from her body. Gideon's arm around her waist and his big body filling in the space between her legs was the only thing that kept her from sliding into the water like dark chocolate from a hot fountain.

"Right answer, sweetness. I think you should be rewarded." Covered in sweat, panting with the exertion of a long distance runner, she pushed a few syllables through her dry throat.

"More." He chuckled, pushed her legs impossibly wide and buried his head. The long, slow lick of his tongue across her nub had her pushing up off the tub.

"I believe I juiced my peach just right." She felt the slide of three fingers stretching her as he increased the sucking pressure on her pleasure center.

The sounds falling from her lips echoed in the room like a dozen different animals answering their mating call.

"Gideon, I can't..."

"That's the point, love. Let it happen." A ripple of pleasure began in her core as his teasing strokes transitioned to firm, circular motions over her nub. Raw hunger and passion surged in her veins, centered over her clit and then exploded. Gideon's name fell from her lips as tremors of unparalleled ecstasy filled her body.

Limp, satiated, and ready for more Lina sank into the cool water. Eyes closed she let her head fall back, swallowing the urge to beg for a second helping. This time minus his clothes. Gideon stood and discarded his wet jeans, placed an arm around her upper back, behind her knees and scooped her up.

"Where are you taking me?" She could barely keep her eyes open.

"To our bed."

Gideon placed her in the center of the bed. Crawling in behind her, he wrapped his damp muscle around her back, cradling his erection in her full backside and pulled her into his body.

"We're wetting the sheets."

"Get used to it, sweetness. Get some rest and I'll wake you up in three hours for round two." She gave him a throaty laugh in response. Her body was spent and she knew she'd sleep like the dead if he didn't wake her.

"Lina, I want you to stay with me."

"I want to stay with you, too, but..." He pulled her earlobe between his teeth.

"No buts, you'll have a key to the house in the morning." His offer was late in coming, because he already held the key to her heart.

Lina would stay with him. Everything he ever wanted he had because of the woman lying asleep in his arms. She believed in his vision for the clinic. Heck, she'd helped him make the WWR clinic a sustainable reality. She believed in him. He was worthy in her eyes. Lina knew of the man he had been and accepted the man he was now. If only he knew who was after her and why? Lina depended on him to keep her safe. He'd followed up with the police, looking for a link between the two incidents at Lina's place. The roses had been dipped in pig's blood, but no roses were found at the scene tonight. Two and a half weeks and no leads on Lina's stalker.

Gideon listened to Lina's slow, steady breathing relishing the feel of her soft, womanly curves against his body. The flood lights at the corner of the neighbor's house came on, streaming yellow-white light through the shears he'd forgotten to close. He threw off the top sheet, preparing to exit the bed. Lina had a long day and he didn't want the light to disrupt her sleep. The last thing he wanted to do was leave the bed, but he'd be curled around her before her body heat dissipated off his skin. A grating sound from the patio caught his attention. He swung his feet to the carpet and stood.

A low hung shadow passed at the glass door, halting him in place. The muscles along his back tightened in anticipation, just as an object came crashing through the bedroom window. Gideon sprang into action covering a sleep roused, screaming Lina with his nude body. The object slammed into the lamp closest next to Lina, the contents on the table flew in varying directions as ceramic shrapnel rained down onto the bed. The glass shattering triggered the house alarm, its high pitched screech filling the air. Reaching for the bedside table, he hit the *Stay* button on the portable alarm control attached to his key ring. The alarm had camouflaged the attacker's movements. The cordless phone, now off the hook, made a steady beep from the carpet. Gideon listened for signs of a second attack, separating the sounds of a predator from nature.

The neighbor's chocolate Labrador bellowed several hoarse barks from over the back fence. Snatch, the neighborhood's Russian blue tom cat released a cacophony of meows in response. What he didn't hear were footsteps. Who were they dealing with? The man was experienced at this cat and mouse game. And he was sure the culprit was male. From his position on the bed, the framed large brick projected at close range spoke to strength.

"Shh, baby. Listen carefully. I'm going to slowly ease my weight off you and move down the bed. I want you to roll onto the floor and stay close to the bed frame."

"What about you?" She whispered.

"Stay low, I will give you the okay to move." Gideon pressed his hands into the mattress, before pressing upward and rolling onto his left elbow. He used the length of his body to shield Lina. He had been thinking seduction and she was in danger. "Go now." Lina rolled from the bed onto the floor.

The motion light from the neighboring house had gone dark. The barking ended moments earlier. Glancing around, he studied the moonlit night for signs of a lurking attacker. He listened. The hum of night creatures in their melodic song greeted him. This attack was over. He knew with certainty the next was close at hand.

"Gideon, what's happening?"

"Somebody threw something through the patio door." He responded as he eased to the floor beside her. Their shoulders touched.

"I think he's gone, but I'm going to check out the rest of the house." Gideon pushed to his feet and Lina grabbed his hand, attempting to follow.

"Stay down, Lina. I'll come back once I know the house is secure." He couldn't see her face clearly, but she hesitated. "Don't worry, sweetness. I can handle anyone that enters this house."

"I know. Hurry back to me." He played a hundred scenarios in his head of Lina telling him she would stay. That she'd always be here with him. But nothing compared to her soft entreaty for him to come back to the safety she provided for him.

"You know I will." Slowly she released his hand. He grabbed a pair of sweats and a T-shirt from the chest at the foot of the bed.

As quiet as a Reaper, Gideon crept through each room in the house. As he suspected the attacker was gone. This guy was dangerous whoever he was. Gideon had left that part of his life in the past. He wasn't a killer anymore. But for Lina, he would be whatever she needed him to be.

"We can't stay here." Gideon said when he entered the bedroom.

"This guy is tracking you. He's familiar with Shell Cove." He reached down to her, offering his hand.

Gideon could feel the tremors racking Lina's body. He'd failed her. Gently he scooped her up and cradled her in his arms. He sat on the bed, holding her close to his chest.

"I don't have anywhere else to go other than my mother's."

"Don't worry. I know a place where the Navy Seals would have a hard time getting at you."

"Where's that?"

"I'm taking you to Waverly Falls."

"That better be on the other side of the freeway. This human turd stalker is not running me out of town."

"Waverly Falls is my hometown in West Virginia."

"Why there?"

"I can keep you safe there." He placed a kiss of assurance to her head. "Jacob will love you." She looked skeptical. "I want you to meet him."

"I want to meet him, too." Her eyes cast to the left. It was obvious meeting the Rice family wasn't high on her priority list.

"Lina you are important to me. I have told you this many times. My feelings for you are real."

"Okay." Not the acceptance he hoped for. Eyes trained on her, he ran his fingers through his hair.

"What I'm doing is the only way I know to express my feelings. If it's too much, too soon, then tell me what you want me to do." He released a deep breath. "I want you to accept our relationship, Lina."

"I do, I am."

"You say the right things and you behave as if we are together. But, I need to know you accept me, you accept us in your heart and mind." She nibbled the corner of her lip, as her hand soothed over the back of her neck.

"Stop that," Gideon said in frustration.

"Why am I not good enough for you, Lina?"

"Gideon, that is not true. You are everything I could want. But, every time I get my hopes up over a man, I get sucker punched. Be patient with me. If what's happening between us is real then everything will work out."

"You are a romantic. Lina, relationships take work or nothing falls in place, but chaos and disappointment."

"You sound like you're speaking from personal experience."

"Maybe I am."

"I see you have your own story of heartbreak. Care to share?"

"One day I will, but not now." It appeared that the threat had passed. Standing, he placed her on her feet. Moving to the chest, he pulled out a pair of sweat pants and a T-shirt and passed them to her. She pulled the shirt over her head. It hung down to her thighs. Even at her height, she had to double roll each pant leg to keep the material from dragging on the floor. Dressed in his clothes, Lina looked like she belonged to him. He liked the look.

"We're leaving town tonight. I'll call the clinical staff and tell them to reassign my patients." Thanks to Lina's ingenuity, the added group therapy sessions and redesigned scheduling templates the clinic's productivity had increased with the current staffing model.

"I don't run away from a fight."

"We're not running, but you don't have to run into the melee waving a big stick at every turn. It's okay to walk away. I get the whole, independent woman thing, but you are in real danger, and I'm here."

"For how long, Gideon?" He took in her unreadable expression. This take on the world attitude made her vulnerable, but he understood the self-preservation.

"Lina," he reached out caressing her cheek, before closing his fingers around her nape and pulling her close, "I'm with you for better or for worse.

This guy is escalating, we need time to formulate a defense. We will come back when the repairs are completed on both our places."

"Who is going to oversee the repairs?"

"My brother, Thane owns a construction company. I contacted him about your place while you were in the tub. He has connections and will take care of everything."

"You have brothers?"

"Yeah, five of them."

"You never mentioned them before."

"There wasn't a reason to discuss my family before now." The expression on her face was none too pleased with him.

"Listen, my family situation is complicated. I have five brothers. I'm the second oldest. Jacob and Emma didn't have any children of their own. She died five years ago." He ran his fingers through his hair, uncomfortable with the discussion. This was a can of worms that they did not have time to mull over. "Can we not do this now?"

"Fine," she said, with her chin lifted in a stubborn tilt, "I'm not leaving town with some guy without seeing my mother."

"Lina." She held up a hand, giving a flat palm to stare at.

"You are not changing my mind. Go grab your Clark Kent bag while I get my purse. I'll meet you by the door."

"You're not leaving my sight. Wait for me and we will gather your things from the guest room and leave together."

CHAPTER THIRTEEN

Bernadean James had the front door open to her brick rambler before she and Gideon exited the car. Lina walked into her mother's arms and buried her head in the teal fluffy robe she had given her nearly a decade ago. She swore her mother kept every speck of lint, paper, or God awful artwork she'd ever given her. Feeling the familiar press of her mother's kiss to her hair, Lina inhaled deep, breathing in courage and trying her best to push away the fear threatening to overwhelm her. She felt helpless. And she didn't know if she was more terrified of the stalker or relying on the brave Marine at her back.

She was depending on Gideon to always be there for her. What would happen to her when he walked away? She had never run from a fight, but that was exactly what she was doing. Following a man, putting all her hopes and dreams in his hands. The past had taught her to rely on herself.

Her mother was the only person in the world who had never failed her. She and Gideon exited the car.

"Momma, this is Gideon Rice. The psychiatrist I told you about." Lina walked past her mother into the house. Her mother regarded Gideon with a critical eye before letting him enter.

"Hello, Gideon. It's nice to finally meet you." Though her mother had caught a brief glimpse of him at Ava's party, Lina had not formally introduced them. A fact her mother had reminded her of on more than one occasion. Gideon must have passed the initial screening because her mother ushered them into the quaint living room.

"Baby, what are they doing to you?" Tears gathered in her mother's eyes.

"I'm alright, Momma."

"Lina, you have to get help. You can't handle this on your own."

"I'm not trying to. Gideon is taking me away…"

"No," her mother said in a stern voice. The look of disapproval was reminiscent of childhood.

"Mom, it's just until the repairs are complete and I could use some down time."

"Where is he taking you?"

"Some one-horse, one-road town in West Virginia. If it's anything like I'm imagining, the bad guys will need satellite imagery to find me."

"Lina I called Bishop and…"

"And who?"

"A friend of the family," her mother's tone was low and filled with trepidation.

"Is this friend from my dad's time on the force?"

"He knew your father."

"That's a good idea, maybe he can help the police focus on my case and who's targeting me." Gideon had remained silent after offering a greeting to her mother.

"Mrs. James, do you have any thoughts on why this is happening to Lina?" Her mother looked unsettled and anxious.

"My baby has done nothing for someone to want to hurt her." Tears streamed down her mother's face. Maybe, she shouldn't have insisted that they come here. Her mother reached for her and clutched her tight.

"I'm sorry this is happening to you, baby."

"Bishop will figure this out."

"My sweet baby, always looking for a hero."

"Momma, that's a terrible thing to say."

"No, it is not. Every woman wants her very own hero."

"Lina." She knew by Gideon's tone it was time to leave. Shell Cove was her home, now she was climbing into a car with Gideon and driving to a place she'd never heard of until forty-five minutes ago. She would be totally dependent on him and his family. Were there even any black people in Waverly Falls, West Virginia?

Hugging her mother tight, she said, "I'll call you when we arrive."

"I expect to hear from you while you are on the road, Lina Diane." Her mother gave Gideon a stern look.

"Gideon, I'm grateful to you for keeping my daughter safe, but if I don't hear from my child at reasonable intervals, me and the Triple OG's will be visiting Waverly Falls." Pointing her finger at Gideon like only a mother could, Bernadean said, "Go in the kitchen and write all your contact information on the refrigerator. Include your families address and home phone number. No omitted information, or else." Lina stretched her eyes wide in horror.

"OG's?" Gideon looked at Lina.

She sighed and looked at her mother. "Momma stop issuing threats. You and the Original Gangsters can rest easy. I'll be sure to call."

"Come on you two, get going. Hopefully, whoever is after you won't expect you to leave town so quickly."

"I love you, Momma."

"Momma loves you too, baby. More than I can express in words." Walking them to the door, her mother reached behind the coat rack and came out with her prized possession. She extended it to Lina.

"Take it." Lina looked down and a tear came to her eye.

"It's okay, I have a back-up."

"Is that a mini-me version of BETAS?" Both of them laughed at Gideon's question.

"Let me do the honors." Clearing her throat, Lina took the eight-inch stick from her mother and turned toward Gideon.

"This is BETAS mother, BEYAS."

"BEYAS," he smirked in question.

"Momma's, Beat Your Ass Stick." Lina's height came from her father's side of the family, thus her mother's petite baton. She watched him rolled his eyes heavenward.

"Keep it with you. It's the perfect size to keep with you at all times," her mother said.

Lina kissed her mother goodbye.

They were exiting the driveway when it occurred to Lina they didn't have any snacks in the car for the nine hundred miles to their destination.

"Wait," Lina blurted out.

"You okay?"

"Yeah, I forgot something I need."

"What? I can buy you whatever you need on the road."

"I need something to eat. Food relaxes me."

"I thought that was my job?" Images of their hot tub session flooded her mind and her body heated by ten degrees. Unwilling to step on that landline she changed the subject.

"Yeah, just let me grab some water and snacks for the road. I don't know how well we'll be received in small town America at two o'clock in the morning. It's best to be prepared."

He nodded. Gideon may not have a problem with being seen with an African-American, but she was willing to bet the good folks in small town America were probably not as tolerant as the tourist haven of Shell Cove.

"Be right back." Lina exited the car with Gideon stepping out on the opposite side.

"I don't need your help."

"Not out of my sight." Finding the front door locked they rounded the house, Lina snagged the side door key from its hiding place and entered the dark utility room. She could hear her mom talking.

"You promised to keep her…"

"Momma?"

Deanie's screech rivaled a scolded cat. She dropped the cordless phone, and it clattered on the linoleum kitchen floor, spinning in circles before coming to a halt.

"Lina, you scared the crap out of me."

"Who's on the phone?"

"Oh, it's Bishop."

"Let me say goodbye." Lina reached for the phone. "Hello?"

Silence greeted her, but she knew someone was on the line. Then the call dropped. Her mother stood like stone, eyes closed, her breathing slow and deep.

"He hung up."

"Why would he do that?" Her mother's eyes popped open.

"Cell phone reception is unpredictable. Why did you turn around, baby?" Reminding her of why she'd entered the house.

"Sorry about scaring you. We need some food for the road." Gideon entered through the side door with a fierce look on his face.

"I heard a scream," he said looking to her.

"Oh, I spooked Momma when I let myself in the house."

"I'll pack you a cooler," Deanie said before disappearing behind the open refrigerator door.

Lina smiled up into Gideon's troubled expression. Was he upset because of the delay?

"We'll be on the road in a few minutes." This was more than a road trip, this was a journey of trust. Gideon would keep her safe but could she trust him with her heart?

It wasn't every day you call a woman's mother a liar. Bernadean James was hiding something. The scene in the kitchen replayed in his mind for the first four hundred miles. Marines are trained to think the same in basic, Bishop wouldn't hang up without talking with him or Lina. He knew his sister was in danger. And more importantly, Gideon knew the type of man Bishop was. Regardless of the newness of their relationship a Marine would never walk away from someone in need.

When he parked the Cadillac next to the four pick-up trucks lined in front of the main house it reminded him how much he didn't belong here. He never wanted to return to this place.

He roused Lina from sleep, "We're here."

"Dang it, why did you let me fall asleep. Now, I don't know how to get out of here." Stepping from the car he released the Crossbill bird call Jacob Rice taught him the first month he came to live at the house.

An answering Nuthatch, Tern, and Harlequin calls carried through the air. Only Caleb and D.Wright's calls were missing.

"What was that?" Lina asked.

"A mountaineer text message," he grinned, rounding the car to open her door. "Something Jacob taught us boys to keep track of one another."

"You all make bird sounds?"

"Not sounds, sweetness. We each have a unique bird call. The ranch sits on one hundred acres of mountains, streams, and flatlands. When we hunt, it helps to signal our location."

"You are a true mountain man." It was the first time those words had been directed at him with a touch of pride.

"Is that a problem?" He studied her. If driving through the town had her alarmed, meeting the locals would have her on the next helicopter home. Waverly Falls was quaint enough that it didn't warrant mass transportation.

"Gideon, your name is synonymous with a lot of words in my vocabulary. There isn't a problem with one of them." Their eyes met, and the trust reflected in them, swelled in his chest like she had given him a new lease on life. She had given him her trust.

"Heard what you said about not knowing the way back." Before he could tell her she wasn't leaving, not without him, his father and three of his brothers came riding up on their mounts.

"Are those real cowboys?"

Gideon laughed.

"Come on sweetness, let's get you introduced to the Rice family."

"The country boy gladiators are your brothers?"

"There's a girl that's not too far behind."

His father, adoptive father he corrected himself, was the first to dismount and approach him.

"Glad to see you, son." They both stood at an odd standoff.

"You too." He remembered the child he'd been standing here on West Virginia soil. Unwanted. A hand-me-down kid taken in by Jacob and Emma Rice.

Reaching back toward Lina, he waited until she took his hand.

"This is my…," he hesitated unsure if Lina would be comfortable with the title of his woman.

"Hi, I'm Lina James." Gideon glanced over to find Lina's expression unreadable.

"I'm Jacob. I owe you a big thank you for bringing my son home, young lady." Lina was the only one to laugh.

"These are my sons, Phoenix, Thane, and Ian." Jacob pointed his finger right to left. "Phoenix is the baby of the bunch." Phoenix offered a salute in greeting. With his tanned complexion, striking Native American features and ink black hair to his mid-back he'd always been a hit with the women in town. He looked every bit the survivalist he was. Phoenix was a born hunter. Guns, knives, or arrows. If it was deadly, he'd mastered it.

"Honestly, Dad, you can stop introducing me as the baby. At thirty-one years old no one would mistake me for a baby," Phoenix said.

Lina chimed in, "I can see you're not a baby." She was flirting with his brother. To add fuel to the fire, Phoenix winked at her. Ian and Thane, not to be outdone, added their *I'm a man* roar.

"Knock it off." Gideon growled. He pinned each man with a steel eyed glare, before he looked to Jacob. Jacob, who studied him with a knowing awareness. The weight of his stare had Gideon grinning his teeth.

"Leave your brother's woman alone, boys." He hated that Jacob could read him so easily.

"Oh no, Gideon and I aren't–"

"Where's Caleb?" He blurted out, interrupting Lina before she inadvertently set one of his brothers up for a beating that would be recorded in the history annals.

"He's working on a case. He'll fly in tonight," Thane answered. Caleb was a contract penetration tester. A male escort was the first image that populated into his brain years earlier when Caleb promptly educated him that was the industry terminology for a computer hacker. If he was on the job, a big fish was involved.

Thane dismounted, crossed to where he and Lina stood in front of the car, and shook Gideon's hand. He gave Lina a quick glance from head to toe before meeting her eyes.

"I'm the brother that plays dirty." Lina tilted her head in askance. Gideon ground his teeth. This would be one heck of a visit.

"Jacob told you to leave her alone." He felt fingers curl around his wrist, before Lina's scent filled the air around him. She'd moved in close, pressing into his side. Her physical reassurance calmed the jealous Neanderthal that was about to make a fool of himself. "Thane owns a demolition and construction company." Thin, slender fingers slipped between his and he squeezed.

"Gideon gave me the okay to take care of the damages to your place. I'm leaving for Shell Cove in the morning." At Lina's furrowed brow, Thane grinned.

"Looks to me like the Marine is still keeping secrets."

"There are no secrets. Gideon told me you would be taking care of the repairs. You surprised me by announcing that you are leaving tomorrow." Thank heaven above, that Lina hadn't seen the frown on Jacob and Ian's face.

"It seems I'm the one that is surprised, Lina." Gideon remembered all over again why he hadn't visited in ten years. He didn't want to relive the past. Living life as an open book was best left to preachers and politicians. Looking at the men before him meant his Book of Life had been pulled out of the archives.

Ignoring Thane's comment, Gideon introduced the last of the Rice clan. "The Nordic blonde is Ian. He's the ambulance chaser." Because Ian was an ass and three inches shorter, he rode forward on his mount, flaunting his temporary height advantage.

Tipping his muted black Stetson, "Now, is that any way to talk about the lawyer handling your..." Gideon was at the end of his rope before and this was just the meet and greet.

"Shut up and welcome Lina." He snapped at Ian, but the weight of hardened stares boring into him said every man knew his words were meant for all of them.

"Thanks for not making me feel like a stray," Lina's smile lightened his sinking mood. "I like the Waverly Falls hospitality already." Gideon raked his fingers through his hair, scoring his scalp. This was a disaster. He cleared his throat searching his muttled brain for a subject that would lighten the conversation.

"The Rice family loves strays." Gideon winced when the sting of his statement burrowed in his chest. Lina turned narrowed eyes on him. Heck, her silent reprimand echoed in his ear.

"Mr. Rice, Gideon and I have been traveling more than twelve hours. We're both tired."

"Please call me Jacob and there's no need to make excuses for Dr. Rice," Jacob emphasized the Rice name, reminding him he'd made the decision to change his name to Rice in spite of knowing they were not his family. The lesser of two evils, better to bear the name of your rescuer than the woman who abandoned you.

Gideon had not prepared her for meeting his family. The Rice family was like a multicultural version of *Dallas*. Any minute JR would come walking out of the big house.

A rider approached on a caramel colored horse with a white streak down the animal's nose. Lina was surprised to see a dark skinned woman swing down from the horse.

"If it isn't our head shrink." The foreign accent was another surprise. The woman with a figure and complexion similar to Lina's walked over to Gideon and threw her arms around his waist.

"Welcome home, Gideon. I missed you." *What the flagnoid?* Did Gideon have a big butt, black woman fetish?

"Nai, this is Lina James."

"Hi Lina, my name is Nairobi, but these guys refuse to add two syllables. It's nice to meet you." Lina didn't share the sentiment.

"Thank you, Nairobi. Are you a sister?" Lina was phishing. Hoping this woman was a part of the Rice rainbow coalition.

"Nah, I just work and live here." Lina didn't know what to think. Was Nairobi an old flame? She felt nauseous. Lina must have fallen and bumped her head to leave Shell Cove and follow Gideon to the West Virginia hills. What did she really know about his past? She looked up at Gideon to find him studying her. A furrow formed between his brows.

"You okay, sweetness?" She nodded her head glancing anywhere but at his face.

"Lina and I are headed up to my room. It was a long drive and we're both exhausted."

She didn't say a word. Just followed behind Gideon blindly.

"Tell me what's wrong, Lina. You look like you just lost your best friend." Had she come to Waverly Falls, only to be left behind again?

"I'm achy from the long car ride. Nothing a hot shower won't solve."

Lina walked beside him, as he kneaded her neck muscles.

"I'll fix all your aches and pains after we shower." Gideon led her around the tree line to a red brick mansion that sat in the middle of green grass and mountains for as far as her eyes could see. A billboard with a smiling Jacob was posted in front of the house. The board read, *Elect Jacob Rice for Mayor.* Jacob was running for office. She didn't see that one coming.

Gideon glanced up at the sign, never missing a step. As if it was a routine occurrence for your father to be running for a public office.

A concrete patio with a circle painted in blue and outfitted with strategically placed ground lights caught her eye.

"What's that?"

"It's a helicopter pad."

"Your family owns a helicopter?"

"West Virginia is mountain country. In the winter the roads can be difficult to travel. Helicopters are a necessity."

"Can you fly it?"

"We all can fly, but Jacob and D.Wright are the most skilled."

"I thought your family was poor."

"My family was poor. The Rice's are the wealthy family in these parts."

"Gideon, they are your family. Just because you don't have the same blood–"

"You're tired," he cut her off. "Let's go on in the house. We can talk later." The glare she turned on him said he would not enjoy their next conversation.

CHAPTER FOURTEEN

Gideon felt as if Lina was light years away from him. He watched as she pulled a clear travel bag with personal items from her purse. She examined the contents before dropping the bag onto his king sized bed.

He'd outgrown a queen sized bed before he hit puberty. His room hadn't changed since the last time he'd been home. Someone had updated the comforter from his blue and gray sports team colors to a hunter green. Probably Nai's attempt to keep Emma's memory alive. West Virginia clay and crisp air seemed to permeate the room. Lina, who normally appreciated everything around her, was still absorbed in the contents of her travel bag. He took her shoulders, turning her to face him.

"Lina talk to me." She smiled up at him, but the smile didn't reach her eyes.

"What do you want to talk about?" She asked dropping her gaze to the floor. He loved that she was a terrible liar. She didn't want to talk.

"Whatever is bothering you." Gideon placed a finger under her chin, raising her head until she made eye contact.

"You're upset. Why?" As he studied her face he noticed the frown lines around her mouth.

"I'll be fine." She was upset with him. Why else would she refuse to tell him what was wrong?

"Lina, I know you'll be fine. You can take care of yourself. What I'm asking is for you to trust me with your feelings. Maybe I can help." Getting

Lina to make a place for him in her life was like moving a mountain with a serving spoon.

"Are we going to be okay here?" What the heck did that mean? He pushed a few strands of hair behind her ear.

"You and I are going to be okay wherever we are. Don't ever doubt that." He placed a kiss on her forehead.

"Gideon you tell me we are good. I believe you." He looked into her eyes, trying to find the source of her doubt.

"Something has happened since we arrived that bothered you." She took in a deep breath, nodding her head.

"If my brothers or Jacob are the cause, we are out of here." A confused look crossed her face.

"No, it's not them. I like your family."

"The Rices' are good people," he said. And Gideon meant every word.

"Gideon, why are you so reluctant to accept them as your family?" He felt the stiffness infuse his muscles.

"I'm not reluctant." He bit out. How had this conversation morphed into a talk about family?

"What are you afraid of?"

"Lina, just drop it, okay. You look exhausted and I'm too tired to talk about me and the Rice family."

"Your family loves you."

"Don't you think I know that?" He grounded out.

"If you know it, then why are you scared to love them back?" His heart was pounding in his chest. How had she gathered a lifetime of information on his familial bonds standing in the front yard? Lina was one heck of a psychiatric nurse.

"Sweetness, I would love to spend tonight making you feel good." He was easily distracted by sex, maybe the tactic would work on Lina.

"I have a question for you doctor." He regarded her with wary eyes.

"Ask your question."

"How can a man fall in love with a complete stranger, yet can't find the capacity to love the people that have cared for him for most of his life?" Ah, heck. He'd walked into her word trap.

"Love is a bottomless emotion, Gideon. It doesn't diminish because you're sharing it with more than one person." He pulled her into an embrace.

"I don't want to talk anymore." He held her close. Hoping that what she said was true.

"Now, who's upset?"

He shook his head. "I'm not mad."

"Good, because I still want my massage." Somehow, their conversation had improved Lina's disposition. He on the other hand, had some soul searching to do.

"Take your clothes off and lie down on the bed." He released her when she stepped out of his embrace.

"Okay." He watched as she discarded her T-shirt and sweat pants. Lina reached behind her back and unfastened her bra.

"I'll be back. Get comfortable on your stomach, Lina. It's going to be a long night for you." Gideon entered the adjoining bathroom, found what he was looking for, and returned to find a very naked Lina gracing his bed.

"Did I tell you having large hands makes me a natural masseuse?"

"No, but I can't wait for you to touch me," she grinned. Neither could he.

Gideon stripped down to his boxers before straddling Lina's hips. He poured some oil into his palms, rubbing his hands together before touching Lina's flawless skin. The scent of toasted almonds filled the air, and he grinned when Lina took a big breath in, before snaking into the mattress.

"Relax, sweetness. This will feel good."

A grin split her lips. "It already does."

Gideon couldn't help laughing.

The oil helped his hands glide across Lina's skin. He cupped her shoulders, kneading the tension from her knotted muscles. He played with the dimples above her buttocks, stroking and massaging, until she groaned in pleasure. Smiling, Gideon reveled at how Lina's body reacted as he slowly worked her body.

He pressed deeper into her muscles, drawing out soft moans of satisfaction. "That feels good, Gideon. Don't stop."

"You don't have to tell me twice." He stroked every inch of her body until, her breathing became uneven, her muscles tensed and she cried out his name in ecstasy. He felt like he'd been worked over right along with Lina. Was this how all their discussions about family would end? He hoped so.

Walking down the stairs to find Team Rice around the longest oak table Lina had ever seen in a house brought a smile to her face. How cool was this? For most of her life, she sat at a small rectangular table in the kitchen while her mother cooked. Phoenix, with his dark eyes, to die for lashes and jet colored hair falling past his shoulders studied her.

"Good morning, you two, hope you got a good night's rest," Gideon's father said.

"We certainly didn't," Ian coughed behind his coffee mug. A man she didn't recognized rose from the table and crossed the room to Gideon. Both men stood surveying one another, before the stranger threw his arm around Gideon for a brief moment, then stood back. He was a lean man with piercing green eyes, golden brown waves, and frameless glasses.

"It's good to have you home Gideon." Expecting the customary *it's good to be home* response from Gideon, Lina watched as the room's occupants fell into quiet at Gideon's lack of response. Lina glanced around the room taking in the different measures of disappointment and frustration on their faces, but the pain and sadness in Jacob's eyes spurred her into action. Pasting a smile on her face, she placed her right arm around his waist. Initiating physical contact with Gideon was something she rarely did, then action garnered the desired response. He turned lowered his head, holding her captive in a heat gaze as a thick arm pulled her close to his side. She had his attention. With increasing pressure, she dug her nails into his right flank, until he got the message. He pushed out a low hiss through clenched teeth.

"Thanks Caleb." Gideon's reply was appropriate, but his voice was blunt. "What time did you get in?"

Caleb choked on his coffee, as Nairobi busied herself studying the ceiling.

"Thane told me you are a nurse. I could have used a little mouth to mouth just then," Caleb said while grinning at her. Lina's mouth fell open.

"I'll give you fist to mouth resuscitation. You want it now or later?" So this was the life of a large family, jealousy, threats, strained conversations, and accusations around the breakfast table. She loved it.

"I'm Caleb by the way. Been awhile since you lived in the main house. Guess you forgot the walls are thin." Lina had the decency to blush, but it was invisible to the naked eye. Gideon glared at every person in the room. His face hardened as he noticed Phoenix was staring at her.

"Phoenix, I hope you have the number to your medicine man because he should start heading this way."

"Why is that big brother?" Gideon visibly bristled at the words big brother.

"Let your eyes roam my woman again." Lina felt herself being pulled. Her back made contact with Gideon's chest.

"I have a question for your woman, but I don't want to offend her." Lina felt her spine stiffened. Here it comes. Rejection. Was his family questioning his choice in her? He would doubt the connection they shared if his family disapproved of her. She would be alone, again. Never one to walk away from a fight she gave Phoenix his opening.

"What's your question?" she heard herself ask. He took a slow drag from his coffee mug.

"You got any sisters?"

"Sisters?"

"Yeah, that don't mind gettin' a little Indian in them." His wide grin was pure devilment.

"Phoenix!" Lina looked up to find a red-faced Jacob.

"We must've dropped you out of the saddle too many times. Head into town and stop by my campaign office. Talk with Fallon about increasing my social media presence."

"How about I use social media to contact Fallon?" Phoenix's face held a wicked grin.

"That wouldn't get you out of the house and away from your brother's… guest," Jacob said. Phoenix crossed the room. She jumped when he placed a quick kiss to her cheek.

"Man…," Lina said touching her cheek.

"I like your spirit, Lina. Welcome to the family, lil sis." Gideon growled at Phoenix from behind her.

"Medicine man," Gideon ground out. But Phoenix had placed his cup in the sink and was at the door.

"Don't forget about my request, lil sis." Phoenix tossed up a salute before walking out the door.

"Is the mountain cabin available?" Gideon asked no one in particular.

"Yep, you'll need fresh linens and some food." Jacob responded as he placed his coffee mug in the sink.

"Everything still in the same place?" Gideon asked.

"It's home, son. Home doesn't change."

"Lina and I are moving out today." Her eyes flew up to Gideon's.

"We just got here. I don't want to be in the middle of nowhere."

"Don't worry. The cabin is at the back of the property and the foot of the mountain." She knew uncertainty was reflected on her face. "We'll have more privacy." She lowered her head in embarrassment remembering all the knowing looks she got when they first entered the kitchen.

"Thane can drive up enough supplies to last you a couple of days," Jacob spoke up.

"Lina and I left in a hurry. I need to borrow a truck."

"We kept your truck tuned-up. It's in the rear barn." Jacob gestured behind him. "The keys are on the pegboard by the door." Gideon's arms around her waist stiffened. The tension level in everyone's face had increased by fifty percent.

"We won't be gone long. We need clothes. Lina needs a descent pair of shoes." She looked down at her dust covered sandals.

"Lina you can shop in my closet." Nairobi said. Lina opened her mouth to refuse, but Nairobi held up a hand. "Before you refuse, we have two women's clothing stores in town. Unless you like an array of sunflowers, butterflies, bumble bees and ladybugs across your chest and back, and on your feet you are going to be disappointed."

Since she put it that way, Lina didn't have a choice. "Okay, thanks Nairobi."

"I have skinny jeans in sizes sixteen and up." That announcement brought a smile to Lina's face.

"Perfect."

"Clothes bridges all gaps," Nairobi joked.

"I'm in the loft over the rear barn. Gideon knows where it is."

Again, what the flagnoid?

Lina let her eyes climb the walls of the Rice family barn. It resembled a mini replica of Noah's Ark. She spun in a circle marveling in the vastness of the space.

"What is this place, exactly?" Lina asked.

"It's a bank barn." Gideon stated like that explained everything.

"Oh my goosebumps, rich people have an upgrade for everything." Lina laughed at the absurdity.

A grin split Gideon's lips, before he tossed his head back and laughed.

"You are such a city girl. Bank refers to the type of design, not the owner's bank account. The barn is built into the hillside. The banks of the landscape allow more than one entrance to the second and third levels." Lina nodded her head in understanding.

"This is a lot of space." Lina gave him a quick glance, hopeful that her snooping went undetected.

"Jacob was a large animal veterinarian. There are a lot of nearby ranchers in the area. He's semi-retired now. But most of the folks around here are loyal. He's too kind hearted to turn people away. Nai helps him care for the animals and maintain the out properties."

Okay he was the first to mention her name, this was her opening.

"You and Nairobi seem close."

"We graduated in the same high school year group."

"Right, makes sense. I guess…graduate from high school together, she moves into the loft and your truck is in her barn." Gideon's laughter filled the room.

"You're jealous?" Her feet left the ground as Gideon lifted her in the air and spun her in a circle.

"That happy, huh?"

"Yes, ma'am. It's about time. And there's nothing between Nairobi and me."

"Not now or not ever?" She had learned from experience that to get the correct answer from a man, a woman had to phrase the question exactly. Gideon narrowed his eyes at her.

"This is not a game between us. There has never been any romantic involvement between me and Nairobi. I consider her a part of the Rice family." The way he phrased his response it was like he wasn't included in the Rice family. From Lina's perspective, he did more to exclude himself.

"Don't you mean your family?"

"Jacob and Emma Rice took me in when my mother didn't want me anymore. I am grateful. But we are not family."

"Gideon, that doesn't make sense. You may not share the same blood with your father and brothers but you obviously trust them or we wouldn't be here."

"Let's not analyze…"

"Hear me out." The look on his face told her he was resigned to let her speak, but he wouldn't hear her.

"When we left Shell Cove, you said you were taking me home. Home is not Waverly Falls, it's this group of people that you consider family."

"I don't have…," Lina held up her hand to stop him.

"Why didn't we go to a hotel or some other remote location?"

"Because."

"That's not an explanation."

"Because I know the Rice's will help me keep you safe."

"Why are you convinced they will help? From what I've noticed, you haven't been to visit in some years."

"I haven't been back since sophomore year of college." Lina was doing the math in her head.

"Ten years." Was he insane? He showed up, with her in tow, and he didn't consider them family? Only family would accept this nonsense. But the psychiatric nurse in her would not let her speak the words aloud.

"How many non-family members would open their door to you, with a woman they don't know in tow, after ten years of no contact?"

"Limited contact," he muttered.

"What was that?"

"They call, I answer. I've talked to Ian."

"He's the lawyer, right?" Gideon nodded his head in agreement.

"Jacob has known me since I was born. My mother lived with her folks about five miles up the road. He's a generous man."

"Yes, your father is very kind. I like him." Lina saw the hint of a smile cross Gideon's face before he steeled it away and the hard lines returned to his face. "I don't have a father."

"Look Gideon, my father is gone and my mother refuses to give me any details surrounding his death. I wish a man had volunteered to step in and help my mother, be a father to me. My mother is still alone, and I don't have another sole in this world other than her to call my own. So, if Jesus can accept Joseph, you-Dr. Rice can cut Jacob some slack." He looked floored by her rant. *Good.* Jacob had welcomed them both with open arms and she liked the man. Jacob was the best kind of father. Father to another man's children, what could be more noble?

"I am sorry I upset you."

"Don't sabotage our accommodations," she joked. "As your guest…" The smile fell away from his face.

"You are not my guest. After what happened between us in that bathtub, we need to discuss our relationship. Talk about our future together."

"Yes, we do." *Blood on stone tablet* she reminded herself. Though she acknowledged a part of her wanted Gideon any way she could have him, that approach would damage them both.

"Am I the pause button in your life, Lina?" She was incapable of pausing anything where Gideon was involved. Fast forward was the only button that functioned in her lust filled brain. "The temporary place holder in your relationship journey?" Could the man be further in left field?

"You're asking if I'm using you." Yes, he had been there to keep her safe, but he had to know she loved him. Correction-cared for him. Love was off the table. "The answer is no. I genuinely like you Gideon. I want to be with you. I would never do that to another person." Having to answer this question caused a painful ache in her heart. He of all men, knew her.

"Don't look so hurt, sweetness. I wanted to hear you say that you desire me for the man I am." She breathed a sigh of relief.

"I know you Lina, but I want to know all of you." She stiffened. He was talking about sex.

"Stop minimizing my words. This is beyond our physical relationship. I want you to know me, too. And yes, sharing your perfect body with me is one part of it." She gave him her best *stop playing* expression.

"Your body is perfect for me. I'm a big man and when I grab a hold of a woman I want to feel her touching me everywhere." Her breath came in shallow, rapid pants.

"Put your mojo back in the bottle, mountain man. I'm not looking for a romantic involvement."

"Good. Because you already found me." He closed the distance between them, capturing her face, he lowered his mouth to hers and feasted on her lips.

CHAPTER FIFTEEN

In the daylight, the drive into downtown Waverly Falls was a visit down memory lane he preferred to avoid. Main Street was near deserted, though it was approaching noon. The crisp, chilled air was a stark contrast to the near tropical conditions in Shell Cove. The weather reflected his mood. The sooner he figured out who was stalking Lina, the faster he could leave this place in the rear view mirror. Ned's Country Store looked untouched by time. Lina was in the fitting room. The clothing selection was worse than Nai's description.

"Gideon Spieth?" He stiffened at the sound of his birth name.

"You look just like your mother. I'd recognize you anywhere," Mrs. Nedstetter's thin voice cut like barbed wire.

"Hello, Ma'am. The last name is Rice, now."

"That's right. Emma and Jacob took you in." He ground his teeth as the old wounds re-opened. The older woman ensnared him with a critical eye. All the old insecurities reared their vicious heads. He felt unworthy, less than, just like that.

"You look like you've done well for yourself," she gave a faint smile.

"Graduated from medical school a few years back." The woman's brows disappeared into her hairline. Did everyone in this town think so little of him?

"I had heard something about you getting some education. Jacob must be real proud. You paying him back by making something out of your life."

Where the hell was Lina?

"So, you a real doctor now?"

Did she think he was a witch doctor?

"I'm not sure what you mean, by that."

"Well, my niece tells everybody she's a nurse."

"Nursing is a noble profession." He was going to pull Lina out of that dressing room if she didn't materialize in the next thirty seconds.

"Yes indeed, but she completed a nursing assistant certificate program over at the trade school on Fifth Street." He saw where this was headed.

"I'm a psychiatrist. No trade schools involved for me." Not that he had a problem with trade professions. In healthcare, it required the collaborative effort of every department working together to care for the patient. From the housekeeping staff that carted away infectious material to the surgeon ablating blood vessels. Each one depended on the other. But he didn't feel like getting into that right now.

"A psychiatrist," she frowned. "I guess that's better than nothing considering your background."

"Lina," he yelled over his shoulder. Not caring who heard the throw away Spieth boy bringing the rafters down. She was at his side before he could blink.

"Hey. You should have told me you were an impatient shopper." She brushed against his arm. His tense muscles immediately relaxed.

"Looka here, you must be new in town?" Mrs. Nedstetter's eyes were practically glowing demon red. The whole town would know he was back in town within forty-five minutes.

"Hello, I'm Lina James." A bony hand, dotted with brown age spots shook Lina's hand in a loose grip. The old woman's attention stayed on him as she spoke.

"You got yourself an interesting accent, missy. Gideon Spieth, you come back home with a big city girl?" Lina's back went ramrod straight beside him.

"The county fair is in town. You two should head on over there. You being a big time doctor now."

"Thanks for telling us."

"Nobody gets to see you out by the falls. Folks round here didn't think you would amount to a hill of beans. You should go to the fair. Show off your big city girl."

"Some beans, grow into bean stalks," Lina chimed in. Her pure saccharine smile warmed his heart. He loved it when she was in she-cat mode.

"I suppose you're right."

"We'd better get going, Mrs. Nedstetter," he pushed their purchases closer to the register, since she hadn't tallied one item. She took the hint.

"It was nice talking with you." Yeah, it was as nice as having your teeth extracted with a toothpick. He gathered their bags, guided Lina in front of him, and made a beeline for the door.

"You too, Gideon. Oh, I meant to ask you, what happened to the other woman I met, back..." Gideon slammed the door on the tail end of that statement. Disaster averted.

CHAPTER SIXTEEN

Her breath hitched in her chest when Gideon stepped onto the porch of the cabin. A tanned god, dressed in black from his broad shoulders down to his feet. Faded black denim clung to his powerful thighs. Scuffed, fine stitched sized fourteen cowboy boots looked well worn, a perfect fit. She knew her eyes were wide with female appreciation as she drank him in. She licked her lips savoring the tasty treat in front of her. She was in love with casual, rugged Gideon. He looked at peace. She had never seen him so comfortable in his own skin. She needed a game plan. The cabin was stocked. The Rice clan had left hours ago. And the sexual energy between them was thick in the air. Their day together, had been perfect. Even that horrid old woman couldn't put a damper on her spirits.

The Rice cabin was one of those luxury cabins on the front of a destination spa magazine. A total of four master suites, two on each level with a huge great room and a floor to ceiling stone fireplace. A mountain stream that was more invigorating than her sandy beach alcove completed the front room view. Rolling hills and mountains completed the picture, providing a panoramic frame. Thane's company had designed and built the property. Jacob rented out the cabins for corporate retreats and other business functions. There were two additional rental properties on the ranch but this was the largest of the three. Gideon had warned her that his mountain would rival her beach. He was right. She might have a new favorite. She hadn't believed him until the cool mist from the Waverly waterfall touched her skin. Being here with Gideon, she let the troubles in Shell Cove fall away. Staring across the stream at the mountains in the distance she felt like she could stay here forever.

"I know you love the beach. Now that I've shown you my mountain, what do you think?"

She didn't answer him, instead she went up onto her tip toes, angled her head, and kissed him.

"Thank you for bringing me home with you."

His large hand massaging her breast pushed her to deepen the kiss. She pulled at the hem of his shirt, her hands against his abdomen. She tugged him closer, giving her wayward body what it craved-finally. But, not totally. Lina forced her hands to leave Gideon's skin. Introducing sex into one of her relationships signaled the beginning of the end. And she wanted their relationship to last. Tilting her chin up, she found Gideon studying her. Analyzing.

She liked everything he was doing, but she didn't want him to know that. Before she could look away, he grasped her chin, lifted her head, until their eyes met.

"You left me. Where did you go?" Gideon asked.

"I'm here." Trying to tear her gaze away was impossible with his strong hand supporting her chin.

"I have questions that need answering. Your responsibility is to stay in place and answer them. Understood?"

She nodded in understanding.

"Do you foresee a future for us?" Gideon asked.

"Yes." She gave him the truth. Lina saw a future that included Gideon in it.

"Then why did you pull away?" He was a beautiful man, even with a crease between his brows. He hadn't shaved this morning. Dark stubble covered his chin and continued down his neck. His jaw the perfect blend of angles and rounded lines.

"I think I'm making a mistake, Gideon."

He sobered.

Those perfect angles were replaced by a stiff jaw and even stiffer spine.

"You don't want to take this next step with me." His hand, which had been supporting her chin fell away. This was her out. She could walk away with her heart intact.

"I want you too much," she admitted, unwilling to allow him to believe anything different. Lina felt her heart beat double time at the admission. His arm tightened around her waist and she held onto him as sure as he held her.

"We will be happy together." Tears sprang to Lina's eyes. Her heart thudded in her chest. *Promises*. Her stomach churned. She looked away from him.

"Lina?"

"No promises. We can take this next step together, but no promises."

"It doesn't work that way, sweetness. Our making love signifies our promise to each other." The firm note in Gideon's voice brought Lina's gaze back to those gray storm cloud eyes she loved.

"Why complicate what we have with promises?"

"Because I want all of you," Gideon said, his tone softer. Could she be open to love, again?

"Gideon I want to believe." Oh gosh, her throat felt tight. A buzzing sound filled her ears. This was so not sexy.

"Could you love me?" he whispered. She was sure she already did. Gag order. She wouldn't utter that word bomb. She nodded her head, knowing to keep her lips sealed before he ran for the hills.

"Then let go. Trust in us. Let it happen." She blinked away the sensual fuzz in her brain. What would he think of her if he knew what she wanted to do to him? That she wanted more, too. Storm clouds rolled in those steel gray eyes that she had come to love. This was her last chance. She had racked up so many man-fast violations. She needed a parole officer. Even now, she could feel the length of his erection pressing into her hip. His masculine heat was seductive. She found herself sinking into his muscles. Compelled to press closer to him. If she surrendered to her kryptonite, she wouldn't have the power to resist him. The bang up job she'd done to this point was the subject of psychiatric journals. She had to be crazy to take a chance, but it felt like an alternate form of sanity to give herself to him.

"How do we begin?" She didn't want to mess this up. She hadn't a clue how to build a relationship rooted in trust and love. Gideon stilled in front of her. "Show me." Her voice steady and sure. She inhaled a deep breath and gave in to the all-consuming sensual storm swirling around them.

Gideon's lips were on hers demanding entrance. His hands cradled her face. His touch was gentle. More gentle than the onslaught of tongue pressing into her mouth. Stroking her, devouring her. When he broke the kiss, his heat lingered. Marking her as his. She felt a feather light kiss to her head.

"I know you're accustomed to taking care of yourself, but I will always be here for you." No more words were needed. Enough had been said. They both were walking into this with their eyes open. "I'm going to take care of you."

"I told myself that the next man who professed to care about me would have to carve his feelings on a stone tablet in blood." She gave a soft laugh. "I'm breaking my own rule for you." She curled her fingers into the soft material of his shirt, stroking his chest through the fabric. "Don't break my heart." She pleaded. Fear warred with hope inside of her.

"I won't. My love for you is constant as the sun rising and setting." *Love.* He pushed into her mouth once more and coherent thought fled. Lina felt him pull away before she drank her fill. She sought his eyes questioning why he'd broken their kiss.

"I love you, Lina." She gasped. He'd said the three words she dared not dream of him saying to her. Not even Troy had said those three words to her. Gideon was different from the men in her past. He'd kept her safe. He expected them to spend time together, beyond the bedroom. He'd brought her home to meet his family. Couples that stayed together did those things. Made connections. Blended their lives together.

"I'm ready." She hoped. When he opened the door to the warmth of the cabin, she followed when he took her hand. Closing the door on the outside world, she crossed the threshold to her future.

Tonight he would claim Lina as his own. Every touch she graced him with was akin to erotic torture.

More than he could bear, not enough for him to stop. Lina tried to commandeer a room to store her things when they entered the cabin. She wanted him. He could see it in her eyes. Yet she fought the attraction between them. After their night together in Shell Cove and her admission of wanting him, retreat was not on the menu. He loved her. The woman he would spend the rest of his life with. The woman who would give him children.

Neither one of them felt like eating after they walked the property surrounding the cabin. Gideon grabbed a bottle of white wine, and a couple of glasses from the cupboard. He piled grapes, berries, and cheese onto a platter. He rejoined Lina on the sheep skin rug in front of the fireplace. The sound of crackling wood infused the air. She looked vulnerable curled on her side staring into the flames. Her head propped on her hand, she looked up as he placed the platter on the leather chest near her head.

Lying down beside her, he fused the front of their bodies together, hip to hip. Gideon threaded his fingers through her hair. With his lips mere inches from hers. He trailed a thumb across Lina's kiss swollen lips. He loved her. Told her as much. They would be one tonight, but there was still a wall between them.

"Who am I to you?" He asked.

"You are my lover." There was no hesitation in her answer. Not a hint of tremor laced her words.

"Will I ever be more than your lover?" She moved to turn away. He captured her chin between his thumb and forefinger.

"Yes, it is possible." The gleam of hope flashed in her eyes and a peace settled over him.

"I have one last request for tonight."

"What is it?" She asked, a hint of a smile on her face.

"Say that you want to stay with me. That we will be together." This wasn't manipulation. He would do anything in his power to keep her happy.

"I'm with you now." Lina replied.

"I want you now and for always." He leaned in nuzzling the area between her neck and shoulder. A low moan escaped her lips.

"Gideon."

"For always, Lina" He licked her earlobe, and she shivered.

"I'll stay," came her whisper. To him it sounded like she shouted from the steeple down to the cathedral.

"Good. We are going to seal our deal, starting tonight."

"What do you have in mind, Doctor?"

"A whole lot of nurse-doctor role play." He touched his lips to hers.

"I'm going to taste every inch of you."

"Sounds like a challenge." Her warm breath skirted across his chest and every muscle in his body tightened.

He rose to his full height, taking her with him.

"Take your clothes off." Her eyes stretched wide in surprise.

"A bossy doctor in and out of the bedroom, shocking. I thought Marines took orders."

"Only from senior officers, sweetness. And I'm the commanding officer when we're making love," he teased.

"Let's see if we can change that." And she opened her gingham print shirt. He only caught a glimpse of her red silk bra, before she released the clasp and the bountiful swells of her breasts filled his vision. He sucked in a breath. Sweet heavenly dove, the blood to his brain shot to his groin.

"Asymmetrical warfare?" He questioned with a raised brow. "Bring it on."

He unbuttoned his fly, and his erection sprang free. Her eyes filled with heat and the pulse in her neck drummed with the intensity of a KISS concert. He was rolling commando and his erection sprang free when he released the button on his jeans.

"What else you got under all those clothes, my naughty nurse?" Every cell in his body was standing at attention. His hands shook with the need to plunge into her. Mark her with his scent. Claim her as his own.

"I can't believe I'm getting X-rated in your family's cabin."

"You believe I want you?" She nodded. "Words Lina, you're not the shy type." He knew where he stood with Lina except in this one area. When he told her he loved her. She'd pulled her *avoid the subject* maneuver. This time it was too important to their future. He would have his answers.

"Men wanting my body was never an issue. Will you keep me?" She stood bare before him. Her breasts were pools of milk chocolate with dark chocolate centers. He reached out, swirling his fingers over her breasts. She strained forward, pushing her soft flesh against his hands. The nipples beaded with the lightest stroke of his knuckles.

Palming her breast in his hand, he kneaded the responsive flesh until her throaty moans filled the room. He experienced a touch of masculine pride, when she sank to her knees before him. He pushed her back onto the soft rug, stretching his long body over hers. With deft movements, he undid the button of her jeans. He heard her hiss of breath as he released the zipper and worked her legs free of her pants and panties.

He didn't believe it was possible, but the pulse in his pants increased, and he got harder. He might die of an erection overload before he ever got inside of her.

"I'm not most men. I sure don't want to hear about other men when my junk is on display and you're a visual feast laid bare for me."

"I know who you are, Gideon. There's no danger of me comparing you to another man." She sat forward, gathered the hem of his shirt, and pushed it up, gliding her hands along his torso. Unabashed appreciation shone in her eyes as she slowly divested him of his shirt.

"You believe I love you?" Her hands stilled on his skin. Her nails dug into his chiseled abdomen. She gave a head tilt or maybe it was a nod. For all he knew, she was scratching her ear with her shoulder. No way would he leave his love for her open to interpretation.

"Open your mouth and tell me you believe I love you." Silence.

"Lina, say it or this stops."

"I'm butt naked by the fire. This is our first time having sex, and you're threatening to hold out on the Cricket?" He made quick work of removing his pants and boots.

"Now were both butt naked by the fire." When her eyes zeroed in on his bobbing erection, he about lost his load. The look in her eyes said she knew the truth.

"I can tell you, this is a bad plan." She placed an open mouthed kiss to his abdomen. He shuddered when she gently sucked his skin between her teeth, licking in rhythm with his breaths. A deep groan filled the room. He felt her lips stretch into a smile. His plan would indeed, fail.

"I can promise you I would be incapable of holding out with you naked in my bed every night. With you in my life, I'll never be limp enough to be paired up, rolled into a neat ball, and tucked away in a sock drawer. I have no idea what the term cricket pertains to on your body, but I know I'll love it. Because I love you."

"Stop saying that you love me." She pushed, but he would not budge.

"I can't and I won't. I love you and if you can't accept my love for you we will never get to where I want to take you."

"I think you have the skills to take me all the way, Gideon."

"No joking, sweetness. I know what you're doing and it's not going to work." It was the hardest thing he had to do, literally. He lifted his weight off Lina and rolled onto the carpet beside her. Before he could chastise himself for being the stupidest man on the planet he reached over and pulled Lina into his lap. Taking her chin between his fingers, he lifted her head until their gazes met, "Why don't you trust me?"

"I do, Gideon." He searched her face. Something held her back and it was beyond the boundaries of her man-fast. "I need you." Lina looked miserable at the admission. She didn't want to need him, Gideon realized. Tonight would be a demonstration in trust for both of them. He reached under the sofa cushion and withdrew a condom.

"How did you know that was under there?" She asked.

"I stocked the cabin with more than food and water," he grinned at her. "Lie down and open wide for me." She scrambled off his lap. The speed of her compliance told him she was as eager as he.

He stroked his tongue over her right nipple before cupping her full breast. Taking the taut bud into his mouth. He felt Lina's arm around his neck, pulling him forward, pushing her breast deeper into his mouth. He suckled the hard peak until Lina writhed beneath him.

She moaned, when he lavished equal attention on its twin. He licked his way down to her bare mound leaving a trail of wetness on her skin. When Gideon cupped her sex, easing two fingers inside to test her readiness, she released a low hiss of pleasure.

"Yeah, sweetness. You are ready for me." He couldn't hold out much longer either.

He tangled his hands in her hair. He pulled her forward, surging into her mouth. The thrusts of his tongue in sync with the fingers stroking her moist channel.

When her legs fell open wider of their own accord, he pumped into her heated core, until she trembled with desire. Her sultry cries for more entered his psyche fueling his own need.

"Gideon, please. I need you." Her voice was throaty and filled with sexual tension.

"I need you more." He withdrew his fingers and she moaned against his mouth.

He reached down positioning his condom sheathed erection at her entrance. He buried himself inside her in one fluid motion, sinking deep into her drenched sex.

Gideon threw back his head, lips parted in ecstasy. The slow roll of Lina's hips, pulled him deep in to an erotic abyss of friction, heat, and bone deep pleasure. The divergence of soft and hard as he surged into her was the sensual ride of his life. And he was determined to savor every hill and valley until they toppled over the precipice together. Soft sucking noises mixed with the crackling of fired wood. Lina's hoarse cries of pleasure stoked his passion and he began pumping into her in long, deep strokes. He wanted to leave a permanent reminder on her body.

He looked down, Lina's eyes were glazed with sexual pleasure. He moved lower, leveraging his weight, pressing her in the rug, his sweat mingling with hers. Their combined scent drove him to push harder, deeper, and faster.

Dozens of pulsations flooded her quaking sex muscles.

"I feel you getting ready to come, Lina."

He bent her leg suspending it with his forearm opening her impossibly wide and plunged into her silken lining until he couldn't distinguish her body from his.

"Gideon," her tone was unsure, almost panicked.

"I'm with you, Lina. I love you." Staring deep into her eyes, he watched, waiting to see her release. Witness her fly apart because of his lovemaking.

All of a sudden, uncertainty flashed in her eyes.

No. No. No. "Lina, don't hold back," he ground out. "Give me your love." He slammed into her harder, driving her into the carpet. She surged up to meet him thrust for thrust. He wasn't gentle, and neither was she. She curled her arms around his neck. Holding on to him as if her life depended on what only he could provide. He felt her tense beneath him.

"I need to come, Gideon." A low sob escaped her lips when he slowed his thrust.

"You will. When I tell you." She bucked against him and he ground his teeth to maintain his control. "I know sweetness." He pulled out before she registered his action. "Roll over onto your stomach."

She hesitated.

"Trust me, Lina. Stop thinking and feel." Complying with his request she rolled, then moved to her knees. He pressed a hand to her lower back. "Stay down and open wide for me."

The warmth of her generous derriere seared his groin as he blanketed her with his body. He pushed into her welcoming heat with one smooth thrust. The air left her lungs. He felt her walls clamp down on his length working to unseat him.

"Gideon," she panted.

"It's okay. Relax, Lina."

"Good, so good." She said in a low pant. "I need you to move, Gideon." He smiled when she tilted her hips up in invitation.

"We are in this together, sweetness. Just this first time, like this." He placed soft kisses on her shoulder, not moving though buried in her sheath, giving her body the time to adjust to his girth at this angle.

Breaths no longer coming in pants, her muscles relaxed underneath him. He reveled in the sensation of being enclosed in her heat. The tip of his glans brushed her womb. He slid deep inside her, slowly withdrawing and pushed into her body again.

"Gideon, it's too much. I can't keep it together much longer." He increased his speed and force with each push of his hips. Tunneling deep in tandem with her cries of pleasure.

"That's the point. Let go Lina. Don't hold back on me."

"I'm trying not…" He cut her off.

"You're trying to control your response. Let it happen, sweetness. I'll never hold back on you. Give me everything."

Her sex clenched tight around his rock hard erection, preventing his full entry. The feel of her, the pulsations coursing through him as he coaxed her body into surrender, nearly toppled his control.

"Take all of me, Lina. You said you needed me. Were you telling me the truth?" She didn't respond. A soft whimper met his ear.

"I would have your words, sweetness."

"Yes," she moaned. "I need…you. Only you Gideon."

"You have me Lina. I want to hear you say it."

"I have you," she moaned, half screamed. She seemed semi-conscious of her responses. Her body writhed beneath his.

"You are mine? Give me the words." He demanded.

"Yes, I'm yours."

"Then give me what is mine, Lina." Her muscles relaxed and he seated himself deep inside her. Branding her with his body. Driving everything he felt, closer to the heart of her. Lina's body surrendered, and she spread her legs wider, giving him full access and he took everything she had.

"Yes, yes. That's the spot, Gideon. Don't stop," she hissed out.

"Come for me." He said close to her ear. He pulled back, and then plunged deep into her quivering sex at the same time he thrummed her hooded nub. The smack of his hips against Lina's prone body filled the room. The sucking sound of sex was loud between their moist bodies.

"Gideon," she screamed.

Lina's sex clamped down on him like an erotic vice grip. His body strained in response. The intensity almost painful as her release ricocheted through him triggering his own. Gideon plunged head first into ecstasy as his orgasm ripped from his body. His semen exploded forward like a rocket launch. As she climaxed he heard her scream and his roar spiral in his ears. He collapsed on Lina's limp body, weak as a newborn colt trying to master its first steps.

"Rest, sweetness." he said kissing the top of her head.

"Lina," he spoke into her hair breathing in her scent, "You are amazing, perfect for me. I'm not letting you go." He squeezed her middle overwhelmed with emotion. He had found his soulmate.

She briefly raised her head to peer over her shoulder in his general direction. Exhaustion and sexual satisfaction etched in her features.

"No more," she croaked before collapsing back to the floor.

He lightly spanked her hip, "There's more, stop all the crazy talk woman." He collapsed onto the floor beside her, pulling her into his arms.

"Sleep. In a few hours, you will look me in the eye and give me your love."

"Whatever you say, Sir." She snorted and he laughed.

"You are going to need your rest for what I have planned."

Lina was asleep beside him. His chest puffed up more when she pressed herself against his warmth and threw her leg over both of his. He realized all he needed was in the bed beside him. Being quiet not to rouse Lina, he rolled to his side, reached for the handle on the bedside table and grabbed him phone. Pressing the power button, he waited for the screen to illuminate, and then he dialed Ian's number.

Hearing his brother's sleep ladened voice was divine pay back for all the times Ian had awakened him in the wee hours of the morning. Gideon spoke before Ian could form a coherent word, "Give her the house." The utter silence on the other end of the phone didn't surprise him. After years of fighting for acceptance, Gideon had won the ultimate prize. The woman he loved was taking him home. Home wasn't a house. His home was with Lina. He finally had a place to belong.

Gideon felt like an insect under a microscope lens. Jacob had talked him into participating in an interview with the local newspaper down at Rice Campaign headquarters. The office was small, but well appointed. The front of the building was a standard glass storefront with a view of Main Street and downtown Waverly Falls. The main office space held eight press wood desks, each with a telephone line ringing. Jacob's office was at the back of the general work force area behind a closed door. The interview would be conducted in the conference room to the far left.

Though he dressed in business attire every day, this was the first time he could see people measuring the fabric of a man. Did he make the cut? Jacob led the way to the interview location. That was probably intentionally. The reporter was a lanky man, in his early thirties with pale skin and medal rimmed glasses. His lips were thin and severe. Thin lipped with glasses walked in front of Phoenix while Gideon brought on the rear.

Once they entered the conference room, Jacob gestured for him to take a seat next to Phoenix at the table.

"These are my sons, Gideon and Phoenix," Jacob said, "they will be with me for the duration of the interview." Jacob smiled at him and Phoenix. And Gideon felt a small ping of pride that after ten years Jacob seamlessly welcomed him back into the fold. Maybe, there was some validity to Lina's argument. Did the possibility exist for him to be a part of the Rice family, and still have enough love to give his own children? He didn't want to misuse the love he had before he was blessed with children.

He wanted to love his children so deeply that they would never have to worry about him giving them up. He would cut off his right arm to keep Lina and any children they had together. Gideon heard his name and it drew him back to the present.

"Gideon, I knew Mrs. Emma. And she talked about you all the time." Gideon smiled at the memory of his adoptive mother. She always had fresh baked cookies on the stove.

"She was a special woman," Gideon replied.

"Yes, she was special, the whole town mourned her death." Ouch. A shiver snaked up Gideon's spine. Phoenix glanced from Jacob to the reporter, and then back at Gideon.

"I don't recall seeing you at her funeral," the reporter said casually.

"I don't live in Waverly Falls," Gideon replied through clenched teeth.

"Gideon is a psychiatrist in Florida. He instituted a behavioral health project aimed at helping combat veterans healing from post traumatic stress disorder," Jacob chimed in. His smile was broad, but it didn't reach his eyes.

"I recall hearing something about that recently," the man replied. No doubt, listening to Mrs. Nedstetter's gossip.

"So, what happened in the Rice household to make you abandon the family?" Gideon saw red. Where the heck had he heard that? Gideon never walked out on anyone in his life.

"Have you lost your mind?" Jacob roared, coming to his feet. "He's my son. If he didn't set a foot in this town in a hundred years, it doesn't change the fact that he's my child. And I love him. This interview is over. Get your crap and get out of my office." Jacob jeopardized the interview for him?

"I meant no disrespect, Mr. Rice." The reporter offered with a shaky voice.

"You disrespected my son. I take that personally." Phoenix held the conference door open, in silence.

"You wanted a story. Write this down," Jacob said pointing at the reporter who now resembled a chastised child. "Nobody messes with my family. Do you understand?" Gideon was speechless. Jacob hadn't hesitated to toss the reporter out on his ear. His brother, Phoenix, had given his support, by opening the door. Would Gideon be this type of father to his own children? How could he have been so blind?

"Yes, Sir," the reporter replied, beating a hasty retreat out of the office.

"I expect to see that headline in print," Jacob called out.

Jacob approached him, placing a hand on his shoulder. "You okay, son?" Gideon looked in the eyes of the man who had raised him. Kept him safe as he grew. Helped him complete his first job application. And what he saw reflected in Jacob's eyes floored him. Love and acceptance. Had it been there all his life, but he refused to see it?

"I'm better than I've been in a long time." Jacob smiled up at him, giving his shoulder a hard squeeze.

"That's good, son. Real good. Keep working at it. You'll get there?" Would he be too late?

One week in Waverly Falls and Lina never wanted to leave. The cabin that had overwhelmed her upon arrival felt like home. Lina turned to face her guest. Ian had stopped by to discuss some business with Gideon, but he'd joined Phoenix and Jacob at the campaign headquarters. She poured a mug of fresh brewed coffee and placed it in front of him.

She grabbed another mug and poured a cup for herself.

"You don't enjoy politics?" Lina questioned as she added a teaspoon of sugar to her mug. She lifted the sugar and cream holders to eye level in offering. Ian shook his head in the negative.

"I enjoy debate, as well as any man. I don't like mud slinging." Lina crinkled her nose in understanding. Dissecting a person's life, in search of leverage for political gain held no appeal for her. She valued her privacy too much to consider a career as a public servant.

"I'm not sure how long Gideon will be gone. You can leave his documents with me. I'll make sure he gets them."

Ian regarded her quizzically.

"You and Gideon seem to get along well." Where was he going with this?

"Yep," she replied.

"You plan on sticking around?" Lina placed her mug on the countertop, giving Ian a *don't go there* with me look.

"Why did you really stop by, Ian?" Lina crossed her arms over her chest and waited.

"Gideon is my brother and I love him."

"But," she prompted.

"He had a lot of scars. Some you can see, most you can't."

"I know about his nightmares, Ian. I'm not afraid of Gideon." He looked surprised.

"There's more. I can see that he cares about you, but Gideon prefers to live in the present." Lina was getting upset.

"Most people prefer to focus on the present and the future. I don't see that as a character flaw, Ian."

"Please don't be angry. What I'm saying is none of us are exempt from our past. We can't put our pasts in a time capsule and start over like it never existed."

"I know that," she hissed.

"You do, but Gideon does not. You should know what you're getting–" The front door to the cabin banged against the rear wall. Gideon's hulking frame filled the door way.

"What are you doing here, Ian?" He growled. Gideon turned hard eyes on her. Lina nearly shrank away, even though he hadn't taken a step towards her. Why was Gideon so pissed?

The banging at the door woke Gideon from the best sleep of his life. It was the door opening that had him out of the bed and on his feet. He was sure the bad guy was back in Shell Cove, but his brothers knew to keep clear of the cabin, so it had to be Jacob.

"I'm coming out."

"I was not coming in, trust me. After all the racket you two were making up at the house."

Gideon closed the door behind him.

"Enough said, what brought you all the way out here at eight o'clock in the morning."

"A little spitfire named Bernadean James called. She said, she'd better hear her daughter's voice in the next twenty minutes or a group of triple OG's are rolling in on us. She promised that I wouldn't like it." His father who was usually reserved, laughed-deep and hearty. Gideon heard Lina's movements in the bedroom. Lina opened the door and his heart pounded in his chest. His woman was gorgeous in the morning after a night of love making.

"I heard everything, get me to a phone. If she said twenty minutes, you are on a timer and her luggage is in the car. You will be sorry if mom rounds up her Ocean Girls book club and starts heading this way."

"A book club?" Both he and his father looked at Lina incredulously.

"Don't underestimate a group of avid readers. Those women read everything from romance to urban fiction and they know a thousand ways to make you bleed." Laughter boomed in the room.

"An all-women gangster book reading club." An image of three, sixty something year old women, decked out in urban gear with their book club logo embroidered on matching t-shirts, bouncing on twenty-four inch rims flashed in his mind. He laughed harder and his father must have had a similar vision. Gideon shook his head to rid himself of the mental image.

"Both our phones were powered off, safely tucked away in the bedside table." Lina looked at him with wide eyes.

Gideon shrugged his shoulders, non-apologetically, "We had an important decision to make."

"I noticed Lina is wearing your ring. When's the big day?" Gideon saw the shock register on Lina's face before she thrusted her hand in the air staring at his ring. The chain around his neck was empty, his mother's ring, now graced Lina's finger.

"As soon as she says yes."

CHAPTER SEVENTEEN

His pulse pounded in his ears. Careful to obey the speed limit, he cruised down the block of the residential neighborhood. He used the heel of his left hand to deliver repeating blows to his temple. The sound of Lina's screams that night had quieted in his head. He hated not hearing her voice. This was his twelfth time driving by the doctor's house. Where had he taken Lina? His Lina. Her car remained in the same parking spot for five days. He'd given up on visiting the condo. It was stupid to attack when she was with him. He should have waited until she was alone, but everyone kept coming between them. The foolish woman had interfered. He didn't like hitting women. They never fought back hard enough.

When he threw the brick, the doctor moved like a trained soldier. He didn't hesitate, he didn't flinch at the sound of breaking glass. It was too dark for him to see Lina, but the man he'd seen clearly. He had been naked. He could hear his own breathing, fast and erratic. His Lina was in bed with another man. Whore. She'd let the doctor shield her body with his bare flesh. Rage blazed hot in his veins.

Damn barking dog and floodlights almost got him caught. By the time the sirens sounded in the distance he was safely hidden in the Range Rover five blocks away. But he'd waited too long to double back. The Cadillac the doctor drove was gone when he jumped the neighboring fence. Now he couldn't find Lina. Exiting the neighborhood he took the entrance ramp to I-95 South.

He needed to think. Taking several deep breaths he slowed his heart rate. The soldier masquerading as a doctor would pay for taking her away. A soldier was a respectable opponent for him. Though he lacked formal combat training, the criminal underworld had trained him as a killer. He was good at killing, enjoyed it most days.

A familiar tune by Boys II Men droned on the radio and he reached to change the station, then the chorus rang out. *You know I love you mama*, the balladeer crooned. He knew how to bring Lina out of hiding. Crossing two lanes of traffic he took the Roosevelt Boulevard exit headed west. He parked his car and waited. He would bring his Lina home.

Her mother had been attacked. The call from Bishop had rocked Lina to her core. Lina and Gideon were in the car eating up the miles headed south. A masked man accosted Bernadean in the parking lot after work. After throwing her to the ground, he proceeded to pour blood on her. Too distraught following the attack, Bernadean was at Willa's house for tonight. When Lina called, Willa informed her that Bernadean had taken a sedative and had finally gone to sleep. They still didn't have the answers they needed to stop the attacks. Because of her, the best mother she could have hoped for had been attacked. Guilt and regret sat like lead weights to Lina's chest. If she had stayed in Shell Cove the attention would've remained on her, rather than involve her family.

The repairs to both their houses were complete and their time in Waverly Falls had come to an end. Janna liaised with Thane when he arrived in Shell Cove. According to Janna, she would be pleased with the remodel. Gideon was silent as they entered the Shell Cove city limits.

He was distracted and for the life of her she couldn't understand why.

"Gideon, nothing happened between me and Ian."

"I know that," came his terse reply.

"So, what's with the silent treatment?"

"What did he say to you?"

"He thinks that we are good together and said he was happy you were finally moving on with your life. He said you're stubborn. Which I'm discovering is an understatement."

"Anything else?"

"No." She was hesitant. Gideon visibly relaxed. "What's going on, Gideon? What aren't you telling me?"

"It's water under a very old bridge. Ian and I disagree on how I handled the situation until recently. It has nothing to do with you and me. My past won't stay buried."

"Nothing stays buried. Being a psychiatrist you understand that better than most."

"Everything is taken care of. Change of subject, I know you love living near the water, if you had the option to build a house where would it be?" Lina leaned over the center console stroking his inner thigh.

"Hmm, interesting question doctor. You're asking me to dream build a house with you?"

"I would love to live in Avondale. With its canopy lined streets, historic charm and water views it has everything I would want in a neighbor."

"How about we build the house of your dreams in Avondale?"

"Get out. You would give up your custom built bachelor's pad for me?"

"That ring on your finger means I'm asking you to do a lot of sacrificing for me." Lina pulled back then.

"Yeah, we need to talk about what this ring means to you. I know it belonged to your mom, and I'm honored that you want me to wear it, but…"

"There's no but. The ring belonged to my birth mother. She would pawn it when we needed money. She once told me, no matter what happened, she would always come back for that ring. I found it in the Waverly Falls pawn shop when I was seventeen. So, as soon as you tell me you're ready to get married, I'm going to make you my wife." Oh God, he held onto the hope that his mother would return for him.

"Wow, I'm not…"

"Let's not do this in the car, while I have to keep us alive, by paying attention. We will talk more when we get home."

"You want to get married?"

"Yes, Lina. You sound as if you don't believe me. I don't go around asking for a woman's hand in marriage to fill a lull in polite conversation."

"I'm sorry. I either slept through your proposal or I was in a sexual stupor when I agreed to marry you." She didn't think she would forget her proposal. Was the sex that good? *Yes*.

Gideon abruptly pulled the car off the road. Arm propped on the steering wheel he turned to face her. Though he moved fast his touch was gentle when he touched her cheek.

"You have nothing to apologize for. I'm a moron." Lina regarded him with more confusion.

"My birth family, never had much they could claim as their own. I think I inherited that trait. No matter how much money I made I still felt like I had nothing. Until I found you, Lina. That ring on your finger is mine. It's a part of my soul and I gave it to you because you're a part of me. I'm asking you to spend the rest of your life loving me. And I pray to God that you say yes, because I won't live another day without you." Oh God, she felt tears prick her eyes. She never cried.

"Yes." She whispered. This was her dream come true.

"Yes to everything?" Gideon trapped her chin in his hand. "You gonna be my wife?" She felt his hands shaking.

"Yes."

"You will marry me and we are going to build our home, together." She gave a barely perceptible nod for fear her head would fall off her neck because the earth had tilted on its axis. "Say the words."

"I'm keeping you, Gideon Rice."

When they navigated the service road leading to Lina's condo, Gideon broached the topic that loomed in the recesses of his mind since Lina had agreed to marry him. The last time he'd traveled this road it was littered with police squad cars, convertibles with the tops lowered and a broken down nineteen seventies style camper truck.

"I know you can move back into your place, but I'm asking you to come live with me." She looked at him like he'd hacked her bank account.

"Living together...huh?" He could feel her withdrawing.

"Lina?"

"I heard you. You want the milk in the house, so you promise the cow a ring." Did she think he was trying a bait and switch? That he would promise marriage then not deliver.

"Look at me, Lina." She kept her eyes trained on the road ahead. "We are going to get married."

"When?"

"Look at me."

"You tell me when...we are getting married and I'll gaze in your eyes all night."

"Sweetness, we can live..." She opened the car door and stepped onto the pavement. Shoot, she moved fast. In the time it took him to release the seat belt and open the car door, she was at the stairs leading to her second floor unit. He ran in her direction, Gideon snagged an arm around her waist, hauling her in, close to his body.

"Pick a date." She was stiff as a pipe against his chest.

"Did you hear me?" He squeezed her tight around the middle, willing her to believe in their love, to trust him. "Tell me when you want to be my wife."

"Friday morning." There was an underlying tremor in her voice. He realized it was doubt. After everything they had shared, she doubted him.

"What time Friday?" She spun in his arms, now they stood nose to nose with her on the step above his.

"Eleven thirty in the hospital chapel," her voice had a light, far away quality.

"Why are we getting married in the hospital?" She smiled broadly at him.

"Because, then all the nurses can take an early lunch break to attend our wedding ceremony and Janna leaves next week. I want Ava, Janna, and Rebecca in the wedding."

"Rebecca, too?"

"Yeah, considering how supportive she's been of Ava. She's an honorary sister." Married by Friday. Would his woman ever stop surprising him?

CHAPTER EIGHTEEN

Lina was happy. Her mother was physically unharmed and she was marrying the man of her dreams. Deanie was more emotional than she'd ever witnessed, but she hoped that with time her mother would heal from the attack.

The traffic flow leading onto Shell Cove Medical Center Parkway was slow, but steady. It would be another ten minutes before she reached the medical complex. Lina pressed the audio controls on the steering column until her favorite R & B station tuned in. The morning music mix was one she'd heard before, she began to sing like she was getting paid to perform. Maybe, that's why she didn't see it coming.

A small side paneled sport utility vehicle T-boned into the passenger door of Lina's purple Camaro convertible. Her grip on the steering wheel had slipped away before she realized she'd been hit. The harsh scrape of metal on metal hurt her ears. She felt the pressure of the fiberglass cracking as the car door buckled against the force and velocity of impact.

.   She smelled the stench of burning tire rubber as the other vehicle accelerated. The SUV continued to push the passenger door further into the interior of the car. Just as quickly as it started, the crushing pressure was gone. She remembered yelling for an emergency medical technician to call Gideon. Before she slipped into unconscious she remembered her mother. When Lina didn't arrive for lunch her mother would worry. But it was too late, the dark abyss pulled her in.

A noise from the hospital room's sitting area startled her from sleep. An urgent text message had pulled Gideon down to the emergency room. Had he returned? Straining against the effects of the narcotics, Lina channeled her strength into prying her eyelids apart. She had a new appreciation for the plight of patients who became addicted to prescription drugs as the morphine drip piped into her veins, life colored in a beautiful mind-numbing hue, literally.

She struggled to focus on the figure emerging from the shadows beyond the draped window. When the familiar chiseled jaw adorned with its signature two days of stubble came into view, the breath she inhaled, stalled in her windpipe. She would have fallen over the side if the bed rails weren't locked into the upright position. His caramel colored eyes, the eyes that had once melted her heart, bore into her.

"Candy." *That voice can't be real.*

When her lips parted, she said one word, "Troy?"

"Hey Candy, I'm back." She released the delivery button to the morphine pump with the swiftness of a cobra strike.

Gideon fumed at the man standing before him. This day was worse than Monday mornings before Lina came into his life. An emergency call had pulled him away from Lina's bedside, then Ian had intercepted him before he could return to her. Gideon held onto his control by a thread. A thread that stretched thinner every time he thought about Lina being struck by that SUV. She could have been lying dead on the side of a road. She needed him and he wasn't there.

"Ian I don't care what it takes. You keep her away from Shell Cove. Someone is trying to kill the woman I love. Moments ago I found out my patient is in a coma because someone slipped Galaxy into her drink." Gideon rubbed his forehead with his fingers, trying to ward off the ache in his head.

"I don't have time for...her shit, Ian. Gideon had almost said her name aloud. "Not with everything that's happened in the last twenty-four hours."

"You have to deal with this. You can't ignore your past because you moved to a new city! Technically, she can assess the property before she assumes ownership."

"She can assess my house once I've left it. Not a moment sooner."

"I'll do what I can, but I don't know where she's located at the moment. I've forwarded the transfer of ownership documents to her attorney's office."

"I need you to take care of this for me, Ian. Lina will be discharged later today. I'm taking her *home*."

"Gideon," Ian's authoritative tone pulled him up short. "Tell Lina about her now, before it's too late. Neither of us would be under pressure to make this negotiation happen if Lina knew the truth. You're giving her the power to hurt you again by keeping Lina in the dark."

"And never the two shall meet," Gideon offered in his own low tone. "The answer is no."

"And why is that...Dr. Rice?" Ian's voice had taken on a more menacing quality. "Was it so horrible having your fiancée meet your family? Did we embarrass you with our hillbilly, man mountain way of treating other people?"

"Heck no, why would you think something that terrible?"

"Because your past isn't tainted. Your perspective of the past is the problem. Lina is stronger than you give her credit for. She's committed to you. She trusts you. Trust her by sharing your life, all of it." Ian said.

"Don't tell me how to handle my woman." Gideon snapped.

"Is that what you're trying to do?" Ian shook head, staring at Gideon with sadness in his eyes. Gideon felt anger pulsing in his veins. It was his responsibility to protect Lina. Even if it was from himself.

"You picked the wrong woman to try and lead around with blinders on. She loves you the way you are. Lina doesn't have a problem with you being adopted or accepting us as your family. But you do. You never wanted to be a member of this family. You rub father's nose in the mud for taking you in, make sure he knows how much you resent him every chance you get."

"You make it sound like I'm ashamed of you. That couldn't be farther from the truth." What a horrible child Gideon must have been for his own mother to walk away from him. The shame was his to bear.

"Aren't you?" Ian ground out.

"I'm ashamed of myself." Gideon said, his voice hitting the walls with the weight of a sonic blast. Ian stood there with his mouth open, like he couldn't believe Gideon's words.

"That's one of the most ridiculous statements I've heard in a while, and I'm a lawyer."

Gideon remained silent.

"You're serious, aren't you?" Ian stared at him, like he was waiting for Gideon to say he was joking.

"Yep," Gideon said.

"You were a Marine for goodness sake, served your country with honor and went on to become a doctor. How can you be ashamed?" A furrow formed between Ian's brows.

"Doesn't change the fact that my mother didn't love me enough to keep me. That I ended up being taken in by a neighbor that felt sorry for me." Gideon stretched his eyes in shock when his brother gripped him by both shoulders.

"Ever consider your mother loved you enough to want to give you a better life? A life she couldn't provide for you." That hadn't occurred to Gideon. He was far too angry at Jacob for making it easy for his mother to leave him. If Jacob hadn't offered to adopt him, his mother would have been forced to figure out a way to keep them together.

"I know the story of your family. After your grandparents died your mother was a young girl left alone to raise an infant. Addicted to drugs, stints in rehab and jail, with you in and out of foster care. Dad respected your grandfather, knew it would break his heart to know his only grandchild had no one to depend on. So he and Mrs. Emma took you in, made you their own. And you hated them for it." Gideon shrugged off Ian's hold.

"It's not that I hate them, but maybe my life would have been different if they hadn't interfered."

"Do you honestly think, mom and dad would have stopped you from seeing your mother if she had returned for you?" Gideon knew the answer to the question and it shamed him to admit the truth. "Let's hear it, doctor of psychiatry."

"No, they would not have forbid her from seeing me."

"Exactly, so pull your head out of your pucker and start treating Dad with the respect that he deserves. He kept you safe, Gideon. Helped you reach your potential. Jacob helped all of us." His muscles went taut as a wave of guilt and shame overtook him. The two emotions, together, shattered the bitterness he'd harbored for years.

"I've been foolish all these years, Ian." He thought back to Jacob standing up for him with the reporter. The ease at which he'd welcomed Lina into his home. Yeah, he'd been a fool.

"I was going to say stupid, but I'm a lawyer. Its time to let the past go, instead of running from it."

"All the time I've wasted. How can I ask him to forgive me?"

"Dad loves you. You're his son. If you stop being a pecker head that would be a massive improvement. Inviting your family to the wedding was a step in the right direction." Gideon released a hearty laugh, because Ian was right. His father was a humble man and when Gideon approached him, Jacob would welcome him. Just like he'd done the first day Gideon arrived on the ranch. Jacob wasn't the problem. Gideon was the stubborn one. Not allowing their relationship to grow beyond that of ward and guardian.

"I'll make things right with Jacob."

"Good. Welcome back into the family, brother."

"It's good to be back." Ian pulled him into a quick embrace and he allowed it. The life he wanted was within his grasp, so why did he feel like it was all about to be swept away? He needed Lina.

Troy Lawson's ink-black curls were shorter than when she knew him. He had been her everything. He'd been on staff in the athletic department where she attended nursing school. Six years her senior, it felt chic for a soon-to-be college graduate to be living with a man who had a job and his own apartment. Looking at him standing in her hospital room was too much.

"You are lucky I'm under the influence of pain killers, or BETAS and I would be prepping you for a hospital bed of your own."

"That's my Candy, always ready to take on the world single-handedly." He smiled then, but it didn't hold her appeal.

"I'm not your Candy. Showing up in my hospital room talking about you're back. Where the hell have you been? Let's start there."

"I've always been close by." He said.

"That's not reassuring, considering I haven't seen you in five years." She crossed her arms over her chest, wincing as her sore muscles protested the movement.

The memory slammed into her. Returning to their apartment, only to notice hours later that his personal items were gone along with the oversized rose gold heart pendant suspended on a sterling filigree chain he'd given her. It was the only piece of jewelry he'd ever given her. He'd said it was the largest heart he could find, because that's what he'd found in her.

"Well, I'm back now and I'll tell you as much as I can about why I left." Three soft dings rang out from the announcement speaker, before an automated voice called a code blue in the emergency room. He gave a brief glance at the door before settling his gaze back to her.

"Tell me why you came back." She raised her eyebrows, waiting for his response. What reason could he possibly give her to justify his return?

"For you." She leaned forward, looking deep into his eyes. His eyes burned with the truth of his words. The more she regarded him the more she couldn't hide her confusion. She grimaced, befuddled by his presence and the truth of his words. Maybe he'd escaped from a psychiatric hospital. Only a lunatic would consider sneaking into a drugged, ex-girlfriend's hospital room and professing his undying feelings for her, five years too late.

"You can't be serious. You stole my heart, Troy." The tremor in her voice was more upsetting to Lina, than the visible shake to her hands.

"Lina, you've had my heart from the moment you activated the emergency exit door alarm in the athletic department."

"I'm talking about the heart necklace you gave to me." He took a step away from the bed, before turning away from her. Would he walk out, now that she had reminded him of the lies between them? He'd left her, no warning, no goodbye, no contact, until today. Lina didn't see Troy turn around, but she clearly saw the sculpted hills and plains of his abdomen because the pale blue collared shirt was unbuttoned. She squeezed her eyes closed.

Everything in the room froze in time. *Don't open your eyes.* She'd caught a glimpse of shiny metal and everything in her rebelled against the pull it had on her.

"Open your eyes Candy. I told you we would always be together." She opened her tear filled eyes and there was no mistaking the rose gold colored heart around his neck.

"Your heart is where it was meant to be–next to mine." Oh God, where was that morphine pump button? She needed a hit of hard stuff because, because this wasn't fair. He left. He couldn't show up five years later, saying they had the double heart locking mechanism. It was hard to see the man that she had once wanted more than her next breathe.

"Troy?"

"I'm here." The sincerity in his tone was more concerning.

"But you shouldn't be." She heard herself say.

"I'm not leaving you again." He moved closer to the bed. She watched in silence as he extended his hand in her direction. Willing her with his eyes to reach for him. His fingers were broad, nails cut short and square, minute scars covered the back of his hand. And she found herself wondering how he received those cuts. He would touch her and all the memories of their time together would come raging back. Confusing her. Troy was her first love.

She could feel the heat of his hand as it approached her cheek.

A shadow moved across the narrow, rectangular shaped window cut in the room's door. A millisecond later the door was pushed wide and there stood Gideon, all six feet five inches of him. The expression on his face was menacing, and ominous.

"Don't touch her." Gideon stormed into the room and crowded into Troy's personal space. Troy straightened to his full height, which was still three inches shorter than Gideon. Both men stood chest to chest.

"What the flagnoid?" She directed at both men. "No fighting over the patient," Lina said, her voice a high squealed sound. Gosh, these two had her behaving like a ditzy girl, instead of a diva.

"I wondered what I would do when I met you man to man," Troy said.

"I guess we both are about to find out," came Gideon's graveled response.

"No, you are not." Lina reached for the remote and raised the head of her bed, her aching limbs opposing each movement.

"Troy, I appreciate you stopping by, but Gideon is here now, so you can go."

"You invited him?" Gideon turned hard eyes on her.

"What?" His accusation cut her deep. Gideon didn't trust her. Did Gideon trust anyone?

"You invited your ex-lover here to see you, the minute I turn my back." Lina felt her brain rattle against her skull. She could hear the blood slow to a crawl in her veins. The pained expression on Gideon's face hurt more than a physical blow. She had never seen him look so vulnerable, yet ice cold. Something was terribly wrong with Gideon. What happened when he left her hospital room?

"That's not true and you know it." She replied in a stern voice. Why would he say something so hurtful to her? "What was the call that took you to the emergency room?"

Gideon shook his head. "You don't want to know. Not right now."

"Tell me. I can handle it." Lina persisted. Why did he insist on shielding her?

"Lina, now is not the time…"

"Just tell me," her voice climbed two octaves.

"Staff Sergeant Hain was admitted to the intensive care unit for Galaxy ingestion. She may have been drugged." The pain that had previously been well controlled, roared back to life, but she held herself still trying, but failing to ward off the sharp, jabs of pain to her side and back.

"Candy?" Troy looked at her, while Gideon looked at them both.

"What the hell did you call my fiancée?"

"No Candy, tell me you didn't agree to marry him." Tears swelled then, she refused to let them fall. Blinking in rapid succession, she held the tears behind a wall of emotion threatening to overwhelm her.

"She did. So, kindly get the hell away from what's mine." Lina saw how Troy's eyes darkened and jaw stiffened before he turned back to face Gideon.

Oh no Troy, don't do this. Lina struggled to sit forward.

"Troy, no."

He ignored her.

"You want to challenge me? Listen carefully, Dr. Rice and you'll discover who Lina belongs to."

"Troy, don't say another word." She pushed herself forward ignoring the pain.

"The condominium she lives in, I paid the down payment, because she loves the water." That wasn't what she expected him to say. Gideon's eyes shot to hers. What was Troy talking about? Why would he say that?

"The designer closet. A birthday gift." Troy continued on.

"Lina, what the hell is going on?" Gideon raged. She wished she knew. If what Troy said was true, her mother had lied to her.

"The custom painted purple Camaro she drives is a gift from me." Gideon's face reddened with fury.

"That's not true, my mother gave me..." Troy turned to look at her with such conviction she knew he was telling the truth.

"And who do you think gave it to her?" She collapsed back on the bed. This couldn't be happening. This was the worst day of her life, then the floor collapsed beneath her.

"The baby that grew in her belly was mine." Troy's eyes blazed, his muscles bunched with his last statement.

"Baby?" She felt Gideon's pain, saw the bleakness in his eyes.

"That's right, everything this woman has I gave it to her." Gideon pointed at her and she felt a spear pierce her heart. His eyes full of questions and concern. Lina's heart broke open. She felt the crack as tangible as a physical wound.

"Go away," she whispered. Troy used her baby as a weapon. How could Troy have taken her sense of accomplishment away from her? He had no right. She'd worked hard to earn her way in the world. To heal. He never came back for her. For them.

"Sweetness, what is he talking about?" Gideon moved toward the bed.

"Both of you go away." Gideon accused her of contacting Troy. Manipulated by two men she trusted.

"Get out, I don't want to see either of you."

"Candy, I'm sorry."

"If you call my woman Candy again, I'll shatter your jaw." That was the last straw. She pressed the call bell. Within seconds a nurse, pushed open the door.

"Did you need something, Ms. James?"

"Yes."

"Lina, don't do this," came Gideon's plea. "Talk to me."

"Please escort these two out of my room. Place a no visitors tag on my door." Lina buried her face in the scratchy surface of the pillow and released a gut wrenching sob. She had her fiancé, the man she loved, removed from her bedside. She pushed back the tears. She never imagined her engagement would start with forcing the man she loved to leave her bedside.

Where was Lina's baby? Had he proposed to a woman who had given her child up for adoption? These were the questions that replayed in his mind as he sat outside of Lina's hospital room. Gideon slid a hand in the pocket of his suit jacket. He withdrew the hard object, cradling it in the palm of his hand.

Troy was gone, which was in the man's best interest. Gideon had to fight his inner Marine to keep from putting that interloper in a chokehold until his existence ceased to be a thorn in his side.

"Dr. Rice, Ms. James has been discharged." He had asked the nurse to give him an estimated time of discharge, there was no way in hell he'd allow Troy Lawson to take his woman home and she was his woman. Lina's room door opened and she stood, though a little unsteady, balancing a plastic bag in one hand.

"You're supposed to be in a wheelchair." He stood, moving forward, but she held up a hand.

"I'm fine. And you are supposed to be anywhere, other than at my door." He took measured steps until they stood less than a foot apart.

"Lina, I'm going to marry you in four days if I have to do battle with every one of your ex-boyfriends since pre-school." She gave him a tentative smile.

"You still want to marry me?" Did she have to ask?

"Oh, yeah, in the worse way." He grinned at her.

"Come here, you." She reached for him and the knotted rope abrading his heart fell away. For an instant, when she stood in the doorway, he thought she might reject him. Instead of moving in her arms, he gingerly scooped her off her feet into the cradle of his arms and carried her to a nearby wheel chair. He watched as she sank down into the chair, closed her eyes, sighing in contentment.

"I love you, Gideon." He was at a loss for words. Had he heard her, correctly?

Gideon was on one knee, bending lower in front of her when she opened her eyes.

"Say that again."

"I love you." Her casual reply to his request held him in suspended animation.

"You love me," he said it aloud, liking how well the words fit together. Like the two of them. Perfect.

"I love you very much Gideon Rice and I look forward to being your wife in four days."

"Good, because I'd hide us in the hills of West Virginia before I let another man have you."

"You're the only man I want."

"Can you stroke my ego this once and let me think you need me."

"You can think that, but I'll never tell."

"Give me your hand." He said before extending his own. When she didn't hesitate, his heart expanded beyond its previous border. She loved him.

He opened his hand, took the object he held and placed it in her palm.

"What is it?" Her eyes shone bright and he had a feeling she knew what she held without him telling her.

"It's what you asked for." He watched as Lina touched the small, oval stone with trembling fingers. "It's inscribed, Lina." He flipped the stone over in her hand. "Read it."

Her lips trembled now as she read the words craved into the stone. He could see tears pooling in her eyes.

"*I love you, Lina.*" Gideon had taken the stone from the river bed before they left Waverly Falls.

"Gideon, it's the most precious gift I've ever received."

"I do love you, Lina, more than life itself." He reached up, cupping her cheek in his hand. "I'll gladly shed my blood if you need me to."

Gideon closed his eyes when Lina turned into his palm, placing a gentle kiss on his skin.

"Let's go home, baby." Lina said.

Music. That's what he heard, because they were going home together. He said a silent prayer of thanks when her fingers closed around the stone and held her closed fist up to her heart. He would ask about her baby when they got home.

"I need to get cleaned up before I talk with my mother."

"Okay, I'll drive you over."

"I'm going alone, Gideon. This conversation is five years overdue." Taking the bag from her, he searched her personal belongings, until he found what he was looking for. He curled his fingers around the wood, pulling the object free of the bag.

"Keep BEYAS tucked some place safe." Lina gave him a slow wink. She slid the short stick between her undies and the waist of her jeans.

"Is that safe enough?" She teased. Grinning when he licked his lips.

"Yeah, that will do. I like the thought of your wood sword on your body."

"May the Force be with me?" He would be with her if she allowed it. The churning in his gut warned that the danger to Lina was closing in.

"You better put some force behind swinging that stick if anyone gives you a problem."

"Yes, Master Gidoda," she laughed. He didn't. Nothing was as it seemed. Each attack was more violent than the last. What would this madman do next?

CHAPTER NINETEEN

Lina felt the doors of a cage slam closed behind her as she entered her mother's house. Whatever happened here today, she would be trapped somewhere she didn't want to be. Lina's hand shook as she regarded her mother in disbelief.

"You knew where Troy was for five years and you didn't tell me?" Her mother sat stoic in her childhood bedroom, which infuriated Lina.

"How could you lie to me?" Her mother jumped as if Lina's words were a slap against her face.

"You were the only person in the whole world I could trust and depend on." The weight of her mother's secret threatened to crush her. "You've been lying to me." Lina didn't stop when tears streamed down her mother's face. At the sound of the back door opening, Lina turned to find Troy striding toward them.

"How did you get in here?" She answered her own question. He knew the location of the spare key. Why wouldn't he? The fact that he had access to her mother's house was an obvious indication of mutual trust. Troy was her mother's confidante. Not Lina. Her own mother didn't trust Lina with the truth.

"Never mind, you both are playing some twisted game that I don't want to be a part of, but it appears I have no choice." She turned narrowed eyes on Troy.

"How did you convince a mother to deceive her own flesh and blood?"

"Bernadean didn't lie to you. She's been trying to keep you safe for the last fifteen years."

"Momma?" Her mother didn't look at her, merely wiped the tears from her blood shot eyes.

"What is Troy talking about?" Still nothing.

"She won't talk to me," she directed at Troy. "Why are you here? I haven't seen you in years. Five years to be exact. Why did you come back?"

"Your mother contacted me after you told her about the roses. She was worried about you."

"Why would she call you rather than Bishop?"

"Because fifteen years ago she received the same message before your father was killed." Finally her mother broke her silence.

"I knew when you came home with Troy, trouble had darkened our door once again." Her mother swung her attention to Troy. "I begged you to stay away from my daughter, but you wouldn't. Now, I might lose her, too." Lina lowered herself onto her knees at her mother's feet.

"Momma, I'm upset because you've been hiding the truth from me. I'm not a child, I can handle whatever it is you're not telling me. Just tell me everything."

"How does a mother tell her only daughter that her father was a corrupt cop?" Lina swayed. She didn't remember much about her father because he was rarely around, but he couldn't be a dirty cop. Not her father.

"Or that I have known Troy since he was a boy." Okay, she really did feel faint. But if she hit the floor she would probably fracture a bone.

"Your father worked with Troy's dad on the police force. You were too young to remember them and they didn't live in our neighborhood. When your father was murdered under suspicious circumstances, his surviving family, us, were left without any means of support. Troy's father tried to help." A light bulb went off in Lina's head.

"Troy, did you purposely seek me out on campus?"

"Initially, I watched over you from a distance, then you came through the athletic department and we connected." She was going to be sick.

"Lina, it is not what you're thinking."

"Oh yeah. How do you know that, because I sure don't?" She'd given her virginity to this man. Carried their baby in her body. It was all a lie.

"I love you." He hadn't looked at her. He delivered the words with the ease of a trained actor minus the emotion.

"You don't love me. You feel some misguided since of responsibility toward me," she spat at him. Troy's downcast gaze spoke volumes.

"I love you both and I'm here to help." His words brought little in the form of comfort. The one man he had believed loved her, was merely a protector. A leftover connection from a father she barely knew. Then another thought occurred to her.

Pointing at Troy, Lina said, "You are not here as a family friend. Is what's happening to me because of my father?" He inhaled a deep breath, lips pressed into a thin line.

"You're involved in this somehow...Oh, God." Troy glanced briefly in her mother's direction before, moving toward her.

"You stay back, Troy. I swear I'll go Taebo on your ass," Lina stumbled to her feet.

"Lina, there's a lot of stuff happening that you don't understand," Troy said. Her mother's expression was blank, yet tears continued to flow onto her blouse, the silk fabric darker in the areas soaked with watery anguish.

"Whose fault is that?" Lina directed her accusation at both of them. He looked contrite. His body stiffened as if offended by her question.

"Listen to me Lina." He didn't get to tell her what to do.

"I'll listen when you start answering my questions. Why did she call you? A guy I have not seen in years." There was pain and anger in her tone, but she couldn't disguise her feelings. He had walked away from her and never looked back.

"I'm not some guy."

"No, you're the first link in a chain of heartbreaks." He took on a hurt expression. She would not let herself care about his feelings. She had spoken the truth.

"Candy."

"Stop calling me that. My name is Lina."

"You are Lina to everyone else in the world. To me, you'll always be Candy." She closed her eyes wrestling the memories away behind a wall of hurt. She opened her eyes to find he had narrowed the gap between them. He moved in, his approach was familiar, a reminder of their shared past. It pissed her off.

"Don't come any closer. I'm with Gideon now. We are getting married."

"Marrying Gideon?" Her mother's voice filled the room.

"Three months ago it was Jace Harper," Troy said matter of factly. Her breath froze in her lungs as her eyes widened in shock. How could he know about her private life?

"Believe me Candy. I know every detail of your life."

"Yet, I know nothing of yours. I never knew the real you."

"You know me better than anyone. I gave you as much as I could. Trust me."

"Trust you? How dare you come to my home asking me to give you my trust? I trusted you once. I trusted you with the very heart of me. I gave you everything a woman could give a man."

"And I gave you the same, Candy. It was my baby that grew in your belly. I love you. That will never change. I have always taken care of you." He should not have mentioned the baby. The foundation tilted on the wall of hurt he helped to build in her heart. She couldn't stop the tears gathering in her eyes.

"How can you say that? You weren't there when the baby left me. You weren't there when I needed you to hold everything together. I saved myself. I built my life without you. What have you done? Nothing, but cause me pain."

"Don't cry, Candy. We lost the baby. You never lost me."

"I never had you Troy. Can't you see that?" God, he was as lost as she was.

"That is not true. You own me."

"Loyalty is not love, Troy. You're loyal to my father's memory. You helped my mother provide for me." She should have known her mother couldn't afford their lifestyle without assistance. She'd been blinded to the truth.

"Lina, I stayed away to keep you safe. Being with me put you and the baby in danger."

"How? Why did you stay away so long?"

"I needed time to build my own alliances and establish a network separate from my family's connections."

"What do you want from me Troy?"

"I want us. We had a family together. Me, you, and a baby. We could have that again."

"I can't do that. I have a life that doesn't include you, Troy. How did you know all these details about my life?" Lina turned to her mother. How had she been so blind?

"I told you that I never left you. You are mine and nothing, no one will change that, ever."

"I spent years of my life with you and I never knew the real you."

"You can get to know me, Candy."

"I'm the daughter of a corrupt cop that was killed most likely by the same people after me."

"Your father was not corrupt and I can prove it," Troy's voice echoed off the walls.

"What?" Her mother's voice echoed her own.

"Someone inside the Shell Cove Police department set Lincoln up to take the fall. If he hadn't died in that raid, he would still be working to salvage his reputation." Her mother sobs filled the room.

"I knew it was a lie. I knew in my heart," her mom cried out.

"Lincoln could never betray us, Lina." Her mother smiled at her through tears. So why didn't Troy look pleased.

"Knowing this information puts you in danger, doesn't it?"

"I think someone in the department leaked my connection to both of you." Lina said.

"Oh my goodness, this is going to get worse." Lina blinked several times, trying to contain her rising panic.

"Lina I can keep you safe. Come away with me. We can build a life together."

"No, that's not possible. I am in love with Gideon. I'll be his wife in four days."

"You are not getting married." That was her mother's voice.

"Gideon asked me to marry him and I said yes."

"Lina this isn't a good time…" Troy said. Who did he think he was? He had no power over her decisions?

"Neither one of you is going to tell me who and when to marry. Gideon and I love each other. We make one another happy."

"I made you happy once and I can keep you safe."

"What we had was a lie. And Gideon is more than capable of keeping me safe." Though Gideon fought what came natural to him. The Marine was the essence of who he was. The psychiatrist persona took work, and wasn't his second nature.

"You think that straight laced shrink can protect you better than I can." Troy demanded.

"I do." She believed in Gideon, trusted him. She'd come to rely on him. The thought should terrify her, but it didn't.

"I'm going home." Lina glanced around the room, ensuring she left nothing behind.

"I'll stop by later this evening." Came Troy's quick reply.

"About the condo, you can have it. I don't care what you do with it. Gideon and I are building a new home for our family." Lina grabbed her things to go, but her mother's hand on her arm stopped her.

"Baby, please don't go. I am scared to death that something is going to happen to you. Let Troy help." Her mother said, as she stood.

"No. I know you trust Troy, Momma. You two have a long standing relationship that I haven't been privy to."

"Lina try to understand why I didn't tell you about the connection between your father and Troy." Her mother's eyes pleaded with her.

"I never asked Troy for help. You let me believe we were taking care of ourselves, but it was a lie. I'm just some charity case to Troy. I understand why you chose to keep your secret, but I don't agree. How do you feel about your decisions now, momma?" Lina left before her mother could answer.

All she wanted was to be in Gideon's arms. They could weather this storm together.

CHAPTER TWENTY

Lord in heaven Gideon was furious. He stared at the woman on his door step. Her. Monica represented everything he despised about his past. Lies, broken promises, abandonment, rejection, loss and that was the short list.

"Aren't you going to invite me in, lover?"

"There's no love between us. I'll call you when the house is available." Stepping backward, he moved to close the door. Monica extended her hand, pressing against the door. He saw the furrows between her brows, heard her sigh of frustration, but he was unmoved. Master manipulation was Monica's specialty.

"Gideon…honestly, after all these years and you would leave me standing at the door?"

"Faster than a New York minute."

"Let me come inside, I promise not to stay long."

"You're not staying, at all. Leave me your new number." She gave him a coy smile.

"I would have given you my number if I thought you would return my calls."

"I wouldn't call you if I was on fire, and the hydrant was spitting gasoline."

Lina's snappy comebacks had rubbed off on him. He should've been with her, not here wasting time with Monica.

"Darling that statement doesn't sound like you. We weren't all bad, together." It pissed him off that she thought she knew him. They were strangers all those years ago, and he certainly didn't want to know her now.

"Leave your number, Monica. Ian will call you." She touched his arm and he flinched.

"Why are you giving me the house?" His connection to Monica would end the moment he walked away from this house. Now, he and Lina would build the home of their dreams. The home where their children would grow to adulthood, knowing they were loved and wanted. A vision of his life with Lina, flashed in his mind. Yes, that was all he wanted. And he finally had the love and acceptance he desperately wanted.

"It's what you asked for." As if conjured by a force set against him, his Cadillac with Lina behind the wheel rounded the wall of verdant hedges that obscured the front portico. She didn't take her eyes off him and Monica as she pulled the car to a stop. Lina approached them with a confident stride, an extra swing to her generous hips with each step-she was in full diva mode.

Her eyes were radiant with love and trust as she reached the front door and stopped adjacent to Monica. She gazed from him, to Monica, then she regarded him with a frown.

"Gideon, why are you standing guard at the door?" She asked before turning to Monica to introduce herself. "Hello, I'm Lina."

"Pleasure Lina, I'm Gideon's wife, Mrs. Rice. You must be the... housekeeper?" Gideon's brows slammed together at Monica's comment.

"Ex-wife," Gideon interrupted immediately. But it was too late. A blank, yet deadly expression covered Lina's face, then she smiled at Monica.

"Actually, I'm Gideon's fiancée," Lina said sweetly. "It's a pleasure to meet you."

Oh hell, Lina was going to kill him once this was over.

Her fiancé was another woman's husband. Gideon said he would never let her fall. He hadn't. She had fallen all by herself and hit her head on every step on the way down, before she face planted at the bottom.

"Ex-wife." Gideon's voice was loud and abrasive. The neighbors on the next block had ringing ears, but his words were a whisper compared to the repetitive gong of *I'm Gideon's wife.*

"I can see my husband still prefers to compartmentalize his life." Bruised, broken, and betrayed, she would not crumble. Her emotional damn was in the red zone, rupture was unavoidable, but not yet. A final gesture for the woman who'd risked her heart and lost. One last performance before the curtain fell.

She moved closer to Gideon, knowing he'd touch her. Predictably, his muscled forearm circled her waist, anchoring her to him. Swallowing the urge to push him away, she stood tall before casting her eyes down at Monica Rice. Doing her best Cookie Lyons impression, Lina plastered a smirk on her face and started her performance.

"You are no surprise to me, boo-boo. I'm wondering why you are here." A steel fist gripped her heart and squeezed. The longer she stood with Gideon at her back and Monica Rice at her front, the sensation intensified. So, this was what it felt like to die of a broken heart? She'd tried to save herself, but in reality she'd provided the hunter with the ammunition to deliver the mortal blow.

"I came to see my house." Like a tumbler in a lock the pieces fell into place.

"Gideon, honey, you and Ian forgot to tell me…I'm sorry I've forgotten your name."

"It's Mrs. Rice."

"Her name is Monica and she likes to be difficult. My ex-wife of five years decided to visit unannounced." He was forthcoming with the information, after the fact. She felt Gideon squeeze her shoulder. She knew what he wanted. Reassurance. Solidarity. No way would she crumble in front of either one of these people. But she would crumble. She felt the pressure when Monica had announced herself, then the crack formed when Gideon confirmed, he was married to this woman. Pain and hurt thickly oozing through the fissures in her soul. Sucker punched again. There would be no recovery this time. She was done.

"Monica, why don't you start upstairs, while we tidy up the master suite?"

"Honey, would you care to join me?" No this heifer didn't.

"I'm not your husband, just go already," Gideon gave Monica a frustrated wave of his hand. As soon as Monica disappeared up the stairs Gideon took Lina in his arms.

"Sweetness, I'm so proud of you." He kissed her forehead. She laughed at the irony. She recalled a time she wanted to massage his kiss into her skin.

"Funny, I don't feel like I've reached a historical milestone or a major achievement." She busied herself rearranging the personal items she had scattered around the chest of drawers. Gideon followed her into the bathroom.

"Monica is here to cause trouble."

"What power does Monica have to cause you trouble, Gideon?"

"I'm giving her the deed to the house, so we can build a life together."

"Oh, really?" She gave him her best "I'm bored" expression. Carting more lotions, potions and foolish notions toward the sink, she released her arms, and the pile fell onto the countertop in a messy heap.

"What are you doing?"

"I'm staging for my performance. What about you?" Came her casual reply.

"Lina, I'm sorry I didn't tell you about Monica, but your tone is a little concerning." Gideon was staring at her now.

"I thought it the perfect blend of I don't give a flip about what you think, what you do, or what you want." He grabbed her arm, spinning her to face him. His warm cedar scent engulfed her, before his breath caressed her cheek.

"We are getting married at the end of this week." She heard his tale of the ring she wore on her finger replay in her head. The metal seemed to heat, burning her skin. She dug her nails into her palms stopping the sensation.

"You sure about that? I mean, you're already married."

"Divorced. And stop with the verbal jabs."

"Consider yourself blessed and very lucky that I haven't punched in that lying mouth of yours." She pushed past him. Reaching into the drawer that held her lingerie, she pulled out four silk scarves. She tied one to each bedpost, and then draped a black leather bustier over the mahogany trunk at the foot of the bed.

"What the heck?" Turning to a wide-eyed Gideon, she smiled.

"That ought to be enough, now let's go check on your wife."

"Ex-wife." He said through pursed lips.

"Whatever," she tossed over her shoulder. Lina called to the other woman. "Monica, we have plans for the evening…"

"Of course," came the terse reply. "I'll check the other rooms, and then be on my way."

"Thanks," Lina cooed, as she threw an arm around Gideon, placing a light kiss on his shoulder. "Woman to woman, you know how antsy a man can be when he has a special night at home planned."

Monica grimaced. "Yes, I suppose." Monica walked past them, but stopped short of the master suite. "Gideon, you kept all the decor the way I like it." Lina stiffened. That little jab would leave a bruise, she thought.

"You can keep it. Lina and I are going to trash everything."

"Pity, it took us months to select the furnishings for each room."

"It's not my style." Came Gideon's frank reply.

"Yes, I can see for myself your tastes have changed," she gave Lina a once over, distaste reflected in her eyes, before entering the bedroom. In under sixty seconds, the fast click of Monica's heels exiting the bedroom drew their attention. With tight lips and a red face Monica stated, "I've seen more than enough."

My work here is done. Permanently.

"Monica, let me see you to the door." Pleased with her closing act performance. Lina added a bonus scene to her act. "Can I get your phone number, there's a list of things I can tell you about the house, for example, the walls are tissue paper thin, and…" Monica held up a hand.

"That's not necessary, my attorney will contact Ian."

"You sure, boo boo?" She said with a plastered on smile

"Quite."

"I appreciate you stopping by. Don't we, honey?" Lina turned to Gideon.

"Hell no." He spat out.

"Gideon, the language." Lina closed the door and stood still. Maybe if she remained still, her world would stop spinning off its axis.

"What was all that?" Gideon prodded.

"It's a woman thing, you wouldn't understand."

"You are even more beautiful when you're fighting alongside your man." Her man? She didn't know he was married. She didn't know they had to leave his house.

"I never imagined I'd have to fight, especially over the man I agreed to marry." She slid his ring off her finger and held it out to him. Gideon stared at the ring. Horror and alarm clear in his stormy gray eyes. Eyes she had been foolish to trust.

"You already have a wife."

"No, I don't. I was married, but I never had a wife. Not in my heart the way you are, Lina."

"I don't think your heart condition is legally binding. Take your ring." She slipped the band off her finger, holding the small circle out to him.

"I should've mentioned I'd been married before, but…put that ring back on your finger." She didn't argue. Sidestepping him, she placed the ring on the cocktail table and collapsed onto the couch. Gideon settled beside her on the couch.

"Sweetness." Even now after his betrayal, his voice made her insides tumble over themselves. "I'm sorry I didn't tell you I was divorced."

"I get it now. You don't want a past."

"Because it doesn't matter. I have you now." Oh he had her. She'd delivered herself into his arms with a big, naive bow superglued to her forehead.

"The drive back to Shell Cove. You were afraid Ian had mentioned Monica. That's why you were quiet."

"My life with Monica is over."

"Apparently not, you have unsettled dealings with your wife."

"This house was the last link between us. I told Ian to give it to her."

"I'd rather not go all General Hospital with the two of you."

"This is the last of it. I gave her the house so you and I can move forward with our plans, Lina."

"Your plan, not mine. You told me what you wanted me to know, so I'd fit into the perfect plan you have for your life."

"You agreed to marry me, so that makes it our plan."

"What do you want from me Gideon?"

Her question stopped him cold. Did she not know how he felt about her? Had she been hurt so many times, that she didn't recognize love, his love?

"I want you to love me." Her eyes widened in shock.

"Love me enough that you trust me to make this right. I am finishing this business with Monica once and for all. That's why I told Ian to give her the house while we were in Waverly Falls."

"I agreed to marry the man I thought I knew. You aren't him," she added the eye and neck roll for emphasis.

"You are no different from Jace or Troy. You told me what I wanted to hear, to get what you wanted from me. Well done, Doctor Rice. By far, you are the best I've ever encountered."

"You are comparing me to all the people in your life that don't love you. People that should have treasured you as the precious jewel you are. I'm right here Lina. I love you. I'll always love you. Don't throw away what we have because of my mistake."

"Grabbing the wrong laundry detergent is a mistake. Failing to mention you have a wife is a blatant lie. I can't do this Gideon. It's time for me to leave."

"No." His tone determined.

"What do you mean, no?" She stared at him.

"I mean you are not leaving me. We were fine before Monica arrived unwelcomed at our home."

"Apparently, it's her home!"

"I have explained the situation with my marriage to you."

"Did you?" she narrowed her eyes. "Because I remember walking up to the door and being confused with the maid."

"I apologize for not telling you that I was married before. She told me she was pregnant with my baby. I married her without asking any questions. Later, I discovered it was a lie. I thought we were in love. In the end, I wanted a wife, children, and my own family. She didn't. I filed for a divorce. We were still fighting over my house until I met you. I don't care about the house any more. We'll build a new one, together. This is a misunderstanding."

"I would have to know the facts to misunderstand them. You are a series of illusions Gideon, and I fell for it."

"I made a mistake. Forgive me, please?"

"You were never going to tell me, were you?"

"My marriage ended years ago, I have a new life with you."

"Gideon, I just learned that my mother and Troy have known each other for years. That they have been in communication since the day he disappeared on me."

"I'm sorry."

"When I discovered their betrayal the first thing I wanted was you." She laughed, a bittersweet sound at the irony. "I thought if I could just get home to you, I would be safe from their lies. But I was wrong."

"I'm here for you."

"But you lied, and I don't need another man like you."

"Lina, you can't mean that."

"I...do."

"I am not losing you. I'm not losing us because of an ex-wife. She is my past. You are my future." He cradled her face in his powerful hands.

"I love you Lina. Please focus on my love for you. Not on old hurts and disappointment. I want to be here for you. I want to wake up and snuggle into your warmth. I want you to wake up every morning to find you wrapped around me like a second skin." She pulled his hands away from her face.

"You taught me to pick my battles. Fighting with an ex-wife that obviously has feelings for her husband is a battle I'll leave for another woman." She pulled the phone from her purse and keyed in a number.

"I am not her husband," he continued. His tone was dark, but then gentled, "I'll be your husband in four days."

"Don't count on it, slick," she said with her hand covering the phone receiver. "Janna, stop whatever you're doing and come and get me. I'll be waiting outside of Gideon's place."

"Don't leave me. We can work through this hiccup." She studied him for a brief moment before giving him a slight nod. Lesson learned from Jace, apply honey not salt.

"Sure, let me put away my props in the bedroom. I need a moment by myself," she said before standing up, pulling her spine tall. He pulled her into his body, cradling her face in his hands. She felt the slide of his tongue against her lips. The familiar rush of warmth in her veins, heating her insides as he savored her mouth. She couldn't give what he wanted. Not now.

He pulled his lips away from hers, searching her face.

"Lina, I love you."

"I know you do." She wrapped her arms around him, holding him tight. "And only God himself, loves you more than I do." She released him. Stepping back, she grabbed her cell phone and disappeared from his sight. She had spoken the truth. She would never love anyone more than she loved Gideon.

Lina could see the light of hope in Gideon's eyes. Thank God he hadn't tried to stop her when she stood to leave the room.

She retrieved her overnight bag from the closet. She cleaned up the bed before clearing out the drawers he'd given her. Lina took one last look around their bedroom, and then put the bag on her shoulder.

The smile on Gideon's face fell away when he spotted the luggage on her shoulder. She heard him suck air into his lungs.

"Lina, no." He moved toward her and she held up a hand.

"I held you to a higher standard, but I should not have." To be with Gideon, she'd broken every rule she'd set in place to protect her heart. He'd convinced her he was different.

"Lina, give me a chance to fix this." He pleaded.

"I'm sorry, Gideon. I can't be your wife."

"You are still in danger. You promised you would stay with me. I will keep you safe." His jaw hardened.

"I can keep myself safe and I don't want you." She needed him like she needed her next breath. The hurt in his eyes was a scalpel to her heart. But, she couldn't continue on like he hadn't lied to her. Like the past didn't exist.

"That is a lie. You promised to be mine, to be my wife."

"Yeah…well, those were just words." Turning on her heel, she walked out the door.

CHAPTER TWENTY-ONE

Lina's life was in shambles. She was a revolving door of bad decisions, each one more costly than the next. Her very existence was a series of interconnected lies with the people she cared about the most at the center of everything. Even her home wasn't really hers. It belonged to Troy. Another pathological lie linked to a man she'd welcomed into her heart. She loved her condominium, but she would let it go. Because of her decision to become involved with men she worked with, her job was tied to Jace and Gideon. Gideon owned her heart. She had nothing left to take or to give. Her independence, the life she'd built, all of it was a lie. The pride she took in her accomplishments was an illusion.

"You okay, sister?" Janna asked, feet dangling over the chair arm in Lina's bedroom. Lina released a sigh at the thought of never being okay, again.

"Nope."

"Things will get better, maybe not anytime soon."

"Thanks, Janna. Your nursing expertise is definitely not psyche related." Lina fell back on the bed pillow, arms folded over her face.

"I leave the country in five days. If it'll make you feel better to toilet paper his house, spray paint butt wipe on his front lawn, or throw doggy turds in his pool I'm game." Lina looked at her and laughed, as the tears rolled down her cheeks.

"I have other ideas if those don't appeal."

"I'll keep that in mind," raising her arms enough to make eye contact, Lina recognized that Janna was genuine in her offer to help. Lina was thankful for the light-hearted reprieve.

Janna took what the world offered, never expecting anything lasting in return. Hit it and quit it was her motto. Lina wished she had heeded Janna's advice at the engagement party. *Ride him like Seabiscuit, and then leave him in the stall for the next jockey.* A choked sob escaped as she replayed their conversation.

"Good ideas, all of them." She didn't think she could mend the pieces of her heart this time. A million pieces of shattered dreams, hopes for her future had dissipated with three words, *I'm Gideon's wife.* Promises of a lifetime of forever, gone. A promise of unconditional love, gone. He promised her love, but he lied to her. Kept the details of his life from her. How many times could she be open to love before her actions were considered blatant stupidity? She had the answer, thrice.

"How about I hang out with you tonight?" Janna asked.

"I want to be alone." Lina never thought she would utter those words. She hated being by herself. She'd better get used to it.

"I could make that Hanoi fish with stir fry veggies that you like," Janna coaxed. "Exemption from chopping up the vegetables, since you're all snotty and wet." Janna wrinkled her nose. Even a broken hearted fool needed to eat.

"Sounds like a plan," Lina sniffled. "Hospital food is worse than the patients ever tell us."

After dinner, Lina walked the beach, but it no longer held the illusion of peace and safety. The warm breeze, didn't chase away the bone deep chill. In the past, the crest of the setting sun was nature's usher to the night. Now, she felt violated. Unseen eyes stealing her private moment, sharing in a pain that was hers alone. Looking at the waves rolling in, feeling the foamy coolness soaking underneath her feet Lina let the tears fall. She walked the beach when she needed to think. It used to be her peaceful place, not anymore. She missed Gideon and the mountains of Waverly Falls. Their mountain. Heartbreak was an understatement. Her heart had disintegrated, ashes floating in a watery grave.

Entering the condo, Lina found Janna parked in front of the television with the volume butting up against the noise ordinance.

"Look at this breaking news story happening in Shell Cove. A major drug bust, and the kingpin, a guy that calls himself Sky, has been wounded."

"Sky... as in sky high?" Lina questioned.

"I don't know." Janna replied, not taking her eyes off the television screen. "Girl, they have Shell Cove locked down like Granny Lou holding onto her pocket book." Janna was an adrenaline junkie. Bad boys and cops were right up her alley.

"That's tight." Lina said.

"Keep watching. I'm going to shower, this fishy smell is too much." Janna stood, rounding the couch en route to the guest suite.

The doorbell rang. Lina moved to go answer without taking her eyes off the television.

Opening the door, Estrella stood with a tray of something sweet and gooey in petit dessert cups.

"Chica, you've been missing in action."

"Yeah, that's old news. What's up?"

"I brought you my favorite dessert."

"What is it?" Lina asked reaching for the plate.

"It's a creamed custard."

"Perfect, I just finished dinner." Estrella handed her a petite dessert cup, but didn't take a seat. With the spoon provided, Lina dug into the custard, swallowing two spoonfuls, before gesturing to Estrella. The scene on the television was a modern day Indiana Jones' adventure, cops running, bursts of lights, gunshots rang out and Lina looked on as the news reporter took cover.

"Sit down. There's still some fish left from dinner if you want to eat. I'm watching this police shake down on the news."

"Really, what's happening?"

"Some drug kingpin got raided. Evidently he was wounded in a shootout with the police."

"Is he dead? Do they have his body?" Lina looked at Estrella then, the woman was stark white.

"Estrella, are you okay?" Lina went to stand, except she was dizzy and fell back to the sofa. Her legs were suddenly uncooperative, like taffy in the summer sun. Her mouth tingled and her fingers felt numb. "I don't feel so well."

"Lie down, Chica. Don't try to move."

"Call 9-1-1, Estr..." Lina's words trailed off. It was hard to remember what she was trying to say and more difficult to speak it.

"I can't, Lina. I'm so sorry." She looked genuinely sorry unless it was the drugs coursing through her system. Drugs? Estrella drugged her?

"It was you?" Lina's breath froze in her lungs. Betrayed.

"Sky wants to meet you. Listen to me carefully." Lina felt Estrella's hands cup her face. "Don't upset him." Estrella bent low, propping Lina's limp body over her shoulders. Lina had the woman by fifty pounds and tried to use the added weight to her advantage. She leaned heavily onto Estrella, making it hard for the woman to move forward. The guest suite door opened and Janna stepped out in warm-up pants with a matching jacket.

"Hey, get away from her!" Lina watched as Estrella blocked the path leading to her.

"Janna she's with the drug dealer." Lina tried to say the words louder, but her voice was barely audible. She lay semi-conscious as Estrella charged Janna. Janna, delivered a round house kick that sent Estrella sprawling toward the floor.

"You let the small frame fool you." Janna crossed the room to Estrella, delivering another swift kick to her lower back.

Janna rushed toward Lina, grabbing both her arms. Her body felt heavy. Rising to her feet, even with assistance was taxing.

"We have to get out of here." They reached the front door, Lina tried to carry some of her weight, but the drug's effect had spread.

Janna pulled the door open and the air stalled in Lina's drunken lungs. "Moon." The waiter from Ava's engagement party stood blocking the only exit from her unit.

"Hello, my Lina." That was all he said before he stabbed a syringe filled with clear liquid in Janna's neck. She felt the free fall as Janna's hold on her shoulder loosened and they both fell to the floor. Lina turned her head to see a lifeless Janna lying next to her. Her friend's eyes were open but she wasn't moving. Had Moon killed her? Oh God, she prayed that they both would live. Then she thought of Gideon and how much she loved him.

"Estrella," Moon yelled, "Get up, we are running out of time." Janna, with her smaller weight, was out cold. Lina thanked heaven she carried a few extra pounds. Her curves had interfered with the drug's absorption. Thank you, big butt and hips. She lacked full control of her limbs, but she didn't think she would lose consciousness.

Lina watched as Estrella stumbled to the door grabbing an unconsciousness Janna in a firefighter's carry. Obviously, this was not new to Estrella. Lina felt herself being lifted. Moon carried her down the steps. He smelled worse than a farm animal. But her watering eyes and disgusted nose meant she was conscious and that the drug had not affected her sense of smell. It meant she could have an opportunity to escape.

Where were these two taking them? Would Gideon find her? She thought about her mother and all the terrible things she'd said. Her mother was right. Lina needed help. Who would help her now? Would anyone think to look for her? She'd been helping the enemy this whole time. Where was the independent woman now? The one that had walked away from the very people trying to keep her safe. Instead she had invited Estrella inside, had dined with the enemy, and then Estrella had used her weakness against her.

"Stop." Lina heard a man scream. "Stop, I said." Lina's head rolled off Moon's shoulder to see Jace's pale blue eyes.

"You put them down at once," she heard Jace say. Thank heavens they were rescued. Estrella hadn't moved, but Moon lowered her feet to the ground.

Jace reached for her and that's when Moon pulled something from his pocket and Jace fell to the ground. His body twitched and spasmed, that's when she realized Moon had tasered Jace. Her feet left the ground once more. Both she and Janna were loaded in the back of a van. Silently she called Gideon's name. God please, help us.

CHAPTER TWENTY-TWO

The second Gideon opened his front door to discover Troy Lawson decked out in tactical assault gear, anger shot through his veins. Gideon stood face to face with the man he considered the biggest stumbling block to his and Lina's relationship. Wrong. Gideon and his need to segment his life had sabotaged what he wanted most in life. A life with Lina.

"What the hell are you doing here?"

"I came to get Lina."

"Get away from our home." That wasn't true. His home was with Lina now. Gideon moved to close the door, but Troy's foot blocked it.

"Lina is in danger. I have to find her."

"What kind of danger?"

"The kind that people don't live to talk about."

A broken down camper was parked in his driveway. Gideon narrowed his eyes on Troy, rage coiling deep in his gut. He'd been stalking Lina. Gideon's brain started organizing the facts he knew.

"It was you at Lina's place the night it was vandalized."

"I was there to take her away."

"I saw that camper the day we drove back from Waverly Falls." Gideon bared his teeth. "Whatever you're involved with has endangered Lina."

"I was going to talk to her after you left, but you stopped her on the stairwell. She left with you."

"Oh, heck." Gideon said.

"You've been in the way for weeks." Troy spat. "I promised Bernadean I would keep Lina safe, but every time I came for her. You took her away. Now, where is she?"

"I'll keep Lina safe. She's mine."

"Man, I don't have time to play cowboys and Indians with you. A police bust is going down as we speak. I've been working this case undercover for six years. If anything goes wrong, Sky will hurt Lina. I've been compromised by someone on the inside of the department." That got Gideon's attention.

"Damn."

"Yep, now where is she?" Troy repeated.

"I don't know. We had a disagreement."

"What kind of disagreement, will she be coming back?" Troy ran a hand over his face.

"Not if I don't physically bring her back."

"Let's start at the condo. If she's not there I know her hiding place." Gideon growled low in his throat.

"Look, we can work together to keep Lina safe, but you and Lina have nothing together. You feel me?"

"Oh, I feel you. Now you feel me," Troy rumbled. "I will always be connected to Lina. We made a baby together." His blood ran cold.

"Where is the child?" That pink bag with bows in her closet. It wasn't for future babies, it was for her and Troy's baby.

"We lost the baby," Troy said on a whisper.

"I'm sorry." Gideon said.

Troy nodded in acknowledgment. "Sounds like you and Lina don't have as much as you think if she didn't tell you." That comment pissed him off. Lina hadn't shared her pregnancy with him. He'd kept his marriage from Lina, true. But he loved her. And he knew she loved him, too.

"I am marrying Lina in four days. Nothing will stop me, not you, not Monica. I will conquer death itself to make Lina my bride." Determination and grit in his voice.

"Who's Monica?"

"She was my wife," he ran his fingers through his hair. How had his life come to this?

"In all likelihood, if anything went wrong with the bust neither of us will make it out of this unscathed." Okay that raised the stakes for Gideon.

"My brothers, Ian and Thane are close by. I'll have them meet us at Lina's." Three men wouldn't be enough if the stalker was any indication of the men they were dealing with. "I need to make a phone call." Gideon dialed the number of the one man he knew he could always count on to be there for him.

"Hello," the steady voice on the other end of the phone answered.

"Dad," he heard himself say, "I need your help."

Gideon and Troy approached Lina's parking lot to find, Thane and Ian surrounding a man lying on the ground. Gideon hugged each of his brothers, grateful they had answered the call for assistance when he had explained the danger surrounding Lina. They rolled the man over and Gideon was surprised to see a blotchy, drooling Jace Harper.

"Jace what happened to you?"

"A man took Lina, and they have Janna, too." They were too late. In a panic, Gideon turned to Thane.

"Go knock on the door next to Lina's. The woman's name is Estrella. Ask her if she saw anything." Troy looked at him in stunned silence, and then he started shaking his head like he was warding off an invisible attack.

"I'm on it," came Thane's terse reply.

"The Estrella woman was helping the man take them," Jace responded.

"I left Estrella safe in Peru." Troy said, his tone one of disbelief. "How long has she lived next to Lina?" Troy's voice was strained and filled with anguish.

"Two months, why?" Gideon asked.

"Damn it, he used her as the plant. Can you describe the van?" Troy's face was raw with emotion. The question was directed at Jace.

"Troy, what are you talking about?"

"The dealer that took Lina, his street name is Sky. He calls his right hand woman Star. And his hit man goes by the name Moon."

"So what?" Ian questioned.

"Estrella means star in Spanish."

"It gets worse," Gideon chimed in.

"How, so?"

"At Ava's engagement party, the waiter that offered Lina a glass of champagne. His name was Moon. Means they've been trying to take her for weeks." Gideon curled his fingers in fists at the revelation.

"Maybe you coming into the picture kept them from getting to her, Gideon. They didn't know you were a factor and then you took her away to Waverly Falls."

"But how do we find her?" Gideon questioned. Fear and need to destroy pumping through his blood in equal measure.

"Follow the smell. Yuck." Jace said with a grimace. "The guy smelled like rotten seafood."

Troy inhaled a deep breath and smiled. "I have an idea of where they are holding them, but I can't assemble a team large enough to take the Princessa before they have time to move her. We have to move fast to get our women back."

"Point us in the right direction. My brothers and I will get my woman back."

Chapter Twenty-Three

Moon stood on the helicopter landing deck of Sky's mega yacht. Rotating in each direction, he did a visual survey of the one hundred and eighty foot luxury liner and the lush tree line surrounding the private pier.

"Where are you, Troy?"

He knew Troy would come for Lina. Moon would be ready to bury his blade deep into the man, feeling the life drain from his body. Gutting Troy for his betrayal would be his gift to Sky. Now that he had Lina in his possession he understood the man's desire to keep her to himself.

A smile curled his lips recalling how her soft curves filled his arms. Flames of lust licked at his skin in anticipation. The look of surprise and fear on her face when he'd taken her had his erection pushing against his zipper. He yearned for them to be alone, but he hadn't been prepared for the other woman. Janna. Lovely name, he could have her, too. His pulse leaped with excitement. No, not this time. He understood how jealous women could be. He would not disrespect his bond with Lina by delighting in her friend.

Before their life together began, Lina had to be punished for her infidelity. She didn't have the decency to wait for him, after all he'd given to her. He clenched his fists at his side as rage surged through him. Slicing Gideon Rice's neck would be a gift to himself.

Jarring pain ricocheted through Lina's head when she hit a hard surface rousing her to consciousness. Terror spiked through her when she realized she'd been moved from the van. The air smelled of dead fish, the ocean, and gasoline fuel. Her skin felt clammy and slick with humidity.

Moon had left her exposed to the elements. Would he return? She cast her eyes left then right. No Janna. Mind working, she realized she had to find Janna and get them both off this boat. She tried to sit up, but her hands didn't work. Tears threatened to spill down her cheeks, but she kept them at bay. Stay calm. Panic and fear would only help Estrella and Moon. Inhaling deep in and out, she curled her hands up to view a thin, white nylon rope bound her hands in front of her body. Rope was better than plastic zip ties, not that she knew how to escape either one. But she felt hopeful.

Sounds of the water hummed beneath the call of the night owls. A boat. She was lying on the deck, taken, because she had to do things her way. God, would she ever see Gideon again? He wanted to keep her safe. Love her. Regret, like she had never felt before, had her head curling to her knees. A sharp pain in her abdomen drew her up short. Had she been injured when she lost her hold on consciousness? Where was Janna? Shifting, Lina surveyed her surroundings.

Straining to see her surroundings in the low lighting, another female sized body lay still not more than twenty feet away from her position.

"Janna?" Lina listened for a response, but no sound came from the other person.

"Janna, please." A soft moan reached Lina's ear and she sighed in relief. "I'm coming to you." Assessing the distance to the hull of the boat, Lina rolled until her back made contact with metal. Using the wall at her back, she pushed herself upright. Sweat beaded her forehead and her abdominals ached. Breathing in heavy pants, she scooted herself to a vertical support, grasped it with her bound hands and pulled herself upright. Sucking in a hungry breath, she listened for voices or anything to tell her where she was being held. They were at a pier, privately owned most likely. Taking in the expansive deck and flooring she surmised she was on a yacht. On bare feet, she padded over to the unmoving figure at the far end of the deck.

She reached for her friend's shoulder. After several attempts she rolled the limp body onto her back. Slowly the other woman's features came into view. A scream that never came reverberated in her head. No. Lina snatched her hand away as if fire had seared her skin.

"Estrella?" Panic rose and threatened to spill out of her in a bellow of fear, anger, and desperation. Where was Janna?

Determined that Janna would not pay the price for her folly. Lina gripped the lapels of Estrella's shirt and shook hard. Estrella's head flopped backward like a broken bobble head figurine, before her eyes blinked open. She watched as Estrella struggled to focus, her eye movements jerky and uncoordinated. Drugged. Why was Estrella left on the deck, drugged alongside her? She needed Estrella to make sense of this living nightmare. Her friend turned enemy was her only option to finding Janna and getting the freak out of here.

Estella's dry lips parted to answer Lina's unasked question.

"So sorry," she croaked.

Dismissing the woman's feeble apology, Lina cut to the chase.

"Where have they taken, Janna? Whose boat is this?" Estrella's eyes drifted closed and Lina let go of the lapels she'd been holding. Her head hit the deck flooring with a thud and Estrella's eyes shot open, regarding Lina in disbelief.

Lina shrugged. "Desperate times, require desperate measures. Now, where is Janna?"

Lina gave her five seconds before she grabbed both shirt lapels again, lurched Estrella up, only to let her compliant body fall back to the flooring.

This time Estrella swung a hand at Lina's face—with all the force of a cotton ball.

"Stop doing that, Lina."

Ignoring her protests, Lina batted the offending arm out of striking distance and pulled Estrella as high off the ground as she could manage with bound hands.

"Not sure a fall from this height will give you a concussion, but I'm willing to take the risk."

Estrella began to struggle in earnest.

"Talk," Lina jostled the semi-conscious woman.

"Sky has her," came the soft reply.

"Who is Sky?" Lina demanded.

"He controls the drugs, the women."

"What does he want with us?"

"Not us, just you." Estrella's tone spoke volumes. Now that they had her, was Janna of no consequence to their captor?

"Why? What do they want from me?"

"Troy," Estrella muttered, before she started to cough violently. Even in the shroud of fear, Lina recognized the voice of sorrow.

"What does Sky have to do with Troy or me?"

"Troy moves the money for Sky's organization." Lina's heart stilled in her throat.

"Troy is not a criminal." Estrella was mistaken. Terribly, terribly mistaken. Had to be.

"He'll wish he was when Sky finds him. He's an undercover cop, Lina." The anguish in Estrella's voice pulled at Lina's heart strings.

"No." How long had Troy been undercover? Had he hidden this from her when they were together?

"Almost five years Troy played the part." He'd told her the truth. Estrella coughed again, a protective hand over her ribs. "Sky trusted him until two Galaxy shipments got seized by the cops within four months. So, Sky knew there was a leak within his network."

"Why signal out Troy?" Lina questioned.

"Sky had Moon review everyone's background, again. This time they researched back to childhood. A money trail from Troy to Bernadean James, a widow to a corrupt cop led us to you."

"If you're one of them, why were you drugged and left here?"

"I'm not one of them. I tried to save you from Moon." Estrella stared at Lina with haunted eyes.

"But they have my little sister." A gasp escaped Lina's lips. "Sky turns girls into whores. I had no choice, but I have displeased him."

"You tricked me into thinking we were friends, then you drugged me and handed me over."

"I am your friend, Lina. I tried to stop Moon from destroying your house, from taking you. Moon has repaid my disloyalty."

"What are you talking about?"

"He broke my ribs, then he drugged me." Oh God, if this was how they treated their spies, what did they have planned for her?

"Tell me how we can get off this yacht and I'll get help."

"I'm afraid my darling niece can't help you, Princess." A man's voice sounded behind her.

Lina had heard that voice before. She pivoted on her heel and she came face to face with five large men. Four of them were dressed in black tee-shirts with dark cargo pants. She stumbled backward, before her eyes met with the bluest eyes she'd ever seen on a man. Even in the semi-darkness, his blonde hair was visible. With a wicked facial scar she recognized. Her mouth fell open. A heavy feeling settled in her stomach.

"Bluton Faraday." Bluton Faraday was Sky. The international business man that brought jobs to third world countries? He was a white collar thug and a drug pusher? Disgusting.

"No witty come back for me tonight, Princess?"

"I don't waste my energy dealing with the garbage."

"Explain to our guest, my darling niece, that I do not suffer rudeness well." Lina hung her head on a make believe swivel from Sky to Estrella. Unreal.

"Star is related to me by marriage. Unfortunately, both her parents met with an untimely death, leaving her nine-year-old sister in the custody of her aunt, my wife. Drug addiction does terrible things to a marriage, does it not, Star."

"My aunt never used drugs," Estrella screamed. "You forced drugs into her arm. You are a monster."

"Don't listen to her, Lina. It is wonderful to have you all to myself, Princess. We will have fun together, but business comes first."

"Boss, we are running out of time." Moon stepped out of the shadows taking the spot next to Sky. Six men including Moon, the likelihood of a successful escape dwindled against those odds.

"Moon, have the captain ready the engines. The rest of you keep a look out for the cop." Lina watched as the four men turned away without a word, each moving in a different direction. Rising panic churned in her stomach. She had to find Janna and get off this boat before they left the pier.

"Tell me where I can find your former lover?" Bluton pulled the tail of his jacket open as he spoke. Sky casually stuck his hands in his pants, revealing the butt of a gun. It glinted in the faint light coming from the cabin's door he'd left ajar. The shirt visible behind the gun was covered in blood. As she watched the stain grow larger, so did the knot in her gut. She thought of Gideon. Would she ever see him again?

The night wind blew warm air, thick with moisture across Gideon's face, but fear ripped through him like an arctic blast. Crouched low into the shadows, he and his brothers followed as Troy led them to a private dock along the Saint Dasius River. Crickets' chirps and frog croaks rang out in competition as if preparing themselves for the blood that would be spilled if any harm had come to Lina. The slap of whitecap waves held a steady cadence over the squawk of an occasional bird.

Estrella had betrayed them all. And Moon, a madman had handed Lina over to a killer. His brothers were at his side. Gideon placed a call to Bishop in case there was more trouble. He didn't want anything to happen to his father or future mother-in-law.

His father agreed to stay behind to protect Bernadean. Troy was certain she wasn't out of danger. If her yelling about being kept in the dark about her own daughter was a precursor to the rest of her conversation, his father had his work cut out for him.

According to the news report, Sky had been wounded during a police shoot out with local law enforcement. An injured man was a deadly man. And Lina was at his mercy. Fear coursed through his veins and he prayed that he reached her in time. Killers didn't want to die, but he knew from experience they would take as many people with them into death if backed into a corner.

"Troy are you sure we are at the correct pier? Lina is running out of time," Gideon whispered.

"Look to your left, about fifty yards." Gideon glanced in the general direction. Other than a late model luxury sport utility vehicle that looked vaguely familiar, he didn't recognize anything indicating that Lina was being held in this location.

"That's Moon's Range Rover. And smell the rotten stench in the air." Anxious to get to Lina, Gideon hadn't noticed how foul the air was at this end of the pier. "Moon's family has worked for Sky's since before he was born. His loyalty is legendary. Trust me, Lina is here."

The Marine in Gideon couldn't be contained. He turned to his brothers, "Put every man down hard. We won't have a second chance," he ground out.

"Wait, we need Sky alive, he's the key to..." Gideon interrupted Troy, he was done listening. "Everyone in position, signal when you are ready."

Gideon stayed in a low crouch as he approached the tree line adjacent to the pier. Gideon waited till his eyes adjusted to the darkness and the outline of a yacht with low lights came into view. A tall, dark figure came to stand along the railing. Gideon could make out a man's facial features when a second appeared at the stern of the yacht. With stealth like precision, Gideon unsheathed the hunting knife from his leg strap.

He could take out the first man, but without knowing if his brothers were in position, the second man was free to alert others to their presence.

Gideon hit the ground as the swish of an arrow's release hit his ear. He felt the swoosh of air for a split second as it flew over his shoulder, then lodged in the chest of the man farthest from his location. Without a second thought, he gripped the handle of his blade and hurled it for the last known position of his target. The weight of the bodies, hitting the water sounded loud in the night, but Phoenix's nuthatch bird call rang out loud and true. His brothers would secure the crew and search for Janna. He would find Lina. He would bring his woman home this time.

Pain shot through Lina's forearm as Sky incrementally constricted his grip until she winced in pain. Those blue eyes flashed with lightning before a smile split his lips. He was pleased with her reaction. Lina fisted her hands around the rope and forced a blank expression.

"Take the Princess to my cabin." Lina saw Moon's jaw tightened, but he moved in her direction. The look in Moon's eye's as he surveyed her body had goosebumps breaking out on her skin. Her heart raced at the thought of lying in wait for Sky's arrival. He wasn't the type of man you wanted to find yourself alone with in an elevator.

"Come with me." Moon reached for her arm, but she jerked away from him.

"I can walk."

Sky grabbed her face, digging his fingers into the flesh under her chin. It was difficult to breath and the pain intensified, as he pressed deeper into the soft tissue at her neck.

"You should know, I like my women pliable during playtime. I can drug you now, then Moon can carry you to my bed. The second option, you tell me where to locate Troy and I let you say goodbye to your little girlfriend, and then I drug you. It's your choice." Estrella's warning rang in her ears. No "too stupid, to live" moments allowed. She had to think smarter to survive. She couldn't risk Janna.

"Where are you taking me?" She said a silent prayer that someone would step onto the deck and help her.

"You will stay with me, Princess, but Janna is too old for one of my houses. She'll take a late night swim before we sail for the coast of South America."

"You're going to kill her."

"I would never kill your friend, Princess. That would be a poor start to our relationship." Lina released a sigh of relief. "The sharks will kill her." Lina's heart stopped. "As we speak, chum is being released into the water." He smiled at her then. "We can't have pesky body parts floating up on the beach? This way, there's plenty of hungry fishes at the table."

"Estrella is right. You are a monster."

Sky jerked her up suddenly bringing her face close enough to inhale his sickly sweet scent. He pulled on her hard enough to have her yelp in pain. Moon looked menacing, but Sky's eyes held pure evil. She recognized the sweet stench of Galaxy users. The guy was addicted to his own product.

"After a few hits of my Galaxy in your system, I'll be your God," he snarled. "Take her away." Who would have guessed Moon was a safer choice than this lunatic?

Moon grabbed the rope securing her wrist and led Lina to the open door. That's when she noticed a card control pad mounted where a key lock should be. Moon led her through the door, then turned to close the door behind her. He pulled a digital key card over a control box concealed by a panel and she heard a lock engage. She wouldn't be able to exit the lower cabin without a key card. She watched Moon with a wary gaze as he slid the key into his left front pocket and smiled at her. Moon pushed her against the wall, molding his bulky frame into her front.

"You made me proud, my Lina. You are a quick study." He grabbed her hair, pulling her closer to him.

"Get off of me," she bellowed. Her bound hands were between them and she pushed at his chest. The man was solid as a boulder.

"Shh, my Lina." His Lina? Oh my God, no. "I will never let him hurt you. You belong to me."

"You're crazy," Lina twisted and pushed at him. "I don't belong to you." His face darkened and menace filled his eyes.

"Don't ever call me crazy." He gripped her arms hard and she groaned in pain. "I saw you," he spat. He squeezed her arms, till his nails dug into her flesh. She bit her lip, refusing to cry out and give him pleasure from her pain. Lust shone in his eyes as he studied her.

"I watched him climb in the bathtub with you. You would've screwed him if I hadn't come that night." His lips parted, teeth bared in rage, for a moment he looked like he would tear her throat out. Instead, Moon leaned in close, covering her mouth with his, he forced his tongue deep into her mouth. His tongue was thick and heavy in her mouth. He tasted of beer and stale spices and she had to battle her gag reflex as he probed her mouth.

At the feel of his erection pressing into her groin, a wave of terror crashed into every cell in her body. She was going to be sick. Her knees buckled, and he tightened his hold on her. Unable to bear the pain she tore her mouth away from his bruising onslaught.

"Ouch, you're hurting me."

He stared at her as if her words confused him, but his hands loosened their grip on her arms. The instinct to survive kicked in. She needed a new approach. Her heart dropped to her feet, but she schooled her features into one of submission. "I'm sorry I upset you, Moon. I didn't want his attention. He came after me." Gideon please forgive me for this.

"Apology accepted, my Lina." Smiling he released his grip on her arm. Groaning she rolled her right shoulder as blood rushed into her abused flesh and the pain dissipated.

He moved in closer stroking her hair, then his hand tunneled into the hairs at her nape and his hold tightened. It took every ounce of psychiatric training she'd ever received to remain still. "I have a place set up for you and me. The bedroom is decorated in purple, just the way you like it, except I added white roses, so you will think of me." She'd maintained eye contact until he mentioned the roses. Not wanting to lose the connection, she forced her rapid beating heart to slow down.

"I thought Sky...all the roses were a gift from you?" His face lit with pleasure.

"Yes, I knew you liked them because you are a romantic, like me. I remember the look on your face when I sent them to your mother." The breath froze in her chest.

"What did you say?"

"I was just a boy back then, but I knew your father." A piercing scream filled her head. No, she didn't want to hear anymore.

"I am so sorry you had to lose him my Lina, but Sky doesn't tolerate betrayal."

"What did you do to him?"

"I spared him the torture Sky had planned. Lincoln was always kind to me. I returned that kindness." Calm filled his words as fire filled her belly. He would pay, they all would.

"Your kindness was to murder him," she railed at him.

"Lina, please don't yell. We are getting to know one another. With time, you will learn that if you do what I ask, I am both generous and merciful. Even now, I am reconsidering the severity of your punishment." Punishment? What was he talking about? He released her hair, and beefy arms surrounded her.

"Please, don't." She hated the tremors in her voice, hated that this man had taken her father away. Hated that her mother was right to shield her from this ugliness.

"You're shivering, my Lina." A single tear slid down her face and a sob broke when Moon wiped it away.

"You are grieving for your loss. We share this moment together, my Lina." She would rather die. Gideon, please come for me. You promised.

CHAPTER TWENTY-FOUR

Sky entered the cabin and stood over Lina. Refusing to cower in his presence she straightened her spine. She looked up at him. She would not fail, this was the moment of culmination when all she'd learned about taking care of herself would be needed to save her life. Because no one would keep her from Gideon. She loved him and she would see him again.

"The look in your eyes says you're ready for me." He reached into his pocket and withdrew a syringe filled with clear liquid. With her eyes, Lina tracked the syringe, until Sky placed it on the bedside table next to his key card.

Trying not to panic, at the thought of Sky touching her, Lina spouted the first thing that came to mind. "Let me clean your wound, so you don't get blood all over me."

He stared at her in confusion.

She pointed to his bloody shirt and tried again, "Give me your first aid kit and I'll patch your wound. You've lost a lot of blood."

"This is a scratch, but I like the thought of your hands on me." She ground her teeth together, forcing a smile to her lips.

"I'm a big woman. You are going to need every ounce of blood you've got to handle me." Lust filled his eyes. Biting her lip, she maintained eye contact knowing he would view it as a challenge.

"A willing partner," he crooned. "I like the thought of our first time without drugs." He left the room and entered a capsule shaped door at the rear of the cabin.

Alone for a minute, she shored up her courage. It was now or never for her escape.

"Here you are, Princess." Instead of giving Lina the full kit, Sky had retrieved antiseptic spray, topical antibiotic cream, gauze and tape. The man was no fool, because given the opportunity she'd have knocked his brains out his ear canal with the first aid box. Improvising, she extended her bound hands up to him.

"Untie my hands, please."

"Not a good idea, for either of us. No need to tempt you with thoughts of escape."

"Escape? I thought you said you were a professional. If a psychiatric nurse can penetrate your defenses you might be batting for the minor leagues." A muscle ticked in his jaw and she wondered if she might have pushed him too far.

She had never been so happy to be a plus sized woman in her life. Neither Moon nor Sky had noticed the lumpy appearance to her waist.

Sky studied her with narrowed eyes. Lina smiled, extending her bound hands up to him from her seated position as if he were a deity. The arrogant smile that covered his sadistic face brought bile to the back of her throat.

"Try anything Princess and I will enjoy crushing each one of your fingers."

"I won't try anything." The time for trying had passed. She would do everything to escape.

Sky reached behind his back and returned with a switchblade. Lina jumped at the release of the blade. She never took her eyes off Sky as the rope fell away from her skin. Her wrists ached. Visible bruises and rope burns covered her abused wrists.

"Clean me up, then remove your shirt." Her heart slammed into her ribs.

"Lie down on the bed, please." He made quick work of removing his shirt. Lina sucked in a breath. An angry red circular entry wound oozed blood from his right flank. The wound edges were jagged and swollen. Dried blood covered him from below his ribs to saturate the waistband of his trousers. She dropped to her knees, gathering the supplies in front of her on the bed.

"You're a bullet wound virgin," he teased. "You'll get used to them. Who knows, maybe you'll get one of your own." She refused to look at him, knowing the fear racing through her insides showed on her face. With trembling hands she cleansed and bandaged his wound.

"You have a gentle touch, Princess. No wonder Troy, couldn't let you go." Lina squeezed her eyes shut. Gratitude wasn't a reason to pretend what they shared all those years ago still existed. Storm gray eyes flashed in her mind. *I love you, Gideon.*

"Thank you." She stood only to have Sky come to a seated position.

"Where do you think you're going?" She pointed to the waste bin under the built-in desk unit.

"To throw the bloody gauze in the trash."

She took her time crossing the room, praying for added strength. This would be her last opportunity. The vibrations from the yacht's engines had roared to life during the wound cleanup. Gideon would be lost to her if she didn't get off this thing. Was Janna fighting for her life, while she cleansed the blood from a killer's skin?

"Remove your clothes, Princess."

She froze.

"You said my top." Her voice came out shaky.

"I changed my mind. Come and reward your patient." She hated what she was about to do.

He sat on the edge of the bed, with his legs spread wide. Lina stood in front of him, just out of reach. She turned her back to him.

"Turn around. I want to see you."

"I'm a southerner. We like to leave something to the imagination." Grabbing the hem of her shirt, Lina pulled the material over her head. Letting instinct reign, Lina curled her right hand around BEYAS, then pulled it free from its hiding place. She twisted her body in Sky's direction with a raised arm. He was still smiling when the first crack sounded against his skull. She delivered blow after blow until his body fell limp at her feet.

Quickly, she shoved her hand through BEYAS's blood soaked lariat, securing it around her wrist. Grabbing the syringe and the key card, she stepped over an unconscious Sky.

Lina opened the two doors in the lower cabin, calling out to Janna. God please, let me find her.

Hitting the deck at a dead run, Lina was frantic to find the other woman.

"Janna!" Please answer me. A Crosshill bird call sounded from the corridor in front of her. Gideon had come for her. Hope filled her lungs, then an ear piercing scream filled the night with the intensity of a summer lightning storm. Oh God, that was Janna.

Gideon bolted across the deck in the direction of Lina's voice. The need to protect her burned a hole in his gut.

"Lina!" he called.

"Gideon I'm here." Hearing Lina's sultry tone, he could breathe again for the first time since this ordeal started.

"Somebody help me." Desperation filled each syllable in the lithe voice Gideon recognized Janna's. He picked up speed in the direction of Janna's cry. Close to the railing, Gideon spotted Janna kicking and punching a man twice her size. Gideon charged toward the pair.

Once he was in striking distance, Gideon delivered a staggering kick to the back of the man's knee.

He buckled, before collapsing to the deck, bellowing in agony.

"Janna, get away from the railing." Janna looked up at him, and began to run toward the yacht's center.

Janna yelled something, but he was having a hard time hearing her. The wind intensity increased. He strained to catch a fraction of what she said.

"Chum lake around the boat," she screamed. "Sharks circling." These guys were twisted.

In one swift move, Gideon's legs were kicked out from under him. The impact of hitting the deck rattled his teeth in their socket. Blood coated his mouth where he bit his tongue. An unexpected blow to the side of the head had him rolling right, away from the next punch.

"That was for touching my Lina." What the hell? Gideon shook off the after affects of the head blow.

"You'll never have her," Gideon stated bluntly. Rage covered Moon's face before his roar filled the air.

"I'm going to enjoy killing you. Lina will forget all about you after one night with me."

"No one touches my wife." Lina was his. And he'd fight to keep her until his last breath. Gideon rolled to his side, coming to his feet. Moon was bulky, but Gideon had reach. Standing in a wide based stance, Gideon threw a punch at Moon's face. He drove his fist down, angling for the thin flat bone between the eye and the nose. Gideon felt the bone shatter under the skin. Howling in pain, Moon staggered backward. Gideon saw movement out of the corner of his eye. He braced himself for impact. Lina materialized and jumped into his arms. She showered kisses on his face.

"You came for me." Lina threw herself at Gideon.

"You're mine. I'll always come for you."

"I love you, Gideon."

"Love you more, sweetness." He panted.

"Hey. Seabiscuit and female jockey, let's get off this boat," Janna yelled.

"Princess," came a male voice in a singsong tone. "I'm going to kill you." Lina stiffened in his arms.

"Oh, God, it's Sky. We have to move now." Lina tugged on him.

Gideon stared in horror at a bloody Bluton Faraday, he held a Sig Sauer trained on Lina's back. Bluton was the head of an organized crime ring?

Gideon pulled Lina close, turning them, so his back was to Sky. He heard the round, spring load into the chamber, before the trigger pull.

The heated metal tore through the flesh of his left upper arm, the force of impact knocked the wind out of his lungs.

"Gideon." A hailstorm of bullets started to rain down in their direction. The shots were coming closer. Janna low crawled toward them. Janna screamed, pleading with Lina to run. Gideon yelled for Janna to stay back. He shielded

Lina's body with his own. Images of Sergeant Julianna Torres, her chest covered in blood as she died in his arms, bombarded his mind. He squeezed his eyes tight as the memories assaulted him one after the other. They were behind the fence in Afghanistan, on Marine Corps soil, she shouldn't have needed her Kevlar vest. He'd been close, but not close enough to save her. He would save Lina. Her broken body wouldn't go lifeless in his arms. Tremors racked Lina's body. A river of tears covered his chest. He pressed her tighter to his chest. She was in shock.

"No, Sky!" Moon bellowed. Gideon angled his head in time to see Moon running at break neck speed across the deck, straight for Sky's position. So focused was he on Lina, that Sky didn't notice the other man closing in on his position. Maybe, Moon was the distraction he needed to save Lina. He was losing blood fast. Lina was too terrified to move, but they were seconds away from certain death. Gauging the distance to the life preserver storage box, Gideon pivoted them. The searing pain of hot metal sizzled at the back of his right thigh. He grunted as his leg gave way. A small whimper escaped Lina. Agony registered through his entire body. He would die, but Lina would live.

"I love you more than life," he gasped out. "Trust me." Lina's spine went rigid. He felt her arms squeeze tight around his waist before he threw them overboard. The whoosh of helicopter blades and Lina's screams were the last sounds he heard before the water swallowed them.

Oily, foul tasting water spilled over Gideon like a faucet on full blast. The impact of hitting the water felt like a steel pole driving the hot metal deeper into his flesh. He felt the push of water displacement like a building had been tossed in the water. Murkiness surrounded them, but Lina's arms were sure at his waist. Gideon was disoriented and struggled to maintain consciousness. A spotlight above the water shone bright as a beacon. Gideon kicked with as much force as he could muster for the surface. Suddenly, Gideon felt Lina's hold on his waist slip away.

The water roiled around him as the helicopter blades disturbed the surface water. Gideon felt his strength waning. He breached the surface. Spinning he searched for Lina. Where was she? Taking in a large gulp of air he dove under the water. At the sight of Lina struggling to free her ankle from Moon's grip, he damn near inhaled.

Arms flailing, Lina fought the water, each stroke pulling her deeper under the water.

With one arm useless at his side, he propelled his body through the water, desperate to reach her before all was lost. He wanted to rail at her, scream for her to calm down and use the water for buoyancy. The glint of metal in Moon's hand had Gideon increasing his stroke length. The blade made contact, and blood swirled in the water surrounding Lina's legs.

Lina seemed to surrender, her body drifted closer to Moon. The other man's arms closed around her, like a lover's embrace.

A reflection was all he saw, before Lina jabbed a syringe into Moon's neck and pushed the plunger. A trail of air bubbles left her nose. Lina started to sink away from him. Everything in him rebelled.

Gideon grabbed Lina just as her eyes drifted closed. With the last of his strength he kicked for the surface, breeching the water, like an escape pod jettisoned under pressure.

"Lina, sweetness...open your eyes." For once she listened without challenging him.

"I love you, Gideon." The ladder dropped from the helicopter. "I love you too, grab the rope ladder and climb up, don't look down. I'll be right behind you."

Reaching for the rope, his hand slipped when something large brushed by his leg. He had fought for freedom, and for ten years he was captive to the past. He had disconnected from his family. His unwillingness to accept the bruises and the blessings life had given him had destroyed Lina's trust in him. He'd risked the love of the one woman that gave him everything. For what? He was alone. Rhythmic ripples of water slammed into her left side before he felt the brush of a shark against his leg. Gideon reached for his ankle holster. His blade was gone. Would he live to see Lina again?

Frantic, Lina searched the water line, looking for any sign of Gideon.

"Gideon!" She screamed his name until her throat burned and ached. The familiar green and black interior of the Rice family helicopter humbled her. Gideon's family had come to aid. Phoenix appeared on the yacht's railing, then did a swan dive in the man-made feeding tank. *Please don't take him from me.*

At the sight of a shark's fin, Lina's heartbeat halted in her chest. Where were they? The seconds seemed like hours. The helicopter's light bounced along the yacht's hull then circled back to the water. Phoenix shot out of the water holding Gideon's limp body.

"I see them. They're next to the boat," she yelled over the noise of the rotating blades.

Let them both be okay.

"I'll drop lower, then we'll get out of here," came a deep voice Lina didn't recognize within the helicopter cockpit. Relief flooded through her.

"We have to find, Janna." The helicopter swayed. Lina gripped the seat strap to steady herself.

"Janna Williamson is on that yacht?" His eyes were sharp with concern. Lina stared at the pilot with wide brown eyes and dark skin. Who was he?

"I'm Dawson," the pilot stated at her continued silence. "My brothers call me D. Wright." *Oh my goosebumps.*

Gideon hoped someone got the license plate number of the car that hit him. Every nerve ending in his body screamed in pain. He winced as the stinging smell of antiseptic hit his nostrils. Shifting his arm caused sharp pain to ricochet across his upper back. Increasing frequency of a hospital monitor's beeping echoed in the background. He sucked in a breath, gritting his teeth against the pain. Maybe, he'd been run over by a high speed rail car.

"I swear Gideon Rice if you are trying to die on me, I'll marry Jace Harper faster than the speed of light, I'll give him a house full of pale, big butt babies."

What the heck was she talking about? It wasn't happening on his watch.

Gideon roused to Lina's soulful serene voice at his ear. Slowly his eyes blinked open. Lina had been crying. Even with blood shot eyes, and puffy eyelids, Lina was the most beautiful woman he'd ever seen. He looked down at the bed. His larger hand was encircled in Lina's smaller grip.

"You'd marry Jace, huh? Not even over my dead body," he croaked out. His throat felt drier than clay dirt in the Florida sun. He licked his dry lips. Lina leaned forward from the chair at his bedside. Looking around he took in the neutral colored beige walls, a television hanging from a ceiling mount. A dry erase board mounted to the wall directly in front of the bed, listed RN Tucker as his nurse for the morning shift.

"Drink this." Lina held a turquoise cup with a fluorescent flexy straw to his lips. The cool water coating his throat was better than cashmere.

"How long have I been here?" He remembered the bullets tearing through his arm and thigh. He and Lina going overboard. Memories of Sky's yacht breached the mental fog.

"Three days. You've been drifting in and out of consciousness for the last forty-eight hours." Though she smiled at him, tears filled her eyes. Gideon's chest filled with such love for this woman, he thought he would burst.

"You got your dress ready?"

He was alive and Lina had stayed with him, even when he wasn't aware of her presence.

"What?" She stared at him in disbelief.

"Tomorrow is Friday, our wedding day." He gave her a determined look.

"Gideon, be serious," she said, avoiding eye contact. Had she changed her mind about marrying him?

Against his body's objections, he pushed himself forward, grabbing her chin, "What's changed?"

The stucco beat of his heart, threatened to topple him over. He loved Lina more than life itself. Was she sorry she'd taken a chance on him?

Please God, let her still love me.

"I lost my baby, Gideon." He sat up taller, never breaking eye contact. She looked at him, but it was as if she didn't see face. Her concentration was elsewhere. Did she expect him to walk away?

"Troy told me about the baby." She gasped, mouth open, with wide eyes.

He caressed her cheek. Closing her eyes, she bit her lip and he instantly hardened. There had to be a hospital policy against sporting wood in an open air gown. "I am sorry about the miscarriage."

"So am I. I don't know if I can carry a baby until full-term." The sorrow of loss filled her words. He would give her children. Children she could lavish with love and acceptance.

"Your ability to conceive is not a factor for me making you my wife. You gonna marry me or what, sweetness?" He had to know how she felt.

"After everything that's happened, you are serious about taking me to the altar?"

"As a shark attack. All I need is a suit and to know you love me. Where's my family?"

"Your Dad has been keeping my mother busy. They left for coffee about thirty minutes ago." Gideon smiled to himself.

"I'm glad they worked out their differences. He could use some company."

"Yeah, they get along pretty well, considering the circumstances."

"Have Thane or Ian bring me a suit for tomorrow."

"Ian is dealing with Monica. She stopped by when you came out of surgery." Lina mentioned Monica with a casual tone, hope soared in him that she might forgive him for having kept the truth from her. "Thane is with your father. They're probably at my momma's house. Jacob is keeping her close."

"D.Wright should be back shortly. He had to check-in on base." Lina continued to fill in. Gideon remembered the relief that flooded his system when he spotted the familiar green and black Rice helicopter circling over Sky's yacht. Thank God, he'd invited his family for the wedding days earlier. Without their help he and Lina would be swimming with the fish. "You could've told me D.Wright's first name was Dawson. Janna and your brother know each other well." Lina giggled like a schoolgirl with a secret.

A knock sounded at the door, "Hold up," Gideon yelled and then turned to Lina. "You didn't answer my question?"

"Which one?" Lina tilted her head.

"Do you love me?"

"With all my heart, I love you." She kissed his cheek, then tried to move away.

He cupped her face in his hands, "We are getting married tomorrow, just like we planned." Lina's eyes lit up. She sprang to her feet. Her sweet lips pressed against his, and he forgot all about the pain. The only thing that mattered was the woman in his arms. He slid his right arm around her waist. Pulling her closer, he savored the exotic taste of her. Heat spread through his veins when her fingers skimmed his chest.

At the rapid succession of knocks at the door, Lina broke the kiss.

"Enter," she called out.

An ashen faced Janna walked in, followed by a stoic Troy.

Janna crossed the room, gave him a stiff hug, "Thank you," she whispered in his ear before taking the seat adjacent to Lina. Troy's eyes immediately fell to Lina's before settling on him. Gideon expected Troy to reference his connection to Lina. Gideon knew to the depths of his soul Lina was his. And soon they would be signed, sealed, and delivered into matrimony. She would be his forever.

"It's good to see you awake." Troy's face held genuine concern and Gideon felt his muscles relax. Taking a deep breath, he pushed himself more upright in the bed.

"Thanks, did you get Sky?" Troy's head fell to his chest. He seemed to be having trouble getting air into his lungs.

"Divers recovered Moon's body two days ago. They are still searching for Sky," his voice was barely above a whisper.

Sky was still out there? Would he come back for Lina? Troy responded to his unspoken question.

"Lina and Bernadean are safe. We will find Sky, dead or alive." Lina squeezed Gideon's fingers.

"I'm glad you both are okay. I'd better get back to Estrella." A glint of more than concern flashed in the other man's eyes at the mention of Estrella.

"Is she in custody?" Gideon watched, waiting for Troy's response.

Troy's hands balled into fists at his side.

"Estrella is three doors down the hall from you." His voice was strained. "Her little sister is missing. We think Sky had her relocated to the US, shortly after he brought Estrella to Shell Cove." Gideon raised a questioning eyebrow. What was the importance of the sister's movement?

"Sky forced Estrella to drug me by holding her nine year old sister hostage," Lina offered in a voice filled with sorrow.

"I didn't realize." Troy gave a stiff nod of acknowledgement.

"Well, I should get going," He said after a moment.

Then Troy did the unexpected.

Instead of exiting the room, he approached Lina. Gideon watched as she released her hold on him, turning to face Troy.

"Take care, Candy."

Okay, he could handle the affectionate greeting, but then Troy opened his arms to her. What the heck?

"That's my fiancée," Gideon said on a grunt.

Lina's laughter filled the room, "Yes I am." Lina turned to face her pint-sized friend. "Janna, take a picture of Troy walking out of here. We can post it on the internet that we have no idea of his location following his visit to Shell Cove. None of us can afford a repeat of his kind of drama."

The room erupted in laughter.

The woman he loved gave Troy a sisterly hug before he turned and exited the room. The door closed with a soft thud.

"Call D.Wright. I need my suit for tomorrow."

Janna bristled in the bedside chair. "Don't mention Dawson's name," she said.

Everybody called his eldest adoptive brother, D.Wright. The fact that this stoic little Navy nurse addressed him as Dawson spoke volumes. Curiosity had him.

"How do you know D.Wright?"

"Dawson Wright is the most intrusive man I know," she huffed. This was the most emotion he'd witnessed in the woman since they met weeks ago.

"Is that so?" This was going to be fun.

"Oh…yeah, he's gotten worse since the wild, Wild West show happened on the open sea." The lady doth protest much, he thought.

Did Janna realize when she said Dawson's name her posture relaxed? If Gideon knew his older brother, wedding bells would toll twice in the Rice family.

Lina stood at the altar in the SCMC chapel her hand in Gideon's larger one. She turned to find a tearful Jacob, in the first wooden pew, hugging an equally tearful Deanie James. Lina glanced around the room, flashing a smile at her friends and family. She had everything she ever wanted. Lasting love and family. A huge family.

Lina's wrists were abraded and swollen. Gideon's face was bruised. They both looked like contestants from Survivor. Who would have thought her decision to start a man-fast would result in a trip to the mountains of West Virginia, a hit and run, an abduction, and a marriage to the man of her dreams. Married.

Gideon had stood by her side for their vows, but now he was seated comfortably in a wheelchair with the Shell Cove Medical Center logo.

Graham Hamilton approached with a determined look in his eyes. "Lina, I was looking for one of your bridesmaids. I can't seem to find her." Graham knew Ava, Janna, and Rebecca. Why was he looking for Ava's sister, Shaylah?

"That's Shaylah." He smiled, but she recognized the predator glint in his eyes.

"She told me her name was Yvonne." Lina sighed in relief.

"It is. Her full name is Shaylah Yvonne Walters." When had Graham spoken to her?

"Gotcha." Graham strode away from her without another word. That was odd. She was searching for Gideon when she spotted him wheeling his chair in her direction. He was grinning like a loon. She smiled as the gleam of his platinum wedding band caught her eye. She had everything she ever dreamed of. They would be packing out Gideon's house when he was released from the hospital. Thane had decided to stick around and help them with house plans and designs.

"Lina." Her best friend calling her name halted her steps.

"You are married, before I am," Ava said.

Lina beamed at her.

"You know me. I have no interest in engagements, receptions, or after parties. Give me the man and I'll see you at the altar." They both laughed.

"I should have followed your lead."

"You still can. Where's Logan?"

"Probably looking for a stiff drink on hospital grounds."

"Why is that?"

"I've been selected for deployment," Ava said with cautious excitement.

"Get out! That's awesome news."

"I think so, but it wasn't a hit with Logan."

"Uh oh."

"Logan wants to protect you. Darwin was prior Navy. Ask him to talk with Logan." Lina suggested.

"Ah, Darwin and Rebecca were in a corner kissing before the minister announced you and Gideon, Mr. and Mrs. Rice." She was Mrs. Gideon Rice. Married to the hottest former Marine, now psychiatrist on the planet.

"I noticed."

"Ava, can I steal my wife?" Gideon's familiar scent filled the air. Her nipples beaded at the same time as her mouth watered.

"Of course you can." Ava bent low, throwing an arm around Gideon in an embrace. "Congratulations and welcome to the family."

Lina and Gideon were each other's family now. They were two lone halves, made whole.

"Where have you been, husband?" She would never tire of saying husband to her man.

"Trying to break up a tiff between Olivia Tran and Bishop." Lina quirked a brow in question.

"They just met each other. What could have happened to result in an argument?" Lina would have to find out. She pivoted on her heel, scanning the chapel for her brother.

"I recognize that look in your eyes. The answer is no. Bishop can handle himself. You have more pressing business to take care of." She grinned, looking into the face of the man who had saved her from herself. She loved Gideon and he loved her right back. Ms. Independent had surrendered her heart, knowing she didn't have to take on the world alone. Gideon would always be there for her. Mrs. Independent had a nice ring to it.

"Can I talk you into wheeling me back to my room?" Lina bent low placing a quick kiss on Gideon's forehead. His arm snaked around her waist. When his fingers met with the hard object at her waist he halted.

"What is under your dress, Lina?" Did he have to ask.

"BEYAS, of course. Sky is still out there." She grinned. "And why would I take you back to your room before our reception?"

"We have a union to consummate and a birthday to celebrate. You won't be fasting anytime soon." Stormy gray eyes bore into hers. Love, acceptance, and friendship shone back at her.

"You convinced me. I'll never fast off you, mountain man."

THE END

Turn the page for a sneak peek at
Siera London's Catching Rebecca.

Darwin and Rebecca's story is book three in the Bachelors of Shell Cove series.

CATCHING REBECCA
EXCERPT

Rebecca Lynn Holbrook stood prim and poised next to a Dick. The cream satin shoes the personal shopper provided pinched her toes. Richard Ascot, her father's potential business partner, with his high-gloss gel hair rivaling a solar panel was at her side. She despised the man. He actually wanted people to call him Dick. Dick Ascot. Seriously? Stop the non-sense.

When would this thing be over? The man standing in front of them droned on. For the love of Pete, Peter, and Pierre, was he reciting the remix? Finish, already. She didn't hear a word. It was for the best. Who needed details, when she'd made a mess of her life? She wondered how many people were in this mammoth space with them. She hadn't looked left or right when she entered the room. She kept her focus straight ahead.

A bird flitted across the sky in no particular direction and she longed to feel that kind of freedom. To have her directions be for her own benefit and not that of the Holbrook family empire. Duty to the empire had landed her in this mess.

She wondered what Darwin Masters was doing at this moment. He was the only man in her life that cared about what she thought. She could talk with him for hours or not. Being in his presence made her feel whole. But he was done with her.

She'd rebuffed his advances one too many times. But she only did that for public appearances. For months, she'd left her back door unlocked and welcomed him to her bed, but that had been when she had been dating his brother. Yep, she was pretty twisted. Dating one brother, while sleeping with the other.

"Do you take this man to be your lawfully, wedded husband?" Oh, this was her part of the dog and pony show.

Turn the page for a sneak peek at Siera London's Chasing Ava.
Logan and Ava's story is book one in the Bachelors of Shell Cove series.

CHASING AVA
EXCERPT

Ava stood in the elegantly adorned grand foyer outside of the Coastal Towers ballroom, her feet rooted to the plush carpeted floor. Anxiety kept her frozen with the posed angles of an ill-placed statue. A random assembly of colleagues made eye contact, offered greetings and moved along without a second glance. She should not have agreed to come out tonight.

Straight ahead, she had a clear view of the city's namesake, Shell Cove, and the larger Queens Bay in the distance. A scattering on waterfront mansions, private docks and yachts dotted the waterscape. With her peripheral vision she met with the frown of her best friend.

"Ava Elaine Walters you can not back out. You are two size-seven stilettos away from the party." Lina chided.

Lina James, her best friend from elementary school gave extrovert at new meaning. The two of them couldn't be more divergent. Lina was cocoa to Ava's butterscotch complexion. Ava's petite frame lacked the fluid poetry of Lina's full curves. Lina had the type of figure teenaged boys cut out of magazines and hid under their mattresses. Ava lived her life backstage while Lina chose center spotlight.

She'd allowed Lina to talk her into a group social thingy. Ava had sworn off non-clinical social interaction six years ago. If she hadn't known them before spring semester of sophomore year there was a "no admittance sign" firmly tacked on her inner circle.

Pop tunes wafted into the lobby with every evening gown clad young woman exiting the ballroom. A reliable indication, that the Shell Cove Medical Center party had hit its full swing to Ava.

"It was a mistake to come. Thanks to you and Jace I left the house on a Saturday night. That's celebration enough for me." Tonight would be cataloged as another foolish decision, in a not so comedic list of errors.

"It's a Christmas miracle." Lina rolled her eyes heavenward the hint of laughter reflected on her face.

"Don't worry about driving me back home. Go join Jace inside. The valet can hail me a cab."

"I'm not worried because we are going to sashay through this door together." Lina pointed to the twin ornate brass handles on the twenty-foot high doors.

Ava ground her teeth in frustration. Nothing grated her nerves more than friends and family telling her what to do. The worst part, they genuinely believed she needed direction. The fault lay with her. How had she sunk to making those closest to her feel responsible for her life? It was official. She had baby-bird syndrome. Dependent, too weak to leave the nest. She should have been a nurse in the United States Navy, like her college roommate Jana, but fear kept her tethered to this familiar, costal Florida town. Pathetic.

"We both know what's waiting for you at home." Lina placed her hands on her hips, careful not to crease the fabric. Ever the diva. Hands on her hips meant Lina was ready to drive her point towards a home run.

"How could 'we' know that when I'm not at home?" She smiled at her snappy come back.

Her response earned a "you've got to be kidding me" look, from Lina. Taking her arm Lina led her to the coved seating area away for the ballroom doors.

"I know all about your grandmother's Holy Ghost hook-ups. Let me activate my super powers and predict your future. This, my reclusive friend, is a retelling of the voicemail you received before we picked you up tonight."

Lina paused before raising her elbows and stacking her forearms in an, "I Dream of Jeannie" imitation. Of the two of them, Lina was hands down the Grand Diva of dramatic gestures.

"Granny Lou has invited another borderline social security recipient to Sunday dinner." Ava gave no outward appearance of hearing the statement. Lina continued on. "She's hopeful that you'll show a remote interest in the male species before Jesus calls her back to heaven." At that, her best friend offered an, *I know I'm right expression.*

Did the entire populace know her grandmother had taken on the mission of finding Ava a matrimony eligible man?

Unfortunately for Ava, her grandmother's social circle consisted of the community seniors club and the church auxiliary. Louise Stanton, affectionately known as Granny Lou was e-harmony, match.com, and a well meaning, but meddlesome church mother packaged into five foot two inches of sparky banter and sequined Velcro comfort shoes.

Ava rolled her eyes heavenward, taking in a deep breath. A telltale sign that Lina's assessment of the situation was accurate. Ava loved her family, but she didn't do relationships.

The silence stretched between the two women. Ava squirmed like a toddler in a car seat under her friend's scrutiny.

"Your silent routine doesn't work with me Ava. Which wife-seeking, God-fearing deacon has she invited to Sunday dinner?"

Never one to let you off the hook Lina held an expectant gaze. Ava gave a resigned sigh then offered the name of her would be suitor. "Deacon Hill."

Ava knew the exact moment Lina recalled the porky gentleman. Wide eyes stared back at Ava as Lina's mouth opened and closed several times before she hid her smile with a carefully placed palm over her red velvet colored mouth. Lina would risk her friend's ire by laughing, but never would she suffer an accidental smudge to perfectly painted lips.

"He's the one with the three adult children and five grandkids living in the house." A vestige of humor at Ava's expense shone in her eyes.

"That's the one." Ava curled her fingers against her temples forcing a breath through her pursed lips. A high definition image of the aged, wide girthed man danced a gig across her mental LCD screen and she cringed.

"Save tomorrow's worries for tomorrow. Tonight is about us having fun. This isn't a matchmaking attempt by Granny Lou Incorporated. Come on, Ava please." Lina flashed her million-dollar smile. Ava was unmoved. The queen of improvisation, her friend switched tactics.

Lina's pout heaped on another layer of ever-present guilt, but she couldn't give her family or friend what they wanted. They wanted her to be open, welcome a date with a nice man, and be social. But being social led to meeting new people. Meeting new people, led to making connections. Connecting to new people, especially men, made you vulnerable. She didn't want to be vulnerable. Not ever again.

"Argh, stop making me feel bad, Lina."

"So let me get this straight," Lina stepped closer, their shoulders near touching. "At the tender age of twenty-six you prefer to be alone on Saturday night with thoughts of a dreadful Sunday dinner looming rather than walk into a fundraising gala with me?" As the reality of Lina's words settled between them Ava felt the sadness reflected in Lina's gaze.

"You'll be with Jace." Ava stated matter of fact. "I'll spend the night watching the two of you doing the humpy dance."

"Ewe, I am so not into watchers", Lina said crinkling her nose. Her best friend always kept the mood light.

"You know what I mean. Besides, I think I forgot my ticket." She diverted her eyes to heaven offering a silent *forgive me Lord* but desperate times required desperate measures.

"Excuse deferred. It's your work anniversary. The Shell Cove Medical Foundation covered your ticket price. Now apologize to the Lord for lying," Lina countered with a snap of her fingers. "The ticket is a formality. Your name is on the attendee list."

Ava quickly scanned her mental Rolodex for any plausible excuse that would get her back to the safety of home.

"You can meet some new people tonight. There are other nurses here. They're our peeps, waiting behind these doors." More people entered the foyer, bubbly voices talking one over the other, eager to join the festivities. The rhythmic beat drawing them into the ballroom like a pied piper.

Ava raised a brow in doubt. She wasn't likely to meet a single person. She knew it, so did Lina.

"Stop worrying about everything. It's a party packed to capacity with gray suit wearing administrators. A few pocket protector wearing clinical researchers and a truckload of fashion deficit doctors." Lina fashioned a mock pocket protector in the middle of her leather bustier, then mimicked stuffing it with pens. Ava released a snort of laughter at her friend's antics.

"Nothing is going to happen. Do this as a gift to me."

A gift. She had little reserve left in her emotional tank to offer anyone. Ava needed to gift herself a box of hope. One big enough to drown out the self doubt, the emptiness that plagued most aspects of her life.

Some days the emptiness weighed so heavy on her chest that emotional collapse seemed better than to greet another day of nothingness. The loneliness abated with work. Tending her garden helped, but the emptiness was a stealth army slowly advancing through her existence. It threatened to devour the fragile threads of a new beginning she desperately clung to.

Relationships and connections were out of the question, but the truth couldn't be denied. She was lonely. Tonight was a beacon cast in a sea of endless night. She was all dressed up with somewhere to go. Heck, she was here lingering in the foyer, on the outside catching glimpses of life through the cracks.

She had reason to celebrate. Her Navy nurse commissioning application was complete except for the employer endorsement. The unsuspecting, navy blue, file folder containing her future had been hand delivered to Kathryn Quest, the pediatric nurse manager this morning. Perhaps, one night of fun to capstone the budding joy she felt at having taken this uncertain step would fuel her emotional tank. Only two people knew what she had done. Lina wasn't one of them.

Ava proffered her elbow in acceptance. This was an evening dedicated to goodwill, and she had her best friend to share it with. She worked side by side with several of the attendees. Her safe zones were home and work— everything would be fine. Lina interlocked their elbows, gently guiding Ava to the ballroom doors.

"Okay, I'll take the plunge."

Buy now: http://amzn.com/B00S1KFRGS

Dear Reader,

Thank you so much for reading Gideon and Lina's story. This is my second contemporary romance novel from the Bachelors of Shell Cove series. I truly appreciate your continued support, and someday I hope to tell you face to face the impact you've had on my life.

Here are some ways you can let me know what you think of my novels or to keep in touch with me:

1. Write a review on Amazon, Goodreads, Barnes and Noble, or iBooks. Please consider leaving a review. Book reviews are equivalent to engine oil for a car. Readers reviews help other readers find new authors. Reviews help increase an author's discoverability with search engines, like Amazon.

2. Sign-up for my newsletter at www.sieralondonauthor.com. You will get updates on any new novels, book signings, and giveaways. I have a few deleted scenes you might be interested in.

3. Go to my Facebook page and "like" me. My Facebook family is welcoming and I host a mean Facebook Party. Here's the link: https://www.facebook.com/authorsieralondon.

I'll meet you between the covers. Wishing you all the best that life has to offer.

Happy reading,
Siera

ABOUT THE AUTHOR

Siera London is a Amazon bestselling author who served twenty-two years in the United States Navy before starting her writing career. She knew she wanted to be a writer when she kept searching for interesting topics to write. Siera tried fiction writing first, but when the words of the page bored her to tears, she decided to write what she enjoyed reading. By day, she is a nurse practitioner. At night, she writes sizzling romances with emotion and humor.

Growing up in the Navy, Siera loves to travel. A semi packed suitcase is usually on standby in her closet. A lover of all things culinary, she often tests new recipes on unsuspecting dinner guests. Siera lives in the Washington, D.C. area with her husband, and a color patch tabby named Frie. When she's not writing, she's reading, teaching or volunteering in the local community. She's a member of Romance Writers of America.

Connect with Siera London
Subscribe to my newsletter: www.sieralondonauthor.com
Like me on Facebook: http:facebook.com/authorsieralondon
Follow me on Twitter: http://twitter.com/siera_london

Made in the USA
San Bernardino, CA
13 September 2015